CAMDEN

PITTSBURGH TITANS

By
SAWYER BENNETT

ISBN: 978-1-0881-9780-6

Find Sawyer on the web!
sawyerbennett.com
www.twitter.com/bennettbooks
www.facebook.com/bennettbooks

Table of Contents

CHAPTER 1	1
CHAPTER 2	17
CHAPTER 3	28
CHAPTER 4	41
CHAPTER 5	55
CHAPTER 6	65
CHAPTER 7	76
CHAPTER 8	92
CHAPTER 9	101
CHAPTER 10	115
CHAPTER 11	131
CHAPTER 12	142
CHAPTER 13	152
CHAPTER 14	166
CHAPTER 15	178
CHAPTER 16	188
CHAPTER 17	200
CHAPTER 18	212
CHAPTER 19	224
CHAPTER 20	236
CHAPTER 21	251
CHAPTER 22	263
CHAPTER 23	274
CHAPTER 24	286
CHAPTER 25	293

CHAPTER 26   307
CHAPTER 27   315
CHAPTER 28   325
Connect with Sawyer online   333
About the Author   334

CHAPTER 1

Camden

*F*IRST STEP ONTO *the sidewalk and my foot lands on a patch of black ice left behind from the storm three days ago. Luckily, it's my right leg that slips out from under me and I manage to stay upright, but not without pulling my groin muscle. I grimace and take a tentative step, relieved that nothing seems to have torn. My knee feels solid.*

I curse the grocery store for not doing a better job of clearing the ice from where their customers walk along slowly. So slow that I get passed by a gentleman who's easily in his eighties and yeah… that's humiliating.

The old man turns, his cheeks ruddy from the cold. "Need some help?"

I'm a fucking professional hockey player. I don't need help from an octogenarian. But I'm a polite dude, so I just smile and shake my head. "Had surgery on my knee. Exercising a little caution."

"Aah," he says in understanding. "Better safe than sorry, right?"

"Right."

"Well, good luck with your shopping," he says, eyes

twinkling with what might be a little pride he's in better shape than me. "Once you've got the shopping cart before you, you'll be steadier."

And it gets more humiliating.

"Thanks," I mutter, but I doubt he heard me. He's taken off, disappearing through the sliding doors.

The trip through the market is an exercise in futility. I do as suggested, using the cart for support and make my way up and down the aisles. I wanted to cook some chili but I've had the worst luck. So far, they've been out of ground beef, canned tomatoes and kidney beans. I've managed to add an onion to my cart but my repertoire of recipes is so limited, I'm not confident I can do anything else with it.

"Fuck it," I grouse as I decide not to cook and just grab some cereal. I'm tired from a long day of rehab and it's fucking cold out. I want to get home.

As luck would have it, they're out of my favorite cereal, and even shittier luck, out of my second favorite as well.

Not sure what cosmic forces I've offended, but nothing's going right and it's leaving me feeling unsettled. In fact, a bit of panic swells inside and I glance around the cereal aisle. Nothing dangerous lurking.

I put the onion on the shelf in the empty spot where my Lucky Charms should be. I leave the cart and make my way to the front of the store, deciding to order a pizza for dinner.

It's gotten dark in the fifteen minutes or so I've been in the grocery store. Another wave of anxiety hits and I get the distinct feeling that if I step out of the safety of this building, something bad is going to happen to me.

Sucking in a long breath through my nose, I hold it for the count of two before letting it out slowly on a four count. I read online that deep breathing can help center and calm you, and I've tried it when I'm agitated for seemingly no reason. Honestly, it does nothing for me, but I make myself do it three more times.

"Nothing bad is going to happen," I whisper.

Not sure if I actually believe that, but I can't stay here all night. At some point, they'll kick me out.

I man up and walk past the registers to the sliding doors that swish open as I near them and then out into the blustery cold evening.

Glancing around, I take in the well-lit parking lot and the customers walking in and out of the store. I see my car only ten yards away. Nothing scary out here, unless you count a rogue piece of ice, but I can see the blacktop looks dry and safe.

I feel like a fucking idiot and these instances of fear that come upon me are unexplainable. I have nothing going on in my life that should make me feel this way. Other than a near mishap on the ice, getting shown up by an eighty-year-old man and a frustrating trip around the grocery aisles, nothing's been going on to make me feel out of control.

Everything is fine.

I'm a hockey player.

I have a great job.

Great friends.

A wonderful life.

"I have a wonderful life," I repeat and just like that... the panic recedes. I simply needed to remind myself I've got it good.

Shaking my head, I chuckle and take a step off the curb. I barely get my other foot down before I hear the noise.

It's so loud, I clap my hands over my ears. A piercing, whining, shrieking sound of metal on metal, but no one else seems bothered by it. People stroll in and out of the store.

It gets louder and then the air current seems to change. A foreboding, electric feeling that cranks my anxiety to full throttle. I tip my head back and at first, I don't understand what I'm seeing. Something huge, hidden in the clouds but with blinking lights... right above me and falling fast.

My first thought is a UFO but as it breaches the clouds, I realize it's an airplane. A massive jet hurtling out of the sky, nose-diving straight at me.

I'm powerless to move as I stare at it.

Closer and closer, until I can actually see the pilots inside, their mouths open in what I'm assuming are screams of terror. I lock eyes with one of them and I think I see sorrow in his expression. Not sure if he's sad he's going to die or that he's leaving behind a family, or hell... maybe he's sad he's dropping a plane on my head.

I lift my hand, mesmerized by the aircraft now forty, thirty, twenty... ten feet from me. And...

Bolting straight up in bed, I bark out a cry of horror,

even though I'm instantly awake and know I merely had a terrible nightmare.

It's not my first rodeo… these planes dropping out of the sky dreams happen pretty frequently. I rub my hands over my face, not surprised to find it sweaty. Despite the immediate awareness that I'm safe and sound in my bed, it takes a few minutes for the last dredges of fear to shake out of me. The dream was so realistic and yet, in hindsight, all of it was ridiculous from the start.

My knee is fully healed, no eighty-year-old would beat me in a fast walk, there's no way the grocery store would be out of all of those items and it's inconceivable that a plane would drop out of the sky onto my head.

And yet the terror it produced was as real as if it had actually happened. I thought I was going to die and I wasn't ready to go.

I flop back onto my mattress and stare at the ceiling. The moonlight shining through the window casts shadows from the bare trees outside. I consider doing the deep breathing exercises I did in my dream, in hopes of relaxing enough to go back to sleep. But they don't work in real life either.

Granted, it's only something I've read about and I've never actually had someone show me how to do it, so I'm not sure I'm doing it correctly.

I close my eyes, the first step in returning to slumber. All that does is start a replay loop of the plane falling on me. My eyes pop back open and I watch the tree shadows above me.

Attempting a supposed tried-and-true method, I imagine sheep jumping over the branches and count each one. I make it up to twenty-seven before my mind drifts toward its inevitable path.

Not a dream catastrophe, but a real one.

The first anniversary of the Pittsburgh Titans' plane crash is a month and a half away. While I've been plagued with more night terrors than I can even begin to count, they've gotten worse in the last two months. I have no clue why because honestly, I feel at peace with things.

I grieved, I mourned, I lamented.

I accepted that I was granted grace while others were not.

So why the fuck am I continually plagued by a plane killing me?

And it's not always a plane falling from the sky. Often I'm on the plane and we're in a long plummet to the earth. It's so terrifying, I've vomited coming back into consciousness.

Sometimes I dream that I'm driving down the road and the plane crashes in the distance but the fireball rolls outward and engulfs my car in flames, blistering my skin painfully. I've come out of those dreams slapping at my body to snuff out the fire.

Christ, I'm a mess.

My head rolls on my pillow and I sigh as I take in the time: 4:03 a.m. I know I'm not going back to sleep. Close my eyes and I'll go right back into my nightmare. Sit here with my eyes open, I'll only think about it.

I should get out of bed and do my workout, but I've got no motivation at all. Instead, I nab the remote control and turn on the television. It casts the room into an immediate blue tinge—a good murder mystery is sure to take my mind off falling jets. Maybe even distract me enough that I can fall asleep. I didn't go to bed until a little after midnight and I need more sleep to function. We have a team meeting at eight a.m. and then practice at nine.

After some surfing, I settle into a three-part docuseries about a set of interconnected murders across two states. Some would find it odd I can watch this stuff after experiencing a nightmare, but I've always found true crime shows and podcasts fascinating. I need my mind to be fully engaged in something other than my woes.

Ten minutes in and I know I chose wisely. I'm fully hooked and I forget about planes and friends dying. It doesn't look like I'll fall back to sleep, but that might be for the best anyway.

♦

BLISSFULLY DEEP IN slumber, I swim upward into consciousness because of a noise that penetrates the fog. An insistent banging, almost desperate in nature. I crack an eye, slightly alarmed at how bright my room is, but I'm not sure why that would cause me distress.

Bang, bang, bang.

The other eye opens and I focus on the bedside clock.

Nine forty-one a.m.

That seems awful late for me to still be in bed.

And then it hits me all at once.

Practice!

"Fuck," I groan as I scramble out of bed, twisting up in the sheets and falling to my knees. I had surgery on the left one over a year ago and I've healed well, but that did not feel good.

Bang, bang, bang. "Camden… open the fucking door or I'm knocking it down."

Jesus Christ.

That's Coach West's voice.

I kick the sheets away, jump up from the floor and lurch out of my bedroom. I careen against a wall and stumble into my living room.

Bang, bang—

Lunging for the handle, I twist the dead bolt and throw open the door to find Coach with his fist raised.

I brace for him to scream at me because this is bad.

Very, very bad.

I missed practice and the fucking head coach is on my doorstep. This is so bad, I'm sure he's here to fire me.

Instead, he lowers his hand as his eyes laser focus on me. I can see he doesn't like anything he sees—a disheveled man in his boxers who probably has sheet crease marks on his face, hair standing on end and sleep gunk in his eyes.

"Get some coffee on," he says with aplomb. "Let's chat."

Get some coffee on? Let's chat.

I'm absolutely discombobulated by his composure when any other coach in the league would be yelling right now about what a colossal fuck-up this is. I'm struck mute and frozen in place, the only thing jolting me out of it is when Coach West brushes past me. He glances around and heads toward the kitchen.

"Let me put some clothes on," I mumble.

Coach seems unperturbed by any of this. "I'll figure out the coffee pot."

I turn for my bedroom, my head spinning with the implications of the conversation we're about to have. There's a very good chance I'm going to be fired… released from my contract and the team. Best-case scenario, sent down to the minors.

I hastily put on a pair of track pants and a T-shirt. I use the restroom, wash my hands and then run them wet through my hair in an attempt to look somewhat presentable.

When I make it back to the kitchen, I see that Coach has figured out I don't have a coffee pot but rather a fancy espresso machine. He's either a mechanical genius or he knows his way around one, because there are two cups of coffee on the table. Not so surprising, given that his girlfriend used to be a barista.

Coach West uses his foot to kick a chair out and nods at it. I sit, pulling the coffee toward me, but make no effort to drink it. The rising steam tells me it will remove a layer of skin until it cools some.

I flush with angst as Coach West stares at me. "When you didn't show up for the team meeting, we tried calling, but you didn't answer."

"I must not have heard it." Was I that deep asleep? It's possible since I've been running on fumes.

"You scared a lot of people. I'm glad you're okay."

"I can't believe I overslept," I blurt with a lot more apologies rushing out. "I am so sorry. I didn't sleep well last night so I watched some TV. I thought I would stay awake until it was time to get up but I must've fallen asleep. I guess I forgot to set my alarm clock or maybe I did. I don't know, it's just... that's never happened to me before. I am so fucking sorry. Please don't terminate my contract."

Coach doesn't say anything for a moment but picks

up his cup and blows across the liquid before taking a small sip. When he sets it down, his voice is level but not unemotional. "I'm not sure what I've done that would lead you to believe I'd be the type of person to terminate a player for missing a practice."

Why I feel the need to argue against this is beyond me, yet I point out, "You set very high expectations for your players when you first got here. You said you expected everyone to be on time and at every practice unless somebody was dead or dying."

His lips curl into a half smile. "That is indeed what I said. It's also the reason I'm here. I thought you were dead or dying."

My face flushes hot with embarrassment. It's humiliating. But then something occurs to me. "Why are *you* here? I mean… why didn't you send one of the assistant coaches, or hell… even someone from the administrative offices to check on me?"

Coach West circles his fingertip around the edge of his coffee cup as he contemplates my question. When his eyes rise to meet mine, he says, "Again… a little disappointed you would think I'm that type of coach. First, you know damn well I delegate a lot of shit to my assistant coaches. They're more than capable of carrying on with practice without me being there. But as head coach, I'm ultimately responsible for everyone on this team. And if you were dead or dying, by God… I was going to be the one who found you. I'm not putting that on anyone else's doorstep. But most importantly, the reason I'm here is it's time to have a transparent conversation about what in the hell is wrong with you."

My eyebrows rise. "Excuse me?"

"You heard me. What's wrong with you? This isn't the first conversation we've had. Your play has been off. And now you're missing practices."

"A practice," I clarify hesitantly, not wanting to piss him off but not willing to be labeled as someone who's routinely late.

Coach inclines his head as if to say *touché*. "I still want to know what's wrong. You may think you're hiding it, but you're not. And if you want to keep your position on this team, I suggest you give me a good reason to help you figure out how to accomplish that."

I don't know where to begin to tell him all the things that seem wrong, so I pick up my coffee and take a sip. It immediately scalds the top of my mouth but I swallow it, burning my throat along the way.

When I set it down, I say, "I'm having a little trouble sleeping. That's all."

"Are you self-medicating? Drinking? Is that why you overslept?"

"No, Coach," I exclaim, leaning forward in my chair. "I'm not doing that. Only having some bad dreams is all."

"Because if you were self-medicating, the league has great resources to—"

"I swear I'm not doing drugs or drinking alcohol to help sleep."

He nods and I see he accepts my declaration at face value. "Okay, then... let's move on. Why are you having trouble sleeping?"

That is the million-dollar question, isn't it?

And one I haven't bothered to try to answer yet.

To fill the silence, Coach prods me. "When we last talked about your level of play on the ice, you said you were having some family issues. Is that it?"

My mind buzzes, trying to remember exactly what I said. He did indeed call me on the carpet about my play not being quite up to par. I think I did tell him I was dealing with some family issues, but that's not the truth. I mean, there's some truth to it... but they're not the root of my sleepless nights.

I choose to be vague. "My family isn't keeping me up at night."

Coach West settles back in his chair, taps an index finger on the table. The way he's looking at me is daunting, as if he can see deep into my soul.

"Is it because your friends and teammates and coaches died in a plane crash?"

I flinch.

And it's noticeable.

"Are you having nightmares about plane crashes?" he asks, and I feel the blood leaving my face.

Coach West takes it in and nods with understanding. "Did you get therapy after the crash?"

I shake my head. "Not really. We had to see someone for an evaluation, but that's all I did."

He knows what I mean by *we*. Coen Highsmith, Hendrix Bateman and I are called the Lucky Three. The trio of players who weren't on the plane. The ones who escaped death and the ones who should be grateful for the lives we have.

Coach pokes at me without hesitation. "Is there a reason you didn't attend therapy?"

I shrug. "I thought I was handling it fine. I mean… I grieved. I mourned the losses. I asked a lot of whys and why-nots. But I handled it fine. Ask anyone who knows me."

"I'm asking you," he says pointedly.

"I handled it fine," I repeat but there's no hiding my defensive tone. "I don't want or need therapy."

Coach West stares at me a good long moment before giving what looks like a resigned nod. There's a release of tension from my chest, something I hadn't realized I'd been holding in this entire time.

"Okay," he says, pushing up from the table and I rise as well. "I respect you don't want to do therapy. I'd never force that. But I am going to require you to do something."

"What's that?" I ask suspiciously.

"Brienne created a support group for all the loved ones and friends left behind. At first, it was pretty structured with regular meetings. She had a certified counselor there to moderate discussions. Now it's more of a social network. We meet every Sunday afternoon at a different place to get together and talk."

"We?" I ask curiously because Coach West isn't a loved one or friend to any of those who perished.

"Brienne invited me to one of the meetings when I first started. Wanted me to talk about overcoming loss and dealing with grief." He shrugs with a fond smile. "I'm sort of an honorary member now."

Coach West lost his wife to cancer several years ago. He would know all about what it's like to mourn someone. And I knew about the support group. Brienne Norcross, the owner of the Pittsburgh Titans, emailed me, Coen and Hendrix about it. I never replied or went to any meetings.

"I expect you at tomorrow's get-together," he says. I immediately close off, wanting to tell him to go to hell, but he adds, "If you want to keep your position on the second line, you *will* do this."

That pisses me off, but I'm polite when I say, "With all due respect, not sure it's fair to require something like that just to keep my job. I missed one practice."

"Your play has been substandard all season and you know it," Coach says, and gone is the affable man we all know and love. His tone is hard and unforgiving. "Now, one of the reasons I'm a great coach is because I can see beneath the surface and coax out the best in my players. You can sit there and tell me until you're blue in the face that you're okay, but something is weighing on you. If it's not the crash, my apologies. You'll still have a great time at the get-together. You'll know a lot of people. If it is the crash, you can thank me later for pushing you to get help."

"And if I don't go?" I ask, so I'm very clear.

"You'll go down to the third line until your play improves," he says simply. "You get a pass today for missing practice. Next time, you won't enjoy my visit."

"Didn't enjoy this one," I admit truthfully.

Rather than take offense, Coach West grins. "That means I'm doing my job then."

CHAPTER 2

Danica

"TRAVIS," I YELL up the stairs as I bend to pick up three pairs of his shoes from the living room. "Don't forget... I want two extra layers under your coat."

"I know," he calls back, his tone a low drawl of frustration that I'm micromanaging his wardrobe choices.

I smile and place the shoes on the staircase, each pair on a different tread. I'm almost gleeful at the idea of when he comes down, I'm going to make him carry them back up to his room. He hates making the trek up for some reason, despite the fact he has the energy of a thousand battery-packed bunnies.

Same as he hates to unload the dishwasher and roll the trash cans out to the curb.

I turn for the kitchen, intent on filling a travel mug with coffee when I hear his pounding feet on the stairs. Swiveling back that way, I meet him before he can reach the very bottom, pointing to the shoes. "You know the rules... no leaving your shoes in a place that is not your bedroom closet."

"Ugh," he groans in an overly dramatic fashion. "Can't I take them up tonight when we get back home?"

"No, you cannot." I point upward. "Upstairs. Now."

He mutters and grumbles but does as he's asked, because honest to God… he's such a great kid. I get a kick out of all these little battles as Travis ages and matures. The way he's pushing boundaries and rules is a rite of passage.

Or so my sister, Reba, assures me—she has a son of her own, although he's four years older than mine.

Just a few days ago, I was working on a grant proposal at the kitchen table while Travis finished his homework for the evening. He closed his math book and started to head upstairs so he could watch his allotted half hour of TV.

I didn't even look up from my work. "Hey, bud… do me a favor and load the dishwasher?"

"No way… that's your job," he said. "I unload and you load."

I lifted my head and appraised him. I had to bite my tongue not to laugh because he looked so earnest in his evaluation of how things work between a parent and a kid.

"No," I drawled, leveling him with a smile. "Your job is to do every chore you could ever imagine in this house. In exchange, I allow you to have a roof over your head and food in your belly. I merely happen to do a lot of it for you."

Travis rolled his eyes and then I did bust out laughing. But I pointedly jerked my head toward the dishwasher and said, "Go on... load it up for me. I've got more work to do."

And the biggest heart melt occurred when he walked not to the dishwasher but to me to kiss my cheek. "You're the best mom ever. Even if you make me do chores."

Travis hightails it up the stairs with his shoes in hand and I can't resist. "And don't just throw them in there," I yell up at him.

I hear the distinct thump of them being unceremoniously dumped and shake my head.

I'll give him a pass on that one because he's nine years old and the last thing I want to be considered is overbearing. After Mitch died, it was only natural to me to gather Travis in close, but sometimes I went overboard and almost proverbially suffocated him. Not with too much love, born of fear that I could lose him in the blink of an eye the way I lost my husband, but with rules and structure. I thought if I could control my environment, which included keeping Travis in a rigid box, I could keep him alive and safe.

It was only through intense counseling for me individually, Travis individually and then both of us together that I learned to loosen the reins I'd involuntarily contracted inward. It's a victory for me to be content he put his shoes in the closet, even if they're thrown in there without thought or care to keep it neat.

It's also a big deal for me to be able to let him go out and be a nine-year-old without my blanket of protection around him.

God, I know it's silly to think that if I'm not near him he's in danger. But for some reason, I went through a period where I thought Mitch dying in a plane crash was somehow my fault. It was fucked-up thinking, but therapy helped so much.

Doesn't mean that I still don't have my demons scratching to get out, though.

Travis hurtles back down the stairs. I wince because I realize one of his shoes is untied and I have a fleeting image of him falling on the stairs and breaking his neck, but I stuff it away. He reaches the bottom safely and I must have that look on my face... the one that says I'm in fear mode, even if it's brief.

It sucks the life out of me when my son sees it... recognizes it... and then throws his arms around my waist. At nine and with his dad's height, he's able to lay his head on my shoulder. "I love you, Mom."

"Love you too, kiddo," I whisper as I pull him in close. I relish these times, even if it's my basket full of crazy thinking that prompts it. I've been forewarned by

Reba that boys turn into monsters when they hit double digits, so I cherish this while it lasts.

"Come on," Travis says with excitement as he releases me. He rushes to the door and grabs his duffel bag with his hockey gear along with the stick propped against the wall.

He glances over his shoulder at me and the sun pouring in from the side pane of glass makes his blond hair shine. My heart catches because he looks so much like Mitch, right down to the lopsided grin I've loved for most of my life. It's as if I'm staring at his younger doppelgänger, back in the days when we'd go fishing together as little kids.

Travis dashes out the door and the illusion of my dead husband is broken. There's the inevitable punch of pain as the loss hits me—although it's not as strong as it once was—and I move on. I have an amazing son and far too much to be grateful for these days to wallow.

On the way to the outdoor ice rink, Travis chatters about the upcoming start of the youth hockey league. He was slated to begin last year but the plane crash derailed everything. We were both so out of it with grief and then all the ways our lives were disrupted financially, the start of the season passed by without me even realizing. When I mentioned it to Travis, he wasn't interested and my heart bled. He and Mitch had looked forward to Travis playing competitively, especially since the kid had been ice skating since he could walk.

But this year's different. When registration opened, Travis was beyond giddy about joining. I definitely had to tighten up my budget to afford it because hockey is expensive, but the smile on his face was worth it.

Today's just a fun day on the ice with some school friends to scrimmage. It was organized by one of the youth hockey moms whose son is in Travis's third grade class.

As we pull into the parking lot, Travis nearly jumps out of the car before I come to a full stop.

"Whoa there, buddy," I exclaim and he groans with frustration as he looks out the window.

"Mom... they're already on the ice." He looks over his shoulder at me plaintively, poised to throw the door open.

I give him my best mom look. "Give me ten seconds... geez."

He rolls his eyes, and I remind myself only half an hour ago he spontaneously hugged me with words of love. Reaching out, I ruffle his hair. "I'll pick you up at Mikey's house at four p.m. You can use his mom's phone to call me if you need anything—"

"I won't need anything."

"—or want me to pick you up early—"

"I won't want to be picked up early."

"—or because you miss me and want to hear the

sound of my voice."

Travis grins. "You're a drama queen, Mom."

Laughing, I nod toward the rink. "Get going, brat."

He leans backward and offers his cheek. I kiss it and then watch with misty eyes as he runs off to join his friends. He doesn't look back at me once but that's how it should be... a child filled with such exuberance that he can only see what's before him and not the pain of the past.

◆

STONE AND HARLOW are hosting this week's support get-together. Comprised of loved ones—whether by blood or heart ties—who lost someone in the crash, we've unofficially named our group *This Pucking Sucks.* It was formed by Brienne Norcross, owner of the Pittsburgh Titans, about two months after the disaster. She lost her brother when the plane went down and wasn't only grieving the loss of the team but a family member, like many of us.

The group was large when it first started. A lot of the widows and widowers stayed in the area for a while, but slowly, some moved away. Most of the players' wives were transient, having moved to Pittsburgh for their husband's jobs. Some—like me, though—had grown deeper roots.

Mitch moved here at eighteen to play with the Titans. I was only sixteen at that time and it was a miserable two years away from him, but I followed right along after high school graduation. You'd think that would've upset my parents, but to the contrary, they were supportive. They knew I wasn't sloughing off college to "just pursue a boy." They'd watched me and Mitch grow up together and turn from playmates to crushes to dating to falling in love.

I was accepted at Pitt and loved being a student, although admittedly, it wouldn't have been anywhere near as fulfilling without Mitch by my side. I moved in with him and life was blissful.

But then we got hit with the craziest of curveballs… I got pregnant halfway through my freshman year, which sort of put a wrinkle in our plans.

Pregnancy was the last thing we wanted at this young time in our lives, and needless to say, Mitch and I were shocked. I was knocked for a bigger loop when the day following my positive pregnancy test, Mitch came home with a huge diamond ring and proposed. We'd always talked about being soul mates and being together forever, but we never specifically talked about getting engaged, married or having kids. We'd been together for pretty much forever and so it was assumed we'd always continue to be together.

And yet, when he gallantly got down on one knee and presented a ring so outlandishly enormous and sparkly, I couldn't believe we hadn't been talking about those things forever because it felt so natural when I threw my arms around his neck and screamed, "Yes!"

The engagement was followed by a quick but beautiful wedding attended by our families and all the Titans. I quickly learned how to be a hockey wife, having Mitch gone for days at a time. I went through my pregnancy with him by my side as much as possible but there were a few appointments he missed because he was traveling. I'd recently turned nineteen when I gave birth to Travis and Mitch was able to be there. It's my fondest memory of him… the look on his face when he first held his son.

I was able to finish my freshman year at Pitt while pregnant, but after Travis was born, I never went back. Mitch and I decided it was better for me to be a full-time mom, which is a move I've never regretted once in my life.

Almost a decade later and I'm still here in Pittsburgh, even though many of the other wives, fiancées and girlfriends have drifted away. We still keep in contact and even have some support group Zoom calls where we'll all have drinks as we catch up on each other's lives.

But almost every Sunday, *This Pucking Sucks* gets together. Not everyone can make it every time. One weekend we'll have a group of ten and the next it's only two of us meeting for lunch. And it's not only the wives or significant others… it's any family member or friend who shares the same grief we do after losing a Titans member.

Today is special because the team is in town and tomorrow's a home game, so Stone and Harlow volunteered to host at their place. Stone lost his brother, Brooks, in the crash and came up from the minors to take his place on the team.

They live in a beautiful, renovated warehouse a few blocks north of the river, just a short drive from the arena. I'm able to find a parallel spot two blocks down. As I walk toward the condo entrance, I come upon Cannon West getting out of his car. He locks it, pockets the key and nods at the bag in my hand. "What did you bring?"

"A pasta salad. You?"

He holds up a grocery bag. "Mini Snickers."

Laughing, I step into him for a side-arm hug. "That works for me."

The Titans' coach comes to some of our meetings and the very first one he was at, he insisted we call him Cannon. He didn't lose anyone in the crash, but he shows up to support us as someone who has known loss in his life. We chitchat all the way into the building and up the flight of stairs to the second level where Stone and Harlow's unit is on the end. There's already the sound of laughter coming down the hall, and I do love to hear that. Cannon and I share a smile.

Before he reaches the door, he asks, "How's the new job going?"

Excitement and pleasure well up within me. "Oh my gosh… so well. I mean, there's so much to learn but Brienne is a patient teacher."

"She couldn't have picked a better person to head her brother's foundation," Cannon murmurs.

His compliment warms me because I struggle with impostor syndrome every day. From the moment Travis was born, my job was to be his mom. Mitch made enough money I didn't have to work and I never went back to college. My career was to make my son's and husband's lives as good as they could be.

It's been a bit of a struggle since Mitch died—not just emotionally, but financially. Brienne's job offer for me to serve as the director of a new charity she named after her brother threw me for a loop. It came at the perfect time because I was very close to throwing in the towel and heading home to Massachusetts, where my parents were more than happy to take Travis and me in.

But now I have purpose and Brienne is showing me that I can be both a mom and a working woman. She's helping me realize that I can take care of my son in all ways and it's empowering. After the last ten months, it feels good to be capable.

CHAPTER 3

Camden

I KNOW ALL the people here and yet I'm decidedly uncomfortable. When I arrive at Stone and Harlow's, Harlow greets me at the door. She latches onto my arm and drags me into the kitchen.

"Food and drink. Get going," she orders. "Then come join us in the living room."

I load up a plate of various foods that people brought. There's a bowl of Snickers and I'm guessing that's from Coach. While I know he comes to some of these get-togethers, I'm certain he's here today to make sure I showed up.

I didn't bring anything because Coach West didn't tell me to, but Harlow assured me it was okay.

In the living room, I end up by the doors to an outdoor balcony talking to Hendrix and Coen—fitting that the Lucky Three are grouped together.

You'd think such an experience would bond us tightly, but oddly, the three of us don't talk about the crash. Sure, we supported each other in the weeks that followed—saying our goodbyes as we attended multiple funerals and memorials. But eventually, we all sort of moved on, occupied by the easy escape of continuing the season with a new team.

Hendrix and I were able to focus on hockey as the team was rebuilt. Coen, unfortunately, went off the deep end for a while and eventually was suspended. Luckily, he got his shit together over the summer and now he's back, in love and playing better than ever.

I realize their girlfriends aren't with them and I wonder if this is open to only those who lost loved ones. Harlow is present, but she lives here and Stone is hosting. Plus, she was best friends with his brother, Brooks.

"Where's Stevie?" I ask Hendrix.

"Working," he says, dipping a cucumber slice into some kind of dip.

"And Tillie?" I ask Coen.

"She wanted to come but had to get back to Coudersport. She's running a local art show."

Well, that answers that. Apparently, it's open to wives and girlfriends. I notice Brienne here but not Drake, although he's probably spending time with his boys.

It's more than just players who were lost on the plane. I see Boyd Frazer—his wife Jessie was one of our trainers. He's local to Pittsburgh, and I haven't seen him in a while.

There are a handful of widows here. Maggie Pearsall, who was married to Cory, one of our defensemen. She's still in the area because she's local to Pittsburgh as well.

Kateryna Kozar, married to our first-line center, Maksym, is here, both of them from Ukraine. I've seen Kateryna around at some of the postgame parties and knew she'd stayed in Pittsburgh on a work visa with their two daughters.

And Danica Brandt, married to our second-line left-winger, Mitch. It was announced at the Titans' Christmas party that she'd be running a new charity Brienne created and named after her brother called the Adam Norcross Charitable Foundation. It's a fascinating concept and one I'd not thought of before. Its main goal will be to aid dependents of professional athletes and support staff who have either died or become incapacitated and can't play anymore. It's not only for hockey, and it's not just for the United States but a global foundation, and Danica will be running it.

I was happy to hear this and it was good to catch up with her at the Christmas party week before last. Obviously, I know some of the loved ones better than others, but Danica I know well. Mitch and I played on the same line, so we hung out a lot more than some of the other players. Through the years playing together, I've been to dinners at their house, met their parents and other family members who visited and once went with him to visit Travis's first grade class to read storybooks to the kids.

I've kept in loose contact with Danica. She still comes to some of the games, after-parties and team functions as Brienne makes sure to invite all the former team family members. At first, Danica didn't come as I imagine she was lost to her grief. But this season, I've seen her a handful of times and it's been nice to see her smiles getting bigger as time moves on.

Watching Danica now, I don't know exactly how the past year has been for her. I'm somewhat surprised she stayed in the area since it's just her and Travis. I know all her family—and Mitch's, for that matter—are in Massachusetts.

Of course, I never bothered to ask specifically her reasons for not returning home. Our talks have been short, some just in passing at events, but she seems to be doing well as far as I can tell.

Same as me.

"Dude." A hand clamps down on my shoulder and I turn to see Stone. "Coach said you were coming. Glad you're here."

He's clearly surprised by my presence. It's been ten and a half months since the crash and I've never been to one of these nor have I talked to Stone about the crash other than to extend my condolences about his brother.

"Coach sort of mandated it," I say.

Stone's hand falls away and he nods. "Because you missed practice yesterday."

I shrug as I glance at Coen and Hendrix, who stare back at me with no judgment and apparent understanding. But how can they comprehend anything when I don't even know what's happening to me?

"Look," he says, drawing my attention. "You know all these people. No one's a stranger. Nothing to fear. Go hang out and enjoy yourself."

"Fine," I say with a pointed stare, a half-smile on my face so he knows I'm teasing. "But if anyone asks me to share or get touchy-feely, I'm out of here."

Stone tips his head back and laughs. "It's not like that, my man. And there's not a person in this room that you couldn't trust with your sorrow. Everyone understands it. They'd all have your back."

Okay… feeling awkward. I didn't come to discuss my feelings. "I'm good, Stone. Truly."

"Well, I'm not." I blink in surprise at the admission because, for months, he's seemed to be loving life. "Not a day goes by that I don't think about my brother. Not a day goes by that I don't feel guilty for being here on this team when he's not."

"Same," Coen says quietly and Hendrix nods.

I'm rendered speechless by these three men casually talking about continued struggles from the crash. They seem so well-adjusted.

Same as me.

Coen smiles. "It takes a long time to heal from the loss of a loved one. You and I... we lost lots of them on that day. If you need to talk, I'm always here for you. But to ease your mind, this is a social get-together. More camaraderie than anything."

My gaze cuts to Coach West. That's not the impression he gave me but hanging out with people I like doesn't sound so bad. I'm a social guy by nature. Coach is deep in discussion with Brienne about something and it makes me wonder if they're discussing my missed practice. Not really something that would be brought to the attention of the team's owner but Brienne is closely involved with her players.

"Camden." A soft voice behind me has me turning—Danica Brandt. She grins and steps in, arms spread wide for a hug. "It's so good to see you."

I pull her in with one arm since my other hand is occupied with my plate. "Twice in less than two weeks. Must be my lucky day."

Danica laughs, gives an extra squeeze and I release her so she steps back. I notice the guys have meandered off, leaving us alone.

"I'm glad you came," she says, her gentle brown eyes smiling with easy affection.

I nod toward Coen and Hendrix who are catching up

with Boyd. "Guess better late than never, huh?"

She glances over at them and then back to me. "This is Hendrix's first time. Coen's been to a few gatherings this season." That surprises me. I assumed when I saw them both here that they were regulars. She must read that on my face because she adds, "I talked to Hendrix about it at the Christmas party. It came up in conversation and I pushed him to come."

Danica and I talked for a bit at that same gathering and she never mentioned this support group. I mean... I knew about it.

Vaguely.

But since I was never interested in something like this, I sort of pushed it away. I wonder if she could tell that about me, or maybe it came up in innocent conversation with Hendrix so she made the invite.

Regardless, I find myself admitting, "Coach made me come."

Danica Brandt is an incredibly beautiful woman. One of those pretty, girl-next-door types with glossy, caramel-colored hair that complements her olive skin tone and doe-brown eyes. Those eyes soften even more with an insider's knowledge that I might be having struggles because of the crash.

I brace for her push but instead she sweeps a fond glance around the room before she looks at me again. "This is absolutely a safe place for you, not only to talk about your experiences, but also to be silent if you want. Sometimes simply being around like-minded people is enough. So my advice to you? Enjoy reconnecting with old friends."

And just like that, a massive release sweeps through my body and what had been previously pent-up tension floats away. I hadn't realized how scared I was to actually be in an environment where I might have to talk about the crash and my feelings. And while Coen basically said the same thing to me two minutes ago, for some reason, I trust it more coming from Danica.

She sees the relief in my expression, telling me how intuitive she is and gives me a tiny nudge with her elbow. "Easy as pie."

I decide to take her advice and use this time to connect. While we'd talked at the party, it was in a group of people and I didn't get one-on-one. It's been a few months since I've been able to catch up. "What's Travis doing today?"

Her smile breaks wide, revealing two dimples I'm not sure I've ever noticed before, or if I had, they hadn't made an impression. I'm momentarily dazzled. "He starts youth hockey next week so he's at the rink today with his buddies getting in some practice. He's so excited, it's all he's talked about for days."

"Going to be a winger like his dad," I say assuredly, knowing that won't offend but not sure if it will sadden.

I've seen Travis skate, and he's got the same speed and agility Mitch had.

Danica's smile doesn't lessen but I see a brief flash of grief. "That's what he says. He's nervous, though, since he didn't play last year. All the other boys have an entire season on him."

"He's got enough talent to make up for it," I assure her. Again, I've seen the kid skate and handle a puck, goofing off with his dad and some of us on the team enough to know where he's going. "If he wants some extra practice, though, I'm glad to help him out."

"Really?" she asks, the drawl of surprise and gratitude in her voice surprising me. It's the sound of someone who doesn't ask for help often and seems shocked when it's offered.

A flash of guilt runs through me. Have I done enough for her after Mitch died? Did I do enough for any of the loved ones?

"Absolutely. I'd love to help him out. We've got a home game tomorrow and an away game on Wednesday. I could do Thursday afternoon. What time does he get out of school?"

Danica seems dumbstruck for a moment but recovers. "I pick him up at three."

"I'll come by at three thirty to get him and have him home by five thirty. Is that good?"

She nods effusively. "Yes, that would be great. He'll

be so excited. You know I play in the driveway with him, letting him slap plastic pucks at me, but I can't give him pointers the way his dad could have."

I laugh. "You know your fair share of hockey, but I admit… I am a professional."

She laughs in return. "I'll text you our new address."

My brows draw inward. "You moved?"

"Um… yeah," she says, tucking her hair behind her ear. "That house was too big for us, you know."

I do know. They lived in a monstrous custom-built home in a gated community but I wonder if maybe it held too many memories. Regardless, I can see the subject makes her a little tense so I don't delve.

"I get it," I assure her.

"Listen," she says hesitantly and steps in a bit closer. "There's something I did want to ask your help with."

I dip my head closer to compensate for the softness in her tone. "What's that?"

"I'm not good at soliciting but as the director of the new foundation, part of my job is keeping it funded."

"You want money? I'm happy to donate."

She grins at me, dimples popping and fuck… I shouldn't think that makes her prettier. "Yes, I'll take your money but that wasn't what I was going to ask for. I'm trying to secure a big corporate sponsor and the CEO is throwing his sixteen-year-old son a birthday party. He's hinted—quite strongly—that he'd join as a sponsor if I can show him some Titans love."

"Aagh," I drawl with a knowing lift of my chin. "Sure… what can I do?"

"Come to the party with me. Maybe a signed jersey for the kid. Take some pictures with the others, sign a few autographs. It's Saturday and I know it's between home games so it's your time off… it's a big ask and—"

"I'm there," I say, somewhat surprising myself. I cherish my downtime and hanging out at a teen's birthday party isn't my idea of relaxing. "Find out how many kids are there and I'll snag jerseys for all of them."

"Oh no," she says, shaking her head and holding out her palms. "I can't ask you to pay for that."

Chuckling, I put my hand on her shoulder and squeeze. "I'm not paying for it. Brienne will be, but this is her foundation so I know she'll be glad to. You've got to think bigger picture, Dani."

Her nickname just slips out, a testament that I knew this woman far better than I even remembered. Years of playing on the same line with Mitch, dozens of team events, parties, birthday celebrations. Many of her friends call her that.

Mitch did.

"I know," she says with mock self-loathing. "I told you I hate asking for stuff. I don't like being a bother to people."

"Trust me." My hand falls away but I give her an

encouraging smile. "Asking rich people for donations or sponsorships or time in helping isn't a bother to them. It's the price of being wealthy. You need to lose that fear."

Her smile is wry. "I'll remember your advice."

Coach West approaches and when Danica sees him, her smile brightens to full wattage. "Cannon." She jabs him playfully with her elbow. "And I didn't ask you earlier, but I heard you've got a new sweetheart. I need to meet her."

"You will," he says, the husky affection in his voice sounding very right for him. He's had a tough road with losing his wife to cancer but he seems to have found something amazing with Ava.

Coach's gaze comes to me. "Glad you could make it."

As if I had a choice.

I smile, giving a half shrug. "Thought I'd see what all the fuss was about." My gaze drops to Danica. "It's been nice to connect with old friends."

"Very nice," she agrees. "Now, I'm going to catch up with some others. I'll see you Thursday. I can't wait to tell Travis."

"See you then."

After Danica moves off, Coach West turns to me. "See... I told you this would be a nice time."

"No," I reply with an emphatic shake of my head.

"You most certainly didn't say that."

He snorts and glances back toward Danica. "Nice to rekindle friendships, huh?"

"I guess. Travis is starting youth hockey next week. Going to help him out. And I got suckered into helping out with securing a sponsor for the foundation."

Coach claps me on the shoulder. "Trust me… we're all going to get suckered by Danica into doing something at some point."

I watch as Danica laughs in her conversation with one of the wives. "Well, she needs to up her courage to ask. She's struggling with that a bit."

"She'll figure it out," he muses thoughtfully. "She's done a remarkable job of keeping things together for her and Travis after the crash. She's had a tough time but still going strong."

"Yeah." I glance around the room again, and really take everyone in. No one looks sad. Some are in deep conversations, others laugh the way Danica does. But this isn't a melancholy gathering of people sharing their pain.

It seems like people have healed or are healing well. I wonder how much is because of this group of peers that leaned on one another from the beginning.

Would I not have nightmares about planes killing me had I done something early on?

Guess I'll never know but I've fulfilled my obligation to Coach West by attending this gathering.

CHAPTER 4

Danica

TAPPING OUT A few more keystrokes, I finish the email and hit Send. My eyes drift from the desktop screen to the photograph of Travis displayed prominently. I take a moment to revel in the joy that radiates from his smile. It was taken this past Christmas and he had just opened up the brand-new hockey skates he'd wanted.

Christmas was a mixed bag of emotions because it was the first one without Mitch. However, the natural feelings of magic, wonder and excitement of the holiday helped to curb the sadness that he wasn't there to celebrate with us. On top of that, Travis had a bit of an emotional growth milestone that I wasn't expecting. A few weeks before Christmas, he told me he had something serious to discuss and I remember my heart beating madly, wondering what it could be.

Was he getting bullied at school?

Was he perhaps interested in a girl? I thought he was probably too young at nine years old, but you never know. I know Mitch certainly wasn't interested in me in that way at that age.

I imagined the worst and when it finally came, it was pretty bad.

Travis sat across the kitchen table from me. "Is Santa Claus real? And please be honest with me. Some kids at school say he's not."

I was wholly unprepared for that. In a million years, it never occurred to me that he would ask that question. With everything that had happened over the past ten months, doubts about Santa Claus were not at the top of my agenda for things I would need to handle as a single parent.

I'm sure I flubbed it badly, but the one thing Mitch and I always promised ourselves as parents is that we would be honest with our kid. I explained to Travis about the myth, the tradition and the magic of St. Nick. I stumbled over a half-hearted attempt to downplay our deception by calling it a gift of magic we were handing to him.

Travis appreciated the honesty but he was also a little pissed.

A smile plays on my lips as I remember him crossing his arms over his chest. "I can't believe you lied to me all those years about Santa Claus."

He even lifted his hands and made air quotes with his fingers when he said the words *Santa Claus* before tucking them back again in a defensive posture.

My eyes roam over the photograph of my son holding up his new hockey skates, his smile beaming so broadly. It fills me with hope and promise that everything will be okay in our lives. With the gift of those skates, he got over his snit that we had lied to him and had a pretty damn good Christmas, despite the fact Mitch wasn't with us.

I glance around my small office here at the Titans' arena. Brienne set me up in this building to run the foundation as she's doing the majority of her work here—running her family's empire of business holdings, including Norcross Bank. She stepped into her brother's shoes to run the hockey team after losing Adam when the plane went down. While she has a downtown headquarters across the river for all her family holdings, she likes working at the arena in Adam's old office.

Even though she's pulling back from team management and handing the reins to the general manager, Callum Derringer, I suspect she likes being on this side of the river because of our esteemed goalie, Drake McGinn. They outed themselves to the world as a couple a few months ago and I've seen him on more than one occasion sauntering into her office to hang out or eat lunch with her at her desk. They are as cute as cute can be.

It's weird having an office. It's weird having a commute. Being a stay-at-home mom all those years meant I didn't have to battle rush-hour traffic. These days, after Travis gets on the bus to head to school, I make the drive across the river via the 40th Street Bridge to the arena. Even though I work only about five miles from my house, it can take me upward of twenty-five minutes from my Lawrenceville neighborhood to get here.

I don't work every day at the arena by the grace of Brienne. I like to pick Travis up from school so I can maintain some semblance of the normal life he had before his dad died. Oftentimes, I'll work from home to cut out some of the driving and I know very well how lucky I am to have a job that allows that level of flexibility.

And I know how blessed I am to have a job that lets me take care of my son.

So far, working for Brienne as the director of the foundation has been beyond my wildest dreams. It's tremendously difficult work, mainly because I don't know what the hell I'm doing. But Brienne has set up her fair share of charitable organizations and she's walking every step of the way with me. She essentially tells me what to do and then I execute it, which is a great way to learn from the ground up.

Before I can turn my attention to the next item on my to-do list—which is to comb through an Excel database Brienne provided that lists donors who have contributed to a variety of past fundraisers—none other than the boss lady breezes into my office.

As always, she's the epitome of chic and haute couture. Today she's wearing a red, white and black plaid skirt that comes to her knees, paired with a fitted black turtleneck. She has on black tights and a pair of high-heeled Mary Janes, giving her somewhat of a sexy schoolgirl vibe. Her pale blond hair is pulled back into a classic chignon, and her makeup is flawless, including her signature red lips that give her a fifties vibe.

Handing me a folder across my desk, she says, "Those are the résumés of the candidates for seats on the board of directors. I know most of them, but I want you to call and interview each one. It will be good practice for you."

I place the folder on my desk and give a surreptitious swipe of my hands on my skirt because that made my hands sweaty. While I'm confident enough in myself to know I'm smart and capable, I know the people she has inside that folder are all successful businesspeople in a completely different class from myself. I don't mean that in a self-deprecating way. It's just that Brienne is a multibillionaire and the people she associates with, while not in that stratosphere of wealth, are pretty damn rich and accomplished. That also means they can be bold, assertive and bullheaded. She's already warned me that I might be up against people who are borderline rude in my dealings because they don't have time for niceties. And now she wants me to cut my teeth on some of those people.

"Not a problem," I say brightly, even though my stomach turns a bit. I remind myself that I need this job and I'm going to do whatever it takes to make it work. I will make it into a career so I can always take care of Travis.

Brienne winks at me. "I have all the confidence in the world, Danica. I know I picked the one and only woman for this job."

That indeed fortifies my confidence.

"Got plans for lunch?" she asks. "I was going to order a salad to be delivered. You're more than welcome to join me in my office?"

"As lovely as that sounds, I'm going to meet your future sister-in-law at Primanti's."

Brienne's eyes light from within, softening into true fondness. "I'm so happy you and Kiera hit it off."

Kiera is Drake's sister who moved here in October to help him take care of his boys when he travels. I also notice Brienne didn't deny that they'll be related by marriage one day and that makes me wonder if they're talking about tying the knot.

"How about you join us?" I suggest. "You know Primanti's is far better than a salad."

Brienne laughs, wagging a finger at me. "I will not be

tempted by that deliciousness. But I truly don't have time to go anywhere. I've got a meeting at one o'clock."

I glance at my watch and see that I need to head out if I'm going to meet Kiera on time. I stand from my desk and reach into my drawer for my purse. "I'll be thinking of you while you eat your rabbit food."

I come around my desk and grab my wool coat off the back of the door. As I'm shrugging into it, Brienne says, "You should just go home for the rest of the afternoon after lunch. No sense in coming back for such a short time before you have to leave to pick up Travis."

It's on the tip of my tongue to assure her I don't mind coming back, even though she's correct. It would only be for about half an hour. Brienne has chastised me on more than one occasion to stop fighting her when she makes legitimate offers like this.

So I nod and say, "I think I'll do that."

◆

KIERA ARRIVED EARLIER than our arranged time so when I walk in, she's already at the table with our food. Since Brienne introduced us back in November, this has been one of our favorite lunch spots.

Apparently, there was an episode when she first moved here that prompted Brienne to introduce us. Kiera got quite sick while Drake was at an away game and was in a precarious situation because she was too weak to care for the three boys. Brienne was more than happy to help her out but realized that Kiera needed a bit more of a support system. Brienne knew me before the crash since I'd been with the team going on almost a decade. She asked me if I'd mind befriending Kiera, which I didn't, and it turned out I met somebody who, in a very short time, has become a dear friend. We have so much in common but mainly the thing that binds us together is our shared sense of humor.

Which can be irreverent at times.

I wave at Kiera as I move toward the corner table and she gives me a tiny lift of her chin, mid-bite of her sandwich. When I plop down in the chair, she mumbles a greeting around tender slices of pastrami, layered with french fries and coleslaw.

I have the same sandwich before me and I immediately start to unwrap it.

After she swallows, wipes her mouth and takes a sip of her water. "Girl... I love what you did with your hair."

I tug on a lock nervously. I've always worn my dark brown hair in one length just past my shoulders but I decided to have some layers cut into it. I'm not sure why... maybe a desire to feel a little different.

"It doesn't look stupid?"

Kiera rolls her eyes at me. "Not even going to justify that with an answer. Someone as obnoxiously beautiful as you has no right to ask such stupid questions."

I snort and pull a french fry free from my sandwich, waving it at her. "Easy for you to say, Miss You Should Have Been a Supermodel."

"Okay, okay… I get it. We're both stunningly beautiful. Which also makes me wonder why we're both depressingly single."

Any other person in the world, including every single one of my family members, would have never said that out loud to me. It's been ten months since Mitch died and no one has ever mentioned the possibility of me dating again.

Finding someone else to love again.

Possibly remarrying.

Not that I'm thinking about that at all. In fact, it seriously has never crossed my mind. I'm so busy trying to give Travis a good life and work a new career, dating and relationships are far enough down on my list of priorities I can't even really see them.

But I love Kiera for not being afraid to say something like that to me. Because sure, one day, I fully expect I will date again.

I imagine I will probably fall in love. While Mitch was my soul mate, I don't believe that we're only allowed one in this lifetime. I love Kiera's courage not to tippy-toe around such things.

"First, you're single because you won't date," I point out.

Kiera's eyes sparkle. "Dating's for romantics. I just want to have a good time. Something super casual with a stud of a man. What's your excuse?"

"I don't have time to date," I say, picking up my sandwich, poised to take a bite. "What's your excuse in not finding a stud of a man to have a good time with?"

Kiera cocks an eyebrow. "Oh, I don't know, how about the fact I have a full-time job and look after three nephews?"

"Oh yeah." I grin mischievously as if that thought had not occurred to me. "I guess we're in the same boat."

I sink my teeth into that first sumptuous bite and groan with satisfaction. Whoever decided on this combination of fries and coleslaw as part of a sandwich is spectacularly brilliant.

Kiera eyeballs me over the top of hers held in both hands. "Booty calls are way easier than dating. A little wham-bam-thank-you-ma'am is truly all we need."

I nearly choke on the food in my mouth and have to take a few sips of water. "Booty calls? Seriously... who even says that?"

"Me," Kiera replies proudly. "I think booty call is a fabulous term."

"Well, that's not exactly something I would understand. Mitch was my one and only."

Kiera's mouth drops open as if she can't believe such a thing is possible but then snaps it shut. "That's right.

He was your first boyfriend so that makes him your first…"

Her words trail off but I understand where she's going. "Yep. I have never been with another man other than Mitch. Thus, I've never had a booty call."

"Did Mitch, like, ever come home from the arena for a quickie?"

"Yeah." I sigh wistfully. "He did."

"Then that was technically a booty call. A monogamous one, mind you, but a booty call all the same."

Laughing, I shake my head. "I feel so progressive."

Kiera looks at me, deadpan. "Well… I have perfected the art of non-monogamous booty calls so if you ever want advice, let me know."

This piques my curiosity and I ignore my sandwich. "Have you had booty calls since coming to Pittsburgh?"

"Yes, I have," Kiera states with a proud lift of her chin and a satisfied twinkle in her eye. "And it was fucking awesome."

"I want to be like you when I grow up," I quip as I pick up my sandwich again.

Talk of hookups subsides and we chitchat about life and all the things. Kiera's one of those women I could sit and talk to for hours. Our conversational topics range from sex to world politics to cheesy movies. We spend a lot of time comparing notes on raising boys since she's so involved with her nephews.

When we're finished, we gather our trash and deposit it in the bin. Outside, I button my coat and turn my collar up against the chill. The sky is dark gray with the smell of snow coming.

"Let's get the boys together soon," Kiera says. "Maybe Travis can do an overnight."

"He'd love that." I glance at my wristwatch. "I've got to get going to make the carpool line. He'll be furious if I'm late since he's going skating this afternoon with Camden."

"Really?" Kiera drawls, a blond eyebrow cocking up high and a quirk on her lips that tells me she's making something of this that isn't there.

"He's a friend. I've known him a long time and Travis knows him. He offered to help out since Travis is starting youth hockey next week."

"That's awesome," she says as we walk down the block toward the parking garage. She hooks an arm through mine. "I have noticed that Camden is unbelievably handsome."

She's not wrong about that. He's got dark blond hair he wears longish with crazy flips all over. It looks like he just got out of bed, but in a stylish way. He wears facial scruff all the time and I'm not sure I've ever seen him clean-shaven.

Maybe at Mitch's funeral.

That douses me with cold water, the combination of

considering how handsome Camden is but with the blunt reminder my husband died less than a year ago.

It's almost as if Kiera senses my mixed feelings. She squeezes her arm around mine reassuringly. "There's absolutely nothing wrong with you admiring a man for his looks."

I sigh and squeeze her back as we move along the sidewalk. "I know. And I love you to death for trying to normalize those things for me. Not one other person in my life has ever broached the idea that there could be something for me after Mitch. And I'm not saying that's Camden... just thank you for reiterating there's nothing wrong with moving on."

"There's not. Besides, you're not moving away from Mitch. He'll always be a part of your life. Maybe consider it, like, you're opening the door to add to your current life."

"I'm not ready for that quite yet."

"But there will be a time when you are," she reminds me.

I stop and face her. "How do I know when it's appropriate?"

She shrugs. "I expect you'll know in your heart."

That's far too vague to help but I also think she's probably right. Regardless, it's not on my agenda at the moment. Not out of respect to Mitch or what we had—I know he'd expect me to find happiness, even with someone else.

Right now, I've got too many things going on to consider a romantic relationship.

CHAPTER 5

Camden

DANICA AND TRAVIS live in the suburb of Lawrence-ville in a pretty redbrick row house with black trim around the windows. While the neighborhood is nice, well maintained, and in a safe area, it is a gigantic step down from the home they owned in Edgeworth, which is one of the most affluent communities in the Pittsburgh area.

I'm able to find a parallel spot a few houses down from hers. If I had to guess by looking at the outside, she lost about three thousand square feet as well. Danica mentioned their other house was too big for the two of them, which I'm not sure I buy. She and Mitch built that massive house with the idea of having it as a social hub for Travis as he got older. There was an incredible game room in the basement and a beautiful pool for summer fun. Mitch and Danica always envisioned their house as the place for Travis and all his buddies to hang out.

I jog up the five steps to the top of the stoop and

knock on the door. Within moments, Danica opens it. She's in a pair of dress pants in dark charcoal with a blue satin blouse. Her feet are bare but it looks like I caught her after her workday. Her makeup is subtle but it's really not needed when those dimples are the only thing you see when she smiles. "Hey... come on in. It's freezing outside."

I wipe my feet on the outdoor mat and step into the small foyer. As she closes the door behind me, Danica says, "We just got home. Travis is upstairs getting changed. You want something to drink?" I follow her through the living room to the kitchen. "I can make you some coffee."

Shoving my hands in my pockets, I look around their home. "I'm good."

It had been a long time since I'd been to Danica and Mitch's Edgeworth house but I can immediately tell that none of the furniture I'm seeing is from their former home.

"This is a nice place." I bring my gaze back to Danica as she pulls a couple of bottles of water from the fridge. "Definitely more convenient for your new job at the arena."

Danica nods. "That's a plus but it's actually more convenient to Travis's school. With me working now, it's nice that he can take the bus if needed."

"He goes to a private school, right?"

She puts the water in a small drawstring satchel and tosses in an apple from a bowl on the counter. "Harrington and it's wonderful. Travis has excelled there."

I move closer to a bookshelf with knickknacks and picture frames. I peruse the various shots, most of which are of Travis, when Danica comes to stand beside me. I shoot her a glance as her gaze roams over them with a fond smile.

Focusing on one, I point to it. It's of a boy and girl standing in a backyard covered in mud as they grin at the camera. The little boy is missing his front tooth. "Is that Mitch?"

Danica laughs. "Yeah... he was probably about seven in that picture. I was only five. We were catching earthworms so we could go fishing."

That shocks me and I look closer at the photo.

And yeah, that's Danica. "Were y'all neighbors or something?"

"Yup. Our backyards butted up against each other's and there was a big hole in the chain-link fence. We would always slip through and play in each other's backyards. Our moms were good friends, passing recipes over the fence type of thing. Mitch's dad would take us fishing and we did everything together, particularly in the summers. We happened to live in a neighborhood that was mostly older, retired folks so we were the only kids within a several-block radius. We had no choice but to be friends."

Laughing, I turn to face her. "Please tell me you got Mitch to play dolls with you."

Danica laughs and shakes her head. "Mitch lucked out. I was the classic tomboy."

I sort of knew that Danica and Mitch had dated in high school but I didn't realize they'd known each other far longer. That's a pretty neat story.

I give another quick look at the photo before grinning at her. "Dating since the tender age of five years old."

Danica snorts and turns from the bookcase. "Hardly. We were buddies for many, many years. Mitch didn't look at me like I was a girl until I turned fifteen. That's when the braces came off, the acne cleared up and my boobs finally started to develop. I was a late bloomer."

I bark out a laugh, imagining a funny image of Mitch one day walking into a room and seeing Danica for the first time as a young woman. He probably was wondering what the hell had happened to her. She probably flashed those dimples at him and it was all over.

"By the way," I say as she grabs the satchel, presumably to give to Travis, "I got the information you texted me and all the jerseys have been ordered. I'll have them in hand on Saturday morning."

"I cannot thank you enough for doing that," she breathes out. "I think you'll pretty much guarantee me the sponsorship."

"I don't mind helping at all," I assure her.

"Do you want to meet me there?"

She's talking about the birthday party I agreed to go to with her so she can hopefully secure a big corporate sponsorship for the foundation. Brienne came through for me and managed to get eleven Camden Poe jerseys that I can hand out and sign at the party.

"How about I pick you up?" I suggest, trying to suppress a laugh. "It's supposed to snow and no offense but men drive better than women."

Danica's eyes go round, her mouth drops open and she backhands me in the stomach. "Wow... I had no clue you were so sexist."

I maintain a straight face. "I'm just saying... if you look at the statistics—"

She puts her hands on her hips and glares at me. "I'll have you know I was born and raised in Massachusetts and I guarantee you I can drive as well as you can in the snow."

There's no holding back the laughter and I lift my palms in peace. "Fine, fine, fine. I've been put in my place."

Which I really haven't. I only offered the ride in case she preferred to carpool, but I didn't want her to feel obligated. That was a good way to do it and I never once had a hesitation over teasing her. That's a testament to my knowing her and I think I sort of forgot that we had a decent friendship over the years before Mitch died.

Danica rolls her eyes at me, her lips quirking upward.

"Shoot me a text with the address and what time you want me there."

"Will do," she says, then turns toward the foyer as the sound of thundering footsteps from above grabs our attention.

Travis comes flying down the stairs, skids across the wood floor and careens into the door before turning our way.

Danica moves to him, handing over the satchel. "I packed you some water and a snack."

"Mom," he drawls in slight annoyance. "I don't need that."

"But you'll take it anyway," she chides as she kisses him on the head. He tries to pull away, and I expect he's at that age where parental affection is "gross."

Travis shoots me a shy glance.

"You remember Camden, don't you?" Danica asks.

I hold out my fist. "'Course he does. I think I last saw you at our game against the Vipers in early November, right?"

Danica, Travis and several other widows and kids came to the game for a special remembrance ceremony between the first and second periods.

Travis taps his fist against mine. "You played a great

game. Got an assist."

I blink in surprise that he'd know such a thing. I don't even remember how I played that game off the top of my head.

"I like memorizing statistics," Travis says.

"My kid is a whiz with numbers," Danica says proudly, causing Travis to flush with embarrassment.

"Okay, whiz kid. Let's get going. Drills wait for no one."

Travis runs to the door, shoves the snack bag his mom gave him into a hockey duffel and slings it over his shoulder. He looks back at me expectantly.

My gaze moves to Danica and she rests her hand on my forearm. "Thank you again for doing this."

"Anytime," I say.

♦

TRAVIS HAS NATURAL talent and I suppose it's in his DNA. I reserved some private ice time at a local complex that has four different rinks. I also brought small cones and set them up for him to do skating and puck-handling drills.

The most recent one has a long line of ten cones spaced about three feet apart. The goal is for Travis to move the puck left to right and back again through the cones as he skates over them.

So far, he's done three rounds and his time has improved with each pass. He's flawless around the cones.

I glance at my watch. "We need to get going, buddy. I don't want you to be late for dinner."

Travis skates to the starting point. "Can I go again?"

"Fine," I drawl, as if I'm put out, but I'm impressed he wants to keep going. I reset the timer on my watch. "Once more. Ready. Set. Go."

Travis takes off and I depress the button that starts the second hand ticking. He maneuvers the puck through the cones with a fluid grace that's impressive to watch on a nine-year-old. When he reaches the end, I stop the timer and call out the result.

Travis pumps his fist because he's almost a full second faster.

"That was fantastic," I praise as I bend to pick up the nearest cone. "That's a great drill to keep practicing. It sharpens your reflexes and also helps you improve your bursts of speed."

"Can I try it just one more time, Camden? I know I can beat it again."

I groan inside because I'm truly ready to go but the excitement on his face plays me for the sucker I am. "Okay. But this is the absolute last time."

"Yes," he cries out jubilantly and skates back to the starting point.

I don't think the kid can beat his last time because it was pretty good and I know he has to be getting tired.

But damn if he doesn't surprise me when he shaves off another half second. He skates over and I turn my watch so he can see.

His eyes light up and he says, "Well, scratch my back with a hacksaw."

I'm startled by that phrase and my eyes snap to his. It's something Mitch would've said.

It's something Mitch *did* say, and often.

Stolen from one of the old Titans' radio announcers who had a bunch of great one-liners that made absolutely no sense. The announcer would yell them out after a goal and they're funny as hell. That announcer retired years ago but Mitch loved repeating those lines whenever something amazing happened.

He must have taught Travis all of them and it's a bit of a punch to the gut—a mixture of sadness wrapped in delight that Mitch is living on within his son.

I clear my throat of the emotion. "Let's pick up these cones."

As we sit side by side on the bench changing out of our skates back into street shoes, I indulge several kids asking for autographs. I take a couple of pictures while Travis patiently waits.

When we finally walk out of the arena, he looks up at me. "How cool is it that people ask to take your picture?"

I grin because only a child would think that is the height of being cool. I personally like the adoration of sexy women, which comes with the territory of being a professional athlete, but I admit, "It's pretty damn cool."

"I remember everywhere we went with my dad, people would want to take a picture with him."

"No surprise. Your dad was an amazing player."

"Yeah," Travis says softly as we exit the arena. "I know."

I drop my arm over Travis's shoulder. "Come on. I promised your mom I'd have you home by five thirty for dinner, which means we have about enough time to grab a quick ice cream and ruin said dinner."

Travis laughs. "She's going to be so mad."

I'm willing to risk it. "She'll be mad at me, not you. I got this one, kid."

CHAPTER 6

Camden

G RAHAM BALE IS the owner of a franchise of gyms located throughout Pennsylvania, West Virginia and Ohio. While I've never worked out in his facilities, I certainly know all about them as they're well branded and plentiful. They're massive buildings outfitted to accommodate any type of workout you could imagine, from powerlifting to yoga. Each gym has an indoor and outdoor pool, saunas, café, physical therapist and chiropractor. It's all sleek chrome, glass and fifteen-dollar smoothies.

Graham and his wife, Lindsey, have a son turning sixteen and to commemorate this event, they're throwing a party the likes of which I've never seen.

At least not for a kid.

A large tent is set up on their spacious back lawn with heat piped in to keep it toasty on this blustery day. I certainly don't know what sixteen-year-olds these days are into, but I can most assuredly say I would not have been interested in this type of party.

While it's not black tie, it's about as dressy of an event as you can get without a tux. All the men—including the birthday boy, Holden, and his ten friends—are wearing suits and ties. There are plenty of adults as well, the women in cocktail dresses.

In the center of the tent is a cherry-red Ferrari with a big bow to match the paint on the car. This answers my question as to why the party is outside rather than inside their fifteen-thousand-square-foot mansion. Large, round tables that seat ten are placed around the edge and a five-course meal is set to be served later. At one end of the tent is an ostentatious four-tiered birthday cake complete with a model Ferrari on top and a separate table to hold dozens upon dozens of gifts. But really, what more could a kid want than a new Italian sports car for his sixteenth birthday?

There's a fully stocked bar from which the liquor flows freely to the adults and waiters circulate with hors d'oeuvres and champagne.

Soft music plays from obscure speakers and everyone mingles, including the sixteen-year-olds, offering sturdy handshakes and air kisses.

It's all so refined and polite, and frankly... just weird for a boy's birthday party.

"I kind of thought there would be, like... video games or paintball," Danica says out of the side of her mouth as we stand along the inner periphery. "I mean...

what sixteen-year-old wants this for a birthday party?"

I can't help but chuckle, nodding toward the car. "I think the kid got exactly what he wanted. I'm guessing this party is for the parents' benefit, not the birthday boy's. A way to show off to all their friends how rich they are and how lucky their child is to have them as parents."

Danica snickers, covering her mouth with her hand.

We've been here about an hour and were greeted at the front door by a woman with a clipboard and an earpiece who looked stressed to the max. I assume she's the event coordinator because she had us wait inside until we could be formally announced to the partygoers. It was a little awkward as we entered the tent to polite applause, although to my relief, the boys were excited to see me.

For about half an hour, I took pictures not only with Holden and his friends, but with adults from whom I received three separate requests to attend birthday parties for their kids. I declined, stating this was a special favor owed.

They can all assume the favor is to Graham Bale, but it's only to Danica.

After the pictures, I signed each jersey. Holden simply dropped his onto a chair and then ushered his friends over to look at—but not touch—his new car.

"What did you do for your sixteenth birthday?" Danica asks.

I have to search my memory for a moment. "My parents let me go to a Drake concert with two of my friends. I had a special one a.m. curfew and that was a big deal."

"Yes... that right there. That's what sixteen-year-olds should do, not stand around eating canapés with elevator music playing in the background."

Laughing, I glance down at her. As always, she's beyond pretty but she's completely underdressed in wool slacks and a thick sweater. We weren't told this was a fancy soiree. "What did you do?" I ask.

"My mom took me and my best friend on a weekend trip to New York. We went shopping and saw a few shows."

I nod, totally seeing Danica doing that. "I guess when you're filthy rich, concerts and weekend trips to the Big Apple are underrated."

"Apparently," she mutters, her gaze drifting over to the host of the party as he talks to a group of upper-crust-looking older men.

"How's the new job going?" I ask.

Danica gives a one-shoulder shrug. "Good, I think. At least Brienne seems happy with my work. It's a bit overwhelming, though."

"Because you've never put together a brand-new charitable organization before?" I tease with a nudge of my elbow.

Danica laughs, wry huskiness roughening the sound. "Well, there's that. But this is actually the first job I've held since I moved to Pittsburgh."

I'm not sure if that surprises me or not. I know Danica was a stay-at-home mom like many of the hockey wives are but she always seemed to be busy doing stuff. I know she was on different committees and she frequently seemed to be organizing things. "I imagine it's a bit harrowing... learning how to be in the workforce while trying to absorb everything in an unfamiliar field."

"Thank God for people like Brienne. I know she gave me this job somewhat out of pity."

I shake my head. "No... no way. Brienne doesn't hand out pity favors. She would've never brought you on if she didn't think you were capable."

"Yeah, you're right. I've learned there are lots of things I didn't think I was capable of until Mitch died."

I don't have a lot of experience regarding the intricacies of marriage. My mom died when I was only ten so I was raised by a single dad. He ran our household with the precision of an army master sergeant, which he actually was. My mom was a stay-at-home mother, the same as Danica. Her duties centered around making sure me and my brothers, as well as my dad, were well taken care of. When she died, gone were the home-cooked meals, warm hugs and bedtime stories before being tucked in.

Granted, my dad could change all the household smoke detector batteries in under ten minutes, which included carting the ten-foot ladder up and down the stairs, but he couldn't hug us. He could fix a leaky pipe but he could barely manage more than canned chicken soup for dinner. My dad was skilled with house maintenance but a failure at emotional intelligence.

Which... a sudden thought strikes. "You need any help around the house?"

Danica frowns, mild confusion on her face. "Um... like what?"

I shrug. "You know... anything need fixing that you might not know how to do? For example, when's the last time you replaced your smoke detector batteries?"

Her expression turns blank. "They run on batteries?"

I roll my eyes at her. "No, they run on sunshine and good vibes. Of course they run on batteries and it's important the batteries are working or else it defeats the whole safety aspect of such things."

She laughs at my backhanded teasing but pinches the bridge of her nose as she shakes her head. "I thought they were hardwired."

"Some are but they have battery backup. When the power is out, they rely on batteries. And I suppose that answers my question. I'll come over and put some fresh ones in for you."

Danica shakes her head. "Oh, no... you don't have

to do that. I'm sure I can figure it out."

I wave her off. "I don't mind."

"You've done enough for me by coming to this thing," she says, nodding toward Holden taking selfies with his car. "Although promise me if I ever let Travis become a materialistic snot like that, you'll throttle me."

My laugh booms a little too loud and several people turn my way. Chuckling, I reassure her, "Your kid is very grounded. No chance of that."

Danica doesn't laugh in response, her attention taken by something across the room. I notice that she worries at her bottom lip while watching Graham Bale as he stands talking to a group of men. "What's wrong?"

She shakes her head, lifting her wrist to eyeball her watch. "Nothing. I just have to go insert myself at some point and secure the sponsorship. I've got the commitment pledge for him to sign and he said he would, but…" Her words trail off, worry pulling her mouth downward as she glances back at them. "He seems so unapproachable."

I know exactly what she means. The dude bought his brand-new licensed driver son a Ferrari, which puts him in a different social stratosphere from Danica. Hell, I make a lot of damn money but I'd never be comfortable hanging with these people. They not only have money but power in this city.

"You know how Graham Bale puts on his pants?" I ask her.

She tilts her head at me, those tawny eyes soft with curiosity. "How?"

"One leg at a time, same as you."

"That's probably the only thing we have in common," she says with a wry smile. "But it's time to put on my big-girl britches and get this done."

"Want me to go with you?" I ask, feeling the undeniable pull to stick by her side for reassurance.

Maybe protection.

For some deep reason, I don't want this to be hard on Danica. The entire point of my coming to this was to grease the wheels for the sponsorship. I had assumed the guy would be so grateful he'd be tossing money at Danica, but in truth, he hasn't acknowledged either one of us.

She shakes her head, hitching her purse up her shoulder. "I need to do this on my own. Wish me luck."

I watch as Danica walks across the parquet flooring that was laid over the grass, her shoulders back and her chin lifted. She might be quaking on the inside but she looks determined and confident.

When she reaches the group of men, Graham Bale keeps talking, refusing to look at her, even though he knows she's there. I know this because I saw his eyes cut to her as she approached.

Danica waits patiently, even as other men converse with Graham.

He continues to ignore her.

I've about made my mind up to walk over there when Danica reaches out to touch his arm very briefly. I can't hear her, but I can see the apology in her expression. She reaches into her purse, and pulls out the pledge form.

A flash of irritation crosses Graham's face but Danica pays it no mind. She hands him the form with a pen and doesn't seem to ask him to sign it but rather tells him.

I'm sure politely, of course.

Graham takes the form and twists to the side to bend over a high-top table to sign it. While he does that, I can't help but grin over Danica's temerity. She introduces herself to the other men in the group, nodding toward Graham as he hands the form back to her.

She continues talking and I have no doubt she's soliciting help for the foundation. Several of the men nod and Danica pulls cards from her purse, handing them out.

Good girl.

When she walks back my way, her smile is smug and her eyes twinkle with satisfaction.

I hold out my fist. "I have no clue what you said but I can tell that was quite the successful little trip you just made."

She bumps hers against mine and it's at that moment I realize she's not only a lefty but that she doesn't have on her wedding rings. I'm not necessarily surprised, but it's what popped into my mind as our knuckles touched.

Danica beams at me. "That felt good. A few of them promised sponsorships."

"You're a natural," I praise.

"Maybe so," she muses, nodding toward the exit. "But I'm about ready to blow this joint. I need to pick up Travis, and this was actually a bit exhausting."

I walk with Danica through the house and out the front door where a valet retrieves our cars. The Bale mansion has a massive half-circle driveway but very little parking so they hired a company to park the guests' vehicles. Danica's comes before mine, a small Nissan that looks new but not the Escalade she used to drive.

There's a moderate snow falling and it's forecasted to continue through the night. I walk with her to the driver's side.

"Thank you again for helping me with this," she says, and to my surprise steps into me for a hug. I wrap my arms around and squeeze her.

"I'm glad to help again if you need me," I offer, and then glance upward. "Drive carefully, okay? The snow is getting heavy."

"I will," she promises as she drops into her front seat. "You do the same."

"Take care, Dani."

"You too."

I close her door and watch her pull out of the drive-way. It was nice doing this for her and I'd like to think that wherever Mitch is right now, he's happy I helped her out.

CHAPTER 7

Danica

PUSHING UP FROM the table, I grab my empty water bottle and toss it in the recycle bin. I bend backward, hands at my hips and groan as the muscles in my aching back bark at me before my spine pops. I've been sitting at the kitchen table working and the chair is in no way ergonomically friendly.

My stomach rumbles and I see it's almost noon. I didn't eat breakfast for no other reason than time slipped away from me. That happens a lot these days with everything I have going on, between managing a full-time job that I'm learning as I go, raising a kid by myself and keeping the house cleaned and meals somewhat planned and healthy. After all of that's done, there's precious little time left and some days I'll forget to eat until dinnertime.

Of course, I'll usually make up for it by overeating something totally bad for me, like a big plate of pasta, because I think I'm starving, then I'll feel like shit. I'm surprised my body hasn't rebelled these last few weeks as

I've tried to juggle it all.

At least I'm getting my water but that's only because I set an hourly alarm on my phone to remind me to drink. I reasoned that this alarm would also prod me to eat as well, but so far that hasn't worked. I'll dutifully pick up my water bottle when it goes off and take several swallows, but if I'm in the middle of something, I find myself saying, "You'll make yourself a sandwich after you finish this one thing."

Three hours later, I find I haven't eaten and my stomach is threatening to eat itself.

I move to the bottom of the staircase and call up. "Travis… you ready for lunch?"

He doesn't respond.

"Trav," I yell louder.

Nothing.

With a sigh, I trudge up the stairs, which is steeply inclined, a trademark of these row houses built in the early 1900s. The steps creak and groan, something that took a little getting used to when we moved in. It was a bit of a culture shock going from our custom-built home to this little two-story row house with an unfinished basement but I've come to appreciate its charm.

Travis's bedroom is the first door on the right and there's a whiteboard attached to the outside that, written in big, block letters, reads DO NOT DISTURB.

I ignore the dire warning and rap my knuckles

against the cheap, pressed-wood door before opening it a bit to peek in.

Travis has his headphones on and he's playing a video game. I step inside and he catches me from the corner of his eye. Taking off the headphones, he says, "What's up?"

"I'm going to make lunch. Since I missed breakfast and you only had a bowl of cereal, I was thinking French toast with bacon. Sound good?"

"Sounds great," he says. "Just yell when it's done."

"Okay," I say with a smile.

Travis spent all morning playing out in the fresh snow that fell overnight. It was only about three inches total but enough that Travis and I were able to build a respectable snowman in the backyard.

In the kitchen, I take out the loaf of fresh brioche and put it on the cutting board. I'm searching for my serrated bread knife when my phone dings with an incoming text. I reach in my back pocket and see it's from Camden, which weirdly causes a rush of giddiness.

Do you have a snow shovel I can borrow?

My brows knit as I try to parcel out why in the world he'd want to borrow a snow shovel from me. I thought he lived in a downtown condo but I could be mistaken. Maybe he bought a house. If that's the case, why wouldn't he just go buy one?

I text back. *Of course.* Then add a smiling face emoji.

The bubble appears and his reply is swift. *Where is it?*

Leaning my hip against the counter, I ponder what in the hell Camden is up to. Nothing comes to mind, so I simply ask, *Why?*

I feel like I've been zapped with electricity when he replies *Because I'm on your front porch and I thought I'd shovel the snow off for you.*

Scrambling for the front door, I toss my phone on the kitchen table as I pass by. Sure enough, I see a hulking figure through the glass panes frosted with ice. I swing the door open and find Camden there grinning at me.

"What are you doing here?" I ask with wide-eyed surprise.

"I'm going to shovel the snow off your steps and stoop. It's a hazard and you could slip and break your neck."

I blink at him. "We don't use the front door. We come in through the back."

"That may be true, but I'll bet you have back steps that need shoveling, right? Plus you have a rear alley garage and I bet there's snow that needs to be cleared away from the door so you can pull out tomorrow. So I'll get that done too."

"Camden," I exclaim, positively overwhelmed that he would be so kind as to think to help me like this. "You don't have to do that."

"Nonsense," he says and steps over the threshold, forcing me back a few steps. He closes the door and looks down at his boots, caked with snow that's melting on my rug, then back to me with a chastened look. "Sorry about that… I would have stomped off the snow first, but since there was snow right up to the door, it was kind of hard."

I snort and shake my head. "You're crazy."

"I'm determined," he retorts. "Where's the shovel?"

"In the garage," I say, throwing a thumb over my shoulder toward the back door in the kitchen. It leads out into a small fenced-in backyard that sits between the house and the freestanding garage off the back alley.

"Perfect." He smiles, movie-star white, straight teeth that have never known the misery of a slap shot to the face.

Making himself right at home, he walks through my house to the back door. When he goes to open it, I finally start coming to my senses. "I'm about to make French toast for me and Travis. Want some?"

"That would be great," he says without looking back at me. "Just yell when it's done."

And then he's gone.

"Everyone wants me to yell at them when the food's done," I mutter, but inside, I'm chuckling.

I'm able to spy on Camden through the kitchen window as he clears snow from my back steps, presumably after he shoveled in front of the garage door, which I can't see from this position.

The bacon is done and I'm about to dip the bread in the egg mixture when he opens the back door. "Mind if I cut through to do the front steps? I'm going to leave some mess behind."

"Of course I don't mind," I say, waving him in. "But leave the shovel out there and kick off your boots. It won't take me long to get this first batch of French toast done and you can eat before you go back out."

"Sounds right by me." He takes off his gloves and knit hat. His brownish-blond hair stands at crazy angles all over his head and the mom in me wants to smooth it down. The twinkle in his brown eyes speaks to his fun-loving nature, something I see every time I look at Travis.

The woman in me is well aware that Camden is no boy, though.

"What do you want to drink?" I ask as he shrugs out of his jacket and drapes it over the back of a kitchen chair.

"Got any coffee?"

"Sure. I'll make a pot."

"I'll make it," he says easily. "Just point me in the right direction."

While Camden expertly works the coffee pot, I dip and drop the thick bread slices onto the electric griddle. As the coffee brews, Camden leans back against the counter, crossing his arms over his chest to watch me cook.

"Where's Travis?" he asks.

I nod upward. "Video games."

"I suppose he spent the morning outside. I saw the snowman."

"That was a joint effort. But I had to get some work done and he was happy zoning out in front of the TV for a while. I'm sure he'll go back out later."

I manage to get four pieces of bread on the griddle when Camden says, "Do you mind if I ask you a personal question?"

That startles me so much, my body jolts. Not that I'm closed off or even put off, it's just… I didn't expect it, especially not with that low timbre of concern.

Turning slightly to face him, I say, "Sure."

Camden unfolds his arms and presses his palms onto the counter near his hips. He glances around the house and then locks his gaze with mine. "Are you doing okay?"

I tilt my head since *okay* is a subjective term in my life. "How do you mean?"

His smile is slightly chagrined. "It's probably none of my business but I can't help but notice the change in your lifestyle since Mitch died. You used to live in a gorgeous home and you drove an Escalade. But now… you're not. So I guess I'm asking, are you okay financially or do you need help?"

Heat prickles and then burns my cheeks. I involuntarily duck my head and turn back to the French toast, using the spatula to lift the corner of one to see how it's doing. Not ready to flip yet, which means I can't busy myself to avoid his question.

My hesitation prompts him to add, "Tell me to back off if you want, Dani. No judgment here. I only want to know if you're okay."

I take a deep breath and turn my head his way. "We weren't quite prepared financially when Mitch died, so I've had to make a few changes."

A frown puckers Camden's face and I'm sure he's confused. He knows damn well what Mitch made as a professional athlete. "What do you mean?"

"We had our wills done and life insurance in place. All that was taken care of, but nobody ever talks to you about the practical aftermath of death. Let's just say, I was woefully unprepared to survive without him."

Camden doesn't say anything but merely watches me with open curiosity laced with concern.

"We obviously had money. You know as well as anyone the salary that Mitch commanded. But we didn't make the smartest choices in our young marriage with what we did with that money. There were far too many bills when he died—all of our extravagances—and with no income, there was no way for me to keep that same lifestyle that you've so aptly noticed is missing."

His jaw tightens slightly. "You sold the house in Edgeworth because you couldn't afford it?"

"If it was only the Edgeworth house, things would've been easier, but we had the beach house down in North Carolina and the condo in Lake Tahoe. Mitch had his flashy cars and he bought me way too much expensive jewelry. So I sold all of it."

"The cars too?" he asks. He's well aware that Mitch had a five-car garage that held an Aston Martin Vulcan, a Lamborghini Urus and a '67 Ford Mustang Shelby. Those were his fun cars. Day to day, he drove a Range Rover and I drove an Escalade.

"The car payments and insurance alone would eat up my current salary. Add on three homes and there was no way to survive."

Camden nods, a slow one of affirmation. "Then it was good you did that."

I look under the corner of the frying bread and deem it ready to flip. With my gaze focused on the task before me, I find it easier to talk. "I could have continued to live off the life insurance proceeds for a few years, but I was looking long term and I knew I wouldn't be able to maintain. I had to boil it down to the most important thing and that was keeping Travis in a good school and starting a college fund." I glance over at Camden, my mouth twisted into a wry smile. "I mean... we didn't even have a college fund for him because we assumed we'd always have enough money we could write a check for wherever he wanted to go."

His return smile is one of understanding. "Hindsight is twenty-twenty, right?"

"Yeah," I reply softly, turning back to the French toast. "I thought we were doing the right things. We put a lot of money into retirement, but that can't be touched without penalty. And we had some liquid savings, but most of our money was in the houses, which didn't have much equity, and those cars were financed and had almost no equity. It's so silly to say it now, but... it just never seemed harmful for us to enjoy all that money."

"I'm curious," he asks, glancing briefly at the coffee pot to see it's still brewing. "Did you ever consider returning home to Massachusetts? I've met your family and Mitch's. I know they would have loved to have you back there. Would have helped take care of you until you got on your feet."

I nod, a soft smile playing on my lips. "I thought long and hard about going back. Hell, I still think about it. My parents and my sister Reba would've loved for me to come home. But we put down roots here in Pittsburgh. Travis loves his school and Harrington is so top notch. I did some math, which I was always very strong at in school and I figured out what I needed to do to make it here. So I sold the houses, the cars, the jewelry and banked the money right along with the life insurance."

The thumb on my left hand absently rubs at my ring finger, the engagement ring and wedding band packed away with the only other piece of jewelry I kept... a locket Mitch gave me for my eighteenth birthday.

"I think you've made some admirable adjustments to accomplish your goals." Camden pushes off the counter and moves to stand beside me. I glance up, finding comfort in his gaze. "I wish I'd known. I feel horrible I didn't know and that's on me. I could have helped. I *can* help if you need it."

Without any volition of my own, my hand reaches out and seeks his. I curl my fingers and squeeze. "You're very sweet but I would never let you. If it makes you feel better, Brienne helped me navigate everything right from the start. She gave me so much advice on how I could get myself in a strong financial position to be comfortable with my decision to stay here."

"She's an amazing woman," Camden agrees, pulling his hand free. "She's done a lot for this entire organization."

"That she has," I say, admiration dripping off my words.

Camden rummages in a cabinet for mugs as I plate the French toast. I quickly dip another batch of bread into the egg mixture and drop them on the griddle.

"I'll get Travis," I say as I set the spatula down.

"How do you want your coffee?" Camden asks.

"Lots of cream and sugar."

"That's not very specific."

I grin at him. "Let's put it this way... you can't put enough in for me."

Camden grimaces. "Got it."

I hurry up the stairs, taking them two at a time. I give a sharp knock and enter Travis's room. Surprisingly, he's on the bed reading a book. My heart does a little flip because Travis doesn't particularly like reading.

His head turns my way. "Lunch ready?"

"Yup. And we have a surprise guest."

"Who?" Travis asks, rolling off the bed.

I choose to be evasive. "Come down and see."

Travis takes that as a challenge and bursts past me, flying down the stairs at the speed of a runaway locomotive. I'm barely to the bottom when I hear him say, "Camden... what are you doing here?"

As I turn the corner, I see them bumping fists.

"I came to help your mom shovel the snow," Camden says as he leans against the counter, sipping at his coffee. "And I'm going to check out the smoke detectors before I leave. I'll teach you how to change the batteries and you can do it next year."

"Really?" Travis says. I'm sure the idea of climbing a ladder has far more appeal than I'd like it to.

"I'll teach you how to shovel snow, too, after we eat."

Travis wrinkles his nose, his reply half-hearted. "Oh… okay."

Camden laughs and his gaze slides over to me. "If you have anything else you need help with on the house, you let me know before I leave. I'll figure out a time to come back and take care of it for you."

"Okay," I say softly, my heart swelling with gratitude. I move to the griddle and nod toward the table. "Sit down."

Travis starts talking Camden's ear off as I load up two plates with French toast and bacon. I stand at the griddle and work on the extra pieces because I certainly know my son's appetite and if Camden's is anything like Mitch's, they'll polish off all of this. I manage to eat two slices myself as I'm cooking.

After we're finished, I clean the kitchen while Travis helps Camden with the front stoop. When they come back in, I'm settling back down at my laptop to get more work done.

They're mid-conversation and I pick up what Camden says as they shut the front door. "… at practice this week, you let me know. We'll work on it when I get back in town."

"Awesome." Travis's face is flushed from the cold but I can see his eyes lit with excitement to be talking hockey with Camden. It causes a tiny pang of hurt in my chest because that's something he's been missing.

Camden hands Travis the shovel. "Do me a favor, bud... put that back in the garage."

"Got it," Travis says as he takes the shovel and I stand from the table.

I slap him on the butt as he passes by. "Great job, kiddo."

"Thanks, Mom."

When Travis is out the back door, I move toward Camden in the foyer. He throws his thumb over his shoulder at the door. "I'm going to head out."

"I cannot thank you enough for coming to do the snow. That was really kind and unexpected and—"

Camden smirks and holds out his hands. "Thank you is fine. And you fed me well, so I might have come out on the better end of the deal."

Laughing, I incline my head. "Well, thank you, then."

"Anytime. We've got three away games over the next week so the schedule is tight, but when we get back, we've got an unprecedented seven days in a row with no games. We'll have practices, but that's a good time for me to come do your batteries so—"

"You don't have to do that," I rush to say, but the look on Camden's face has me slamming my mouth shut.

"Just accept the offer of help, Dani," Camden chastises. "It's what friends do, okay?"

I blow out a breath and laugh nervously. "Okay… fine. I'm not good at accepting help, so double thank you."

"And that garage of yours," he says, nodding once again toward the back door. "It's a death trap waiting to happen with the boxes stacked everywhere. It needs to be organized. I'll help do that too."

I'm silent for a moment, battling my need to be strong and not accept the offer against the woman who actually *does* need help and recognizes a genuine offer when she's presented with it. "I'm really glad we reconnected, Camden. I appreciate what you're doing not only to help me but Travis too. I know Mitch would be so grateful."

"I'm glad," he says and then reaches back for the knob. "Make a list of anything else you might want fixed or whatever. I'll knock it out next week."

I slip my hands into the back pockets of my jeans, rocking forward on the balls of my feet. "Will do."

Camden smiles, nods and starts to turn for the door.

"You know *This Pucking Sucks* is getting together tonight. Coach West is sponsoring and it's at his condo. Pizza party."

"Yeah… he told me at morning skate. But I've already got plans."

Over the last year, I'd forgotten what a good guy

Camden is since we haven't seen each other much and he's sure proved it this past week in the ways he's helped me. But I can tell he's more than a little reserved when it comes to anything to do with the crash. He was ill at ease last week at Stone's place and he's definitely avoiding a return trip.

Still, it's not up to me to pressure him to do anything, so I give him an easy smile. "Sure. No problem. I hope you know you're welcome at all of them."

"I do," he replies breezily. "I better get going."

I lift my hand in silent farewell and Camden walks out as Travis bounds through the back door.

"Did you make sure to lock the garage?" I ask.

"Yup. Can I go back up and play video games?"

"If you give your mom a hug," I say, not in the least abashed to be using bribery for affection.

Travis is in a good mood and he comes willingly, a grin on his face.

"Love you, buddy."

"Love you too," he replies, resting his head on my shoulder. This time next year, he'll be as tall as me.

CHAPTER 8

Camden

T HE CLOCK WINDS down and the buzzer sounds. I'm on the ice with the rest of my second line and since Drake just got a shutout, we all race down to him for a mini-celebration. The San Francisco Bay Brawler fans are noticeably silent as over half of them left during the third period when we were up 5–0.

This was a crushing defeat as the Brawlers were at the top of their division and as we head into the home stretch of the regular season, every game counts.

Coach West and the other coaches leave the ice before the team but wait for us outside the locker room door to give each of us a slap on the back. Coach has a big cheesy smile on his face but then again, so do most of us. It was a fucking excellent game.

"That was solid play," Coach West says as he claps me on the shoulder.

"Thanks, Coach." I walk past him and into the locker room, eager to get a hot shower and then an ice pack. I leveled a couple of hits tonight that have my right shoulder throbbing.

I'm confident enough to say that I played pretty damn good tonight. Compared to how I've been playing, it was a notable improvement. Beyond my solid on-ice performance, one of those five goals was mine after I intercepted a power-play pass. I skated like there was no tomorrow and whipped off a short-handed goal. As I've done every time I've scored since the plane went down, I sent up a silent commemoration to those who died. It's usually just a general recognition of the lives lost, but tonight, for some reason, I thought specifically of Mitch.

Which made me think of Danica and Travis.

I've been pondering them both a lot, mostly because it's mind-boggling to me how well they're doing. Not that I expected them to be mired in misery, but Danica chose to stick it out in Pittsburgh and essentially reinvent her life. It's fucking courageous as hell.

Travis, I expect, has the resilience of youth on his side but I know he misses his dad. Still, he's a great kid and I love helping him out with hockey. I'd like to do more if his mom wants, but I don't want to overstep in any way. I know that by helping them, I feel better inside. I guess that's why Coach wanted me to connect with the support group to begin with, because he figured I'd get something out of it that would help me gain perspective and possibly some peace.

Within an hour, the entire team is showered and

dressed, our equipment loaded on the bus that will take us to the airport. The team plane awaits to take us on the next leg of our West Coast trip, which includes three more games against the Calgary Wild, the Edmonton Grizzlies and the Alaska Blizzard. It's going to be a tough week of flights, hotel rooms and playing against home crowds. The upside is that we have a solid week of no games followed by the last three games of January happening at home.

On the plane, I snag a window seat. The plane is posh with overstuffed captain's chairs that recline with both heat and massage built in. There's always a menu of delicious food and drinks available, served by pretty flight attendants.

It's late as hell but I'm still a little wired so I order a Blanton's neat before takeoff, hoping it will relax me enough I can grab a few hours of sleep.

Bain Hillridge drops into the seat next to me as more players board the plane. A defenseman like me, he came over from the Arizona Vengeance in November. Even though every day of my life is a competition to make first-line status on this team, I've developed a quick bond with Bain.

As he pulls his earbuds out of his backpack, he says, "You were on fire tonight, dude."

I'm not one to be humble and slough it off to a lucky break. I busted my ass to play up to my potential.

"Thanks. Now I have to keep it at that level."

"Everything else good?" he asks. It's with enough innuendo, I know he's talking about the aftermath of me missing practice week before last. I told him about what went down with Coach showing up at my house and insisting I go to the support group meeting.

"It's all copacetic," I quip.

The flight attendant brings my drink and I scramble to flip the tray over my lap. She sets it down and asks Bain if he wants something.

"I'll take some mint tea."

She smiles and turns to fulfill his order and I mutter, "Lame ass."

"Fuck off," he grouses and puts his earbuds in so he can't hear any reply I might lob his way.

I smile as he flips his tray over in anticipation of his tea and settles back into his seat. His head bobs slightly to his music.

Nabbing my phone from the seat pocket in front of me, I check my messages. There's a text from my oldest brother, Caleb. *Great game, bro.*

Caleb's thirty-two and although I'm closer in age to our middle sibling, Christian—we're two years apart—I have more of a bond with Caleb. The six-year age gap between us and the fact my mom died when I was ten made Caleb the go-to person in our household for basic care. My dad was the *go to work, then come home and relax* type. He wasn't a caretaker.

Both Caleb and Christian followed my dad into the army. They're still active duty but my dad retired several years ago and now works as a manager at a lumber supply yard.

Thanks, bro, I text back. *All good?*

While I wait for him to reply, I take a sip of my drink and enjoy the smoky burn as it goes down. I know it's not a great habit but since the plane crash, I've gotten into the routine of having a drink before to ease my nerves before takeoff.

I idly flip through my messages, which includes reading an exchange I had with Danica earlier today. She'd been on my mind so much, I decided to reach out to see how she was doing.

My inquiry was benign enough. *I'm checking to see if you've made a list of things for me to do next week.*

She replied simply with a laughing emoji.

That made me laugh, so I asked a better question. Probably the more important one. *How was Travis's first day of hockey?*

That got a response. *He said it went great. Was really excited about it. A little stressed because the kids are all really good.*

I wrote back without any hesitation. *I'll practice with him if he wants when I get back. I'll text you my schedule.*

You're the best, she wrote back.

I was casual and merely liked her response. I had

been putting my phone away when it chimed again. *Good luck tonight. Kick some Brawler ass. I'll be cheering you on.*

My eyes skim over those words again. The feeling upon reading them was indescribable, same as it is now. Happiness comes to mind but I don't know why. I've had friends cheer me on. Family, for that matter.

But Danica is different because she's a lot like me. She lost a part of herself in that plane crash. She's been to the same dark place I have. If there's anyone who would understand what that day did to me, it's her.

Granted, many others lost the same things. The other widows, mothers, fathers, siblings. The other two surviving players, Hendrix and Coen. Brienne Norcross. They're all like me.

But I haven't connected with them the way I have with Danica. There's no real reason for it. Sure, I was friends with her before but I was closer to Hendrix and Coen. Shouldn't I have felt a measure of solidarity with them the way I do with Danica?

Or is it because of something else?

That's a thought I push way down deep inside because if I have to start thinking about the reasons why Danica would be different from Hendrix and Coen, the obvious answer is unacceptable. Danica is a woman who lost a husband on that plane. It's left her alone in a way that Hendrix and Coen aren't, and I hope I'm not playing into that.

I pray to God this isn't some savior complex I have going on to help me feel better about my own problems.

And even though I have intense distaste over this being such a thing, it's not remotely feasible for me to back away.

I fucking like helping Danica. I might even need it.

Bain nudges my shoulder hard and I twist my neck to look at him. "What?"

He's got one earbud pulled out. "I asked if you're still cool with us doing a little birthday celebration for you next week?"

I cringe inwardly. I hate celebrating my birthday because I don't like the fuss. It wasn't something we did in my family and I'm not big on the spotlight being on me for an extended period. "What were you thinking?"

"Nothing fancy. Maybe we all go hang out at Stevie's bar? We got almost a week off so why not party one night and your birthday is a great excuse."

"As long as there aren't balloons and cake, and I'll kill anyone who sings me happy birthday."

"Are you serious?"

"As a heart attack," I reply. "I don't like that shit but I'm down to hang out. Who all would be there?"

"Whoever you want, dude. It's your birthday."

"Just invite the team and SOs."

"Coaches?"

"Yeah, man. That's cool."

Bain punches me lightly on the shoulder. "Consider me your party coordinator. Any other requests other than no balloons, no cake and no singing?"

I snort at how grumpy and assholish that makes me sound. "Yeah, no puck bunnies."

Bain blinks at me in wide-eyed astonishment. "You're kidding, right?"

I shake my head. "The older I get, the less tolerance I have for that. Plus… they make a fuss and I don't feel like having them hanging all over me."

"You are indeed," Bain says with his lip curling upward, "sincerely… a weird dude. I know no single hockey players who don't love that."

"Now you're stereotyping," I say dismissively.

Truth is, for those first years in the league, I loved the perks of being a professional hockey player. I could have a different girl every night willing to give it up to me. My sex life was not hurting.

These days… it's not something I enjoy.

Not that I don't enjoy sex. Fucking love it. But I think since the crash, I've narrowed my world down to include only those people who I have a genuine connection with.

Like Danica.

My fingers curl and I clench my fists way too tightly at the bothersome thought. I am not interested in Danica in any way other than friendship. More specifically, in being the type of friend Mitch would have wanted me to be to her. I'm making up for a lot of months I could have been helping her.

I have purpose now.

A path forward.

There's no clear answer as to why the path includes Danica but it's the only one I'm seeing right now that doesn't include airplanes dropping out of the sky to crush me.

CHAPTER 9

Danica

OPENING THE BACK door, I glance at my watch. "Shit."

I'm pushing the time, so I drop my purse haphazardly on the counter and toss my keys beside it. A quick jog through the living room and I'm up the stairs, straight into my bedroom where I shed my clothes.

The blouse I wore to the office hits the floor as I kick off my heels, then I shimmy out of my dress pants. I give them a kick toward my laundry basket and start rifling through the clothes hanging in my small closet.

One of the downgrades I made when I sold the Edgeworth house was cutting down my wardrobe. I had five times as many clothes as I could fit in this tiny box of a closet and I donated most. Some had sentimental value, which I kept, while others were high-end labels, so I sold them on consignment. The majority of what's left are outfits to wear into the office and jeans or leggings that I pair with T-shirts, blouses, flannels or sweatshirts.

For this afternoon's agenda, I grab a pair of jeans, a

long-sleeve, waffle-knit shirt and a puffer vest since it's a little chilly outside. I throw the new outfit on and grab a pair of tennis shoes.

When I'm fully dressed, I note that I still have a few minutes. I head into my bathroom to pull my long hair into a ponytail and after considering my face, I freshen up my makeup. I don't wear a lot on any given day, but I brush on another coat of mascara and add some tinted lip gloss.

I stare at myself with censure. *What are you doing, Danica?*

There's a knock at the front door and I jolt.

Camden's here.

I don't know whether I should hate myself. I just rushed home to meet Camden, who's going to change out the batteries in my smoke detectors and help me organize my garage. Not a big deal.

But here I am, staring into the mirror, worried about how I look.

I grab a tissue and wipe the gloss off my lips, but there's nothing I can do about the extra mascara. I toss the tissue in the garbage and race down the stairs, taking a deep breath before I open the door.

Camden stands there and … goddamn it. The first thought that runs through my head is how handsome he is.

That's not exactly a revelation. I'll fully admit I

thought Camden was handsome back when I was married to Mitch, just like I thought many of the players were.

Exactly like I thought many of the wives were beautiful and the kids were adorable.

It's only natural, right? To appreciate beauty.

"Can I come in?" Camden asks and I flush hot at the realization I was staring mutely at him because his messy hair and scruffy beard are way too hot.

"Yes. Yes, of course. Sorry. I guess I've still got work on the brain."

Lie. Absolute lie.

"Busy day?" he asks, stepping across the threshold. He's dressed casual in jeans and a Titans sweatshirt. He's got on a pair of battered black Converse high-tops.

"Not overly. I got some stuff done last night so I could scoot out early to meet you here. I really appreciate you offering to help."

And yes, despite me getting girl stupid over how handsome Camden is, he's actually pushing me to do something I've put off for a long time.

Cleaning out my garage, which means cleaning out some of Mitch's stuff. Camden doesn't know that. I mean, he doesn't know that all those boxes stacked in dangerous towers that could topple at any minute are Mitch's clothes, shoes, books, memorabilia, awards and almost a decade of collected memories. I bet if he did know, he'd never have offered to help.

It's not that I want to get rid of any of it. Quite the opposite, I want to keep most of it, but it does need organizing and I wasn't able to put some of the boxes up on floating shelves above the garage door rails. My goal is to separate the clothing that can be donated, less a few things to keep for Travis, and then clean and organize the garage. Camden's offer to help, along with an unseasonably warm January day—upper forties—and I knew this was the perfect chance to get it done.

"Want to start on the garage or do the batteries first?" I ask.

"How about we do the garage first?" he suggests. He holds up a small plastic bag. "I bought all the batteries but if we run out of time before you have to pick up Travis, I can hang back here and get those done."

"It's a plan," I reply, ignoring the slight thudding in my chest because I realize that Camden smells really good. I take an involuntary step backward.

"All right," he says with a bright smile. "Let's go take a look at the project."

We head out the back door and through the yard to the freestanding garage. It has a standard door to enter from the side and the rolling portion where my car enters faces the alley. I left my car parked on the street so that when we walk inside, Camden will have a good idea of what we're working with.

He glances up and says, "We need to identify what you don't need easy access to and then put those boxes up there."

"Mitch's stuff," I say, and I have to swallow the uprising of sadness from deep in my chest.

Camden faces me, his eyes soft with understanding. "We don't have to do this."

"Yeah… I need to. I would have done it when we first moved in, but things were crazy and I didn't have the help you're offering. I need to sort boxes of his clothes that will go to donation. The stuff I keep will be for Travis one day."

He nods in understanding, glancing around. "Okay… three piles. One to keep that will go up high, one to keep that you need easy access to and that can go on the wall shelves, and one pile to donate. I'll do all the heavy lifting."

It's his crisp words and easy organizational ideas that put me at ease, making this no more than a project that involves some rearranging and has nothing to do with erasing something from my life. There's nothing wrong with getting rid of things like clothes and only keeping those pieces that are drenched in important memories.

For the next hour, we open boxes and separate. Sometimes Camden calls out the contents to me if he's not sure what to do with it.

"There's a bunch of paperbacks by some author

named Johanna Lindsey," he says.

I nod my head toward the donate pile. "Those are old romance books of mine. I read digitally now."

"Romance, huh?" Camden says, picking one with Fabio on the cover, his hair blowing in the wind as he stares down at a busty temptress in his arms. "Any good?"

"Oh yeah," I say as I flip through some old tax returns, deeming them too old to keep. I put them aside as they'll need to be shredded.

"I've got Christmas decorations in these boxes." I look up from my task to see Camden has five boxes before him. "I'm going to put them on one of the lower shelves so you can easily get them down."

"That works." I lift another box onto the counter so I don't have to bend over. I lift the lid carefully, afraid of spiders but luckily it's too cold. Inside I see a bunch of photos I'd printed over the years using an online service. Many I put in picture frames, but I always went overboard and would store the others, promising myself I'd make scrap albums one day.

I pull one of the packets out and flip through them. It's Travis's fifth birthday party. We had it at the house and because he's a July kid, it was a pool party. There are several action shots of Travis and his dad doing cannonballs, kids chasing each other with water guns and a huge sheet cake with Travis blowing out the candles.

Setting it aside, I pull out another envelope and lift the flap cover. I find photos of a winter girls' weekend I went on with some of the other hockey wives to Miami. I think I was probably twenty-one, maybe twenty-two. Some of those wives left when their husbands got traded, others when their husbands died in the plane crash. I flip through the photos of us in sexy dresses, out clubbing for the night. Others with us on the beach, sipping fruity cocktails. That was so much fun and I miss things like that.

The next envelope is a Titans' party. I can't remember what it was for, but everyone's dressed up, the men in suits and the ladies in cocktail dresses. I flip through them and halt on one of Mitch and Camden together.

"Hey… look at this," I say as I pull it free.

Camden comes up behind me, looking over my shoulder as I hand him the photo. I continue flipping through and lo and behold, there's one of Camden, Mitch and Hendrix together. I hand that one back without looking at him, feeling the glossy photo slide from my grasp as he takes it.

I pull the rest of the pictures free and turn to face Camden. I lean back against the countertop as I flip through them. "Here's Brienne and Adam."

Camden takes it, a smile forming. "You should give her a copy of this."

"Totally. And you should keep that one of you and

Mitch."

Shaking his head, Camden hands me the pictures. "No, I couldn't."

"I insist." I take the photos, pull the one of him and Mitch and force it back on him.

He nods almost imperceptibly as he accepts it and my head dips back down as I thumb through others. I share them one at a time as we reminisce.

"This was a charity dinner for the Boys and Girls Club," Camden says. "Remember... someone hired that really weird magician to perform."

"Oh my God," I say, a cackle escaping my mouth. "And remember he tried to use Teemu's wife as his assistant and she freaked out when he told her he was going to saw her in half?"

Camden laughs at the memory. "She didn't speak the greatest English and I think it was a mistake for him to mime what he was going to do with the saw."

I laugh so hard I almost pee, remembering how Motina shrieked. "And then Teemu got upset because he wasn't sure what was going on."

"Apparently they don't have many magicians in Lithuania." Camden chortles.

I drag a knuckle under my eye because tears are forming from laughing so hard and my eyes lock with Camden's. There's a quiet between us right now that feels like the fizz of champagne bubbles. Leftover happiness from good memories buzzing around.

Smiling, I straighten the photos to slide them back into the envelope. "I love good memories."

"Yeah," Camden says gruffly as he turns away, tucking the photo I gave him in the back pocket of his jeans. "Sometimes I forget about them, though."

"It can be hard to pull them forth," I commiserate. "Especially when our thoughts are overflowing with so many other things."

"Hmm," he says, bending over to grab one of the Christmas boxes. He doesn't say anything else and I watch him a moment. He's purposely checking out of the conversation.

"How have you been doing?" I ask bluntly.

Camden places the box on a shelf and faces me. "What do you mean?"

"After the crash. How have you been handling things?"

"Fine. Why?"

I shrug, putting the photos back in the box. "Just curiosity. I mean... we both went through something traumatic. There shouldn't be any reason I wouldn't ask you about it. Or wonder how you're doing."

Camden runs a hand along his stubbled jaw, then tilts his head left and right as if he's trying to release tension. He won't meet my eyes and I'm on the verge of telling him to forget about it. I don't want to push him into anything uncomfortable.

"I'm still having nightmares," he says, and my heart breaks over how tired he sounds. As if he hasn't had a good night's sleep since last February and that admission has done him in.

In addition to the exhaustion I hear in his tone, I can also tell he's skittish about divulging this to me. I could leave it alone but something tells me not to.

"Want to tell me about them?" I ask.

"Not really," he mutters.

"You know I'd understand," I assure him.

"I know you would. But what I don't understand is how you seem so well adjusted and I'm still dreaming of plane crashes."

He sounds so angry toward himself... as if this is a weakness he can't control.

I move across the garage to him, putting my hand on his forearm. "There are no rules as to what's right and what's wrong when it comes to grieving or handling loss. And I can assure you, I'm not totally well adjusted."

"Maybe not," he says, eyes roaming over my face. "But you sure as shit have shown resilience like I've never seen before."

I'm both pleased by his compliment and sad that it makes him feel lower about himself. I'm no psychologist but if I had to guess, I'd say Camden hasn't processed the loss of his team very well. I don't know what he's done over the last year. I know he's continued to play hockey, but past that... has he gotten help?

I know I have. Not only from my support group, but from friends, family and a great therapist. Both Travis and I saw counselors to help wade through our grief, pick up the broken pieces and put them back together again.

Still... there are moments I feel as broken as the night I got the call that the plane had gone down. Those times are thankfully fewer and farther between.

"Did you talk to anyone after?" I ask hesitantly.

"By anyone, you mean..." His words trail off deliberately, prodding me to seek clarity.

"A professional."

"No."

That's it. Just... no.

"Family?" I ask.

Camden makes a scoffing sound. "My dad and brothers aren't exactly the type to discuss feelings."

That's an interesting thing to say. "Why not?"

I'm relieved to see a genuine smile on his face. "They're great... don't get me wrong. It's just, they have this mentality that feelings are stupid and that which doesn't kill you only makes you stronger." He says that with a robotic, nasal tone, as if he's repeating something learned in a handbook.

"Why are they that way?"

"Army. My dad retired and both my brothers are

active duty. They have a mindset that you tough things out. You deal with it and move the hell on. You don't have to air it out to fix it, you only have to be stronger than it."

I find that incredibly sad. "Your mom?"

"Died when I was ten."

And that right there explains it. Camden comes from a family that buries feelings and I'm not sure he's ever been permitted to hurt.

I assess the situation with all the information I've learned and consider the expression on Camden's face. He looks ill at ease and I don't want him to associate bad feelings with spending time with me.

"I'm here if you ever want to talk. But I'm also still here if you don't want to talk about it either."

The relief on his face is instantaneous and it transfers into his smile. "Fair enough."

"Okay… let's get this finished. I've got to head out in about an hour to pick up Travis."

Camden looks at his watch. "I've got dinner plans, so yeah… let's knock this stuff out and then I'll handle the smoke detectors."

Dinner plans?

As in a date?

I want to ask but it's none of my business.

And then something hits me and I'm appalled by how much I'm bothered by it.

What if Camden has a girlfriend?

I suddenly feel terrible for taking up his time. He's got his own life to live. "You know what... I can finish this all later. And I'm sure I can get the batteries in myself. I'm pretty good on a ladder."

Camden frowns. "I'm good to stay for a while. I don't have to leave right now."

"I know," I say, turning my back on him and blindly rifling through boxes. My voice sounds unnecessarily shrill. "I don't want you to waste your time here when you—"

My words are cut off when Camden has my wrist in his large hand and he's turning me to face him. "Did I say something wrong?"

I whirl the rest of the way and he lets me go. "No. Of course not. It's just... you said you had plans and I don't want to disrupt you."

Camden laughs. "Not a big deal. I'm meeting some of the guys for dinner, so I can be a little late."

Oh, sweet Jesus. That's relief coursing through me that he's meeting friends and not a date.

What the hell is wrong with me?

"Speaking of the guys," Camden drawls.

I blink away my thoughts, plastering on a smile. "What's up?"

"They're throwing me a birthday party Friday night. Have you met Hendrix's new girlfriend, Stevie?"

I shake my head.

"It's going to be at her bar. You should come and hang out with us. Stevie's cool and you'll know a bunch of people there."

A trill of excitement buzzes through me. I haven't gone out in a long time, merely to have fun. And it would be great to celebrate Camden's birthday.

"Okay… I'd love that. I'll need to arrange a babysitter for Travis."

"Awesome," Camden says, his grin answering whether he truly wants me there or if he's only being polite. But then it slides a little, not in a way that tells me he's losing his joy but to a degree that I know he's considering something serious. "I'm really glad we reconnected, Danica."

"Yeah," I say softly, emotion threatening to choke me up. "Me too."

CHAPTER 10

Camden

I T'S A RARITY that the season provides almost an entire week without any games. The schedule for the first half of January was heavy with road trips, including a full week on the West Coast where we fit in four games. It enabled us to have this time off—from games but not from practices, team meetings and workouts—and it frankly feels a little weird. Hockey season is always like a nonstop, high-speed train that eats up the distance so fast, you don't know where your time has gone.

It's taken me three full days to settle down, trying to dispel the anxious feeling that I should be doing something or going somewhere.

When my birthday rolls around on Friday, I'm prepared to party down with my teammates. It will be good to cut loose and not have to worry about the consequences of a hangover tomorrow.

To my relief, when I walk into Stevie's bar there are no balloons or streamers, but then I notice a huge banner at the back extended from one corner to another over the jukebox. It reads *Happy 26th Birthday, Camden.*

I suppose that's not so bad.

Stevie's the first person I run into and she hugs me.

"I'm guessing I have you to thank for the banner," I mutter.

"Yup," she replies with a mugging grin as she pulls back. "Bain said you didn't want any decorations, but this is my bar, so my rules."

I incline my head. "Well, thank you for not doing balloons."

She winks at me. "Those might still be coming."

I make my way through the crowd—a mix of Stevie's regulars, mostly bikers and my Titans peeps—receiving back slaps from the guys and hugs from the women. I'm not surprised to see most of the team here, some with their wives or dates. Even the coaches are here, and that touches me they'd come. Of course, having so many days off probably helped since they spend so much time working in our off-hours.

Hendrix materializes before me and his first words are to deny culpability. "Stevie did the banner. I had nothing to do with that."

Laughing, I shake his hand. "She already copped to it."

Someone shoves a beer at me and I see Bain. "Drink up, dude. You've got probably fifty-plus people here who want to buy you a birthday beer tonight."

"Thank fuck we don't have a morning practice," I mutter, tapping the neck of my bottle against his. "Cheers."

We both tip our beers back and that first ice-cold slide of fizz down my throat tastes way too good. I'm totally going to be hungover tomorrow.

Walking deeper into the bar, I circulate to thank everyone for coming. I finish my first beer and someone hands me another. I'm standing at a high-top table talking to Coen and Tillie when I notice a smile form on his face at something over my shoulder.

"Look who's here," he says, nodding toward the door.

I twist around and see Danica coming in. Her long brown hair hangs over her shoulders and she tucks it behind an ear as she glances around nervously. Most of the bikers are sitting at the bar right near the entrance and I can read it on her face... she thinks she might have walked into the wrong establishment.

I weave through the patrons and when she finally sees me, it's relief in her smile.

"You made it," I say in greeting.

She moves to take off her coat and I help her shrug out of it. "Well, it's not every day you turn... wait... how old are you?"

I fold her jacket over my arm, intent to put it at one of the tables with some of the other women's stuff.

"Twenty-six."

"A young pup," she teases.

I'm not sure exactly how old Danica is but I know she had Travis young... maybe in her freshman year of college. She can't be but twenty-seven, twenty-eight years old, but I'm not going to ask. It's irrelevant.

"I'm really glad you came. Come on... let's hook you up with a drink."

I take Danica back to where most of the Titans are hanging, the farthest recess of the bar but on the opposite side of the jukebox so it's not as loud. There are several round tables with chairs plus some standing high tops. To the left are three pool tables and beyond that, a few digital dartboards.

There are hugs from those who Danica knows well... Stone, Harlow, Coen, Tillie and Hendrix. I introduce her to Stevie who she hasn't met yet and they start gabbing.

Coach West and Ava aren't here, but I knew they were taking a quick trip to Charlotte to meet with her boss whose company is based there. Brienne and Drake aren't here either, but Drake's sister Kiera is. She's become part of our regular crowd and fits in well. Drake likes to grumble and warn all the single players away from her but you'd find every one of us fiercely protective of her. She's family.

For the next hour, I spend most of the time making

the rounds among my friends. I willingly accept birthday beers and play a few games of pool with Bain. I watch as a fight breaks out between two bikers near the front of the bar and smile when it's Stevie who wades into the brawl to break it up while Hendrix watches with an uneasy expression. Stevie's a tough chick and she's not afraid to keep the peace. Still, it's a hard pill for Hendrix to swallow since his instinct is to jump in and handle it. I saw this firsthand on a prior visit here.

As time moves on, I notice that no matter where I am and what I'm doing, I've got an eye out for Danica. While she knows a handful of people here, she's meeting most of the new players for the first time. I stand at the ready to swoop in if she's left alone or looks uncomfortable, but on the contrary, she seems to be having a great time. She wears that natural smile I've come to appreciate over the last three weeks since we reconnected, and part of me wants it focused my way.

Since I helped her organize her garage day before yesterday, I feel an even stronger pull toward her. I know it has everything to do with the fact that she broke through a barrier that I've not allowed a single person past since the plane crash. I shared with her about my nightmares, and it doesn't count that I divulged that to Coach West. That was done under duress and fear I'd lose my job.

But Danica somehow presented a safe environment

for me in that small stone garage with a broken concrete floor. Within the confines of that space, she learned that I'm still struggling to accept the crash and that my background plays into it. I told her enough about my family dynamics that she's aware that I'm not someone who puts my feelings out there. She knew exactly when to back off so that I never felt cornered or overwhelmed.

Consequently, I'm like the curious, starved dog. I want to sniff and nudge at her hand to see what other treats she might have, but I'm a bit too skittish to go all in.

"That was nice of Danica to come." I turn to see Bain with another beer in hand for me. I accept it with a nod of thanks. "I assume you invited her."

"Yeah. Figured she'd enjoy being around the team again."

Bain knows I've had a few interactions with her since I was ordered to attend the support group. He knows I played on the same line as Mitch, and I even told him I feel a little guilty for not having done more for her until now.

"I talked to her a bit ago. She sure is singing your praises."

My gaze cuts over to Danica sitting at a table with Tillie while Coen plays pool. Whatever they're talking about has Danica laughing hard.

I don't let a single facial muscle move in response to

Bain's words, denying that it feels a little too good to have her appreciation. It means that what I'm doing for her means something to her personally, and for whatever reason, helping Danica seems to be a balm to my tortured thoughts about the crash. I manage to keep my tone neutral. "She's done an amazing job of rebuilding her life after Mitch died. I admire her a lot."

"I also notice you haven't hung out with her at all tonight," Bain muses.

I turn my gaze lazily to him as if the question doesn't bother me. "Why would I? It's not like this is a date or anything."

Bain's mouth curves upward, his expression knowing. "Never said it was. But it does seem like you're avoiding her."

"I'm not avoiding," I grouse. "She's been busy talking to other people and I didn't want to interrupt."

"If you say so," Bain says blandly before nodding at an empty pool table. "Want to play again?"

No, I don't. I want to talk to Danica and I realize I've been keeping my distance because I didn't want anyone to think poorly of me. I didn't want anyone to think I invited her for any reason other than friendship.

I've got enough beer in me now to remind myself that I am indeed nothing but her friend and it's totally permissible for me to hang out with her. "I'm going to pass," I tell Bain, walking away without a backward glance.

When I reach the table where Danica's sitting, I have to convince myself it's only my imagination that her eyes light up. I plop down in the adjacent chair and Tillie immediately rises. "I'm going to the bathroom and getting another drink. Want one?" she asks Danica.

"Sure, thanks."

Tillie then looks at me. "It's my turn to buy one for the birthday boy."

Even though I have a full one in hand, I wink at her in acceptance. I've got a nice buzz going and don't want to lose it. Especially now that I'm committed to hanging out with Danica a bit.

"Having fun?" I ask.

"Yeah... thank you for inviting me. It kind of feels like old times."

That pleases me to hear because more than anything, I knew she'd appreciate the familial camaraderie that's inherent within the team dynamic. "I'm glad you came. What did you do with the little man tonight?"

"He's staying the night at a friend's house. They're in youth hockey together and they have practice tomorrow. I'll pick him up from there."

"And how's that going? He finished his first week of practice, right?"

Danica's face clouds with uncertainty and she lifts a shoulder. "I don't know. He hasn't done organized sports before so I'm not sure what's reasonable."

"Did something happen?"

"No," she insists and offers a small smile. "Not at all. It's just… the coach is a little intense. Travis is used to his dad playing with him one-on-one and it being fun. Even when you did drills with him, it was pretty lighthearted. But now he feels the pressure to perform and it's mostly from the coach. I watched one of the practices, and he's pretty tough on the boys. Some of the parents like that, though, so I don't know if I'm being too overprotective."

"It runs the gamut when it comes to coaching styles. But the one thing I know, it's not a one size fits all. Some people are motivated by a highly pressurized environment while it can cripple others. A good coach knows how to tailor his style to fit all."

Danica nods. "I offered to talk to the coach and Travis was mortified. I've been forbidden."

I chuckle because I can see Travis doing that. "You only want what's best for him."

"He knows that, but he also dealt with a mom who was way too overprotective after Mitch died. I was so afraid of something happening to him, I became a bit smothering. I learned how to step back a bit but it's hard. I want to fix all his problems because he's had enough bad stuff to last a lifetime."

My hand itches to take Danica's and give it a squeeze but I don't. I would have if we were alone, but with so many eyes on us, I'm not willing to have this look like anything more than an amiable chat.

Doesn't mean I won't offer something, though. "He might not want you to talk to the coach, but that doesn't mean I can't." Her eyes flare. "I'll watch the next practice, and if I see something out of sorts, I can talk to him about it on the sly."

"I can't ask you to do that."

"Sure you can. All you have to do is invite me to watch his practice."

Danica stares at me a long moment and I can practically see the wheels turning in her head. Finally, she smiles. "Okay… I'd like that. And, of course, at your convenience. You've got a lot on your plate, so whenever you can—"

"Tomorrow," I say.

She blinks. "Um… yeah. Tomorrow works."

"Perfect," I say, rapping my knuckles on the wooden top. My gaze shifts left and I notice an empty pool table. "Want to play a game?"

"I'm not that great," she admits candidly. "Not sure I'd be much of a challenge."

"We'll play partners with Coen and Tillie. That will be an even matchup."

The four of us play a few games of pool and I down a few more beers. "Livin' on a Prayer" comes on the jukebox and somehow, the entire bar ends up singing it at the top of our lungs. Danica and I pretend our pool cue is a microphone.

Stevie brings out a big cake and fuck if she doesn't almost set it on fire by attempting to light twenty-six candles. It takes me three tries to get them all out but only because I'm laughing so hard as the guys make lewd noises each time I try.

The cake is demolished in short order and I get distracted by a stray piece of frosting on the corner of Danica's lip. I have to turn away and talk to someone else, and thankfully it's gone by the time I look back.

Around eleven p.m., I feel a tug on my shirt sleeve and turn to find Danica there. She has her coat on, and while I haven't spent the entire evening hanging with her, I find myself not wanting her to leave yet.

I keep that opinion to myself, though. "You heading out?"

"Yeah." She wrinkles her nose. "I'm so lame but it's a late night for me. I've said all my other goodbyes but saved the best for last."

Okay, that feels good to hear. "I'm glad you came. Do you need an Uber to take you home?"

She shakes her head, hefting her purse over her shoulder. "No. I stopped at two beers."

I had noticed she'd been drinking water for a while and that assures me she's okay to drive. I know Danica is responsible and wouldn't risk it.

"Then let me walk you to your car," I say, turning to set my beer on a nearby table.

"Oh, you don't have to do that."

"I kind of do," I say, offering her my arm. "Mitch would come back and straight-up poltergeist haunt me if I let you walk out of a bar by yourself at night."

Danica laughs, as I expected, and links her arm through mine. Somehow I knew that a joke about Mitch wouldn't be offensive but, on the contrary, understood. It says that I know how Mitch felt about his wife and I'm going to honor that.

We head out of the bar and she turns us west. "I'm about two blocks down that way in a paid lot."

As we stroll along the sidewalk, I brace against the chill in the air. I never thought to grab my coat but it's dipped down into the thirties. Is it my imagination or has Danica stepped in closer to me?

Is she cold and seeking warmth or is she worried that I'm cold?

"… starts at ten a.m."

"I'm sorry… what?" I ask, having missed something.

Danica laughs. "Are you drunk?"

"Pleasantly buzzed," I correct her but I'm sure I'll be drunk before the night is through. I will most definitely be taking an Uber home.

"I said Travis's practice starts at ten. I can text you the address."

I consider offering to pick her up but that seems too forward for some reason. Despite the fact I've pretty much pushed myself on her twice now to help out without giving her an opportunity to decline, picking her up at her house to take her somewhere feels too personal.

"Sounds great," I reply. "I'll meet you there."

"Here's the lot," Danica says and we walk past an attendant who's asleep in his booth.

At her car, she fishes in her purse for keys and I'm surprised that when she has them in hand, she moves in for a hug. I'm startled and it takes me a moment to reciprocate. Her arms go around my neck, the keys in her hand jangling as she murmurs, "Happy birthday, Camden."

A simple endearment to a friend and yet it sounds like more.

Or maybe that's the beer.

Regardless, neither one of us withdraws from the embrace and I turn my head slightly so I can breathe in her shampoo.

Fuck… that smells good.

Too good.

She feels a little too nice in my arms and I have no right to be thinking those things.

I loosen my hold on her even though I'm reluctant to pull away. At first, Danica doesn't take the opportunity to extricate herself, so we hold still a few seconds more.

Then slowly, we move apart. But it's so fucking slow that my cheek grazes her temple and I feel the heat of her breath on my neck.

I dip my head for no reason at all and it puts us cheek to cheek as we continue to separate. Christ, only an inch separates the corners of our mouths and if I turned my head just that amount, my lips would touch hers.

We both freeze and I can feel the rise and fall of her chest even under her heavy coat, her breath wafting over me in the same rhythm.

Squeezing my eyes shut, I send up a secret prayer for strength and somehow manage to pull myself free of the hug.

Danica gives a tiny cough as she steps back, her gaze dropping to the ground. I shove my hands in my back pockets and look over to the attendant in the booth, merely to divert my attention somewhere else.

A slight giggle has my attention snapping back to Danica. I raise an eyebrow and she shakes her head as she puts her hand over her mouth, perhaps to shut down another laugh. Her eyes finally meet mine and they're not full of recrimination, even though we came very close to kissing.

Instead, they're alight with humor and I can't help but grin at her.

Just like that, we're back on even footing.

She unlocks her door. "Thanks again for the invite. I had a great time."

"Me too. I'll see you in the morning."

Danica slides into her seat and I don't move until she exits the lot and heads off down the street. Because it's cold as fuck, I jog back to the bar.

Once inside, Bain hands me a fresh beer so no need to hunt down my old one. "Thanks, man."

"Danica get out of here okay?" he asks.

"Yeah."

Bain doesn't say anything, merely stares at me with raised eyebrows as if he expects me to provide further details. It makes me hot under the collar and before I know it, I'm defending myself. "There's nothing there, dude. I walked her to her car to make sure she's safe."

"Okay," he says easily.

"We're just friends," I insist.

"I can see that."

"Then get that look off your face," I growl.

"What look?"

"As if you know a secret about me. There's nothing to know."

Bain nods and takes a long pull of his beer. I think the subject is dropped but then he says, "There's no bro code in effect."

That makes no sense and I turn to him with a scowl. "What?"

"Mitch is dead. She's single. You're single. There is no bro code in effect."

Bro code.

That unwritten rule everyone understands. You don't ever, and I mean ever, move in on a teammate's woman. Even if they're broken up or divorced, you steer clear. Coen broke the rules on one drunken night when he thought a teammate was broken up with his girlfriend and crossed a line. Before he could rectify it, the plane went down and he was burdened with some serious guilt because he couldn't even apologize.

I'm sure the bro code applies to widows as well.

"Whatever," I mutter.

"I'm only saying, if you had an interest—"

"I don't."

"Sure looks like you do to me," Bain retorts and I don't miss the mischief in his eyes. "I think it's evident you both have a connection. Anyone in this bar could see it tonight."

My eyes zip wildly around the room, expecting everyone to be staring at me with the same knowing look Bain has on his face right now.

But no one's paying me any attention and I figure he's pulling my leg.

"We're only friends," I insist and before he can say anything else crazy, I walk away.

We're. Only. Friends.

Nothing more.

CHAPTER 11

Camden

TRAVIS IS PLAYING in a nine-and-under youth league, and while the kid is an amazing skater and has great hands, it's his confidence that needs the most work. I figured that out the day I took him to the rink for drills. While praising him, I noticed that he had a hard time believing the affirmations.

I'd say, "You have a fantastic transition," and he'd automatically assume it wouldn't be good enough to play for his current team. I'm convinced that is because he sat out this past year after Mitch died and needs his confidence rebuilt once he starts playing with a team again.

I meet Danica and Travis at the facility where his league practices. They only practice twice a week—Monday and Saturday—and their games are on Sundays. If Travis sticks with this, those commitments will increase year after year. I know the kid's got enough talent to play at the top tier when he gets older and they practice five nights a week. Travel hockey means he'll be flying to other states for games and tournaments, and it's a hugely expensive commitment.

That's the biggest credit I give to my dad. He might not have known how to show me love, affection and support after Mom died, but he made sure I was able to pursue my passion for hockey. It's the big reason I'm a professional athlete today.

I arrive early, wanting a few minutes to talk to Travis before he goes out on the ice. Danica texted me this morning that Travis was excited I was coming to watch. He has no clue it's to check out the coach so I can give Danica some peace of mind, but that doesn't mean I can't give him a last-minute pep talk.

Waiting by the entrance door, I spot Danica pulling in. Travis sees me through the rear passenger window and waves with a broad grin on his face. He barely waits for his mom to bring the car to a full stop before he throws open the door and bursts from the back seat.

"Hey, hey, hey," Danica calls as she opens her door. "Watch for cars."

Travis stops, looks left, then right and deems it safe to cross the throughway. Danica steps out of the car, rolling her eyes at her son. She's wearing jeans with a red pea coat and white lace-up boots with fuzzy fur around the edges. On her head is a knit cap in the same shade of red as her coat with her long chocolate hair spilling down her back.

I hate that I'm checking her out, but since that near kiss last night and Bain telling me there's no bro code, I'm looking at her more and more as a woman and not the widow of my dead teammate.

Even though I got a little drunk last night after she left the party, I had a hard time falling asleep when I got home. I kept playing in my head how fucking inconvenient this is… having an interest in someone with whom I have no business being anything more than friends. I might not have gotten much sleep but at least I didn't have any planes dropping on my head.

"Camden," Travis exclaims as he reaches me. "Mom said you'd be here."

"I was happy she invited me." I put my hand on his shoulder and bend at the waist. "Wanted to see you do all those snazzy moves you showed me when we practiced."

Travis blushes but I'm pleased to see he doesn't self-deprecate. Perhaps he's already built up some confidence over the last two weeks.

Danica reaches us and I see she's carrying Travis's gear bag and his stick. I take them from her and hand them off to Travis. "Little man… why is your mom carrying all this for you? Show me them muscles."

Travis grins. "Sorry… I normally do. I was just excited to see you."

My eyes cut to Danica who I'm relieved to see is

amused and not offended, judging by the wink she gives me. I'm not sure if she's the type of mom who enjoys catering to her kid, and far be it from me to change things, but if not, then he needs to be a little more cognizant of those things. If he wants to play hockey, he needs to lug his own gear around.

Another mom and kid approach the building, apparently known to Danica and Travis. The women hug and Travis turns his friend to me. "This is Camden Poe."

The other boy's eyes go round as saucers. "Oh wow."

"Hi," I say, holding out my hand for the kid to shake. "And you are?"

"Gabe," he says, gaping up at me.

"Hi, Gabe. Any buddy of Travis's is a buddy of mine."

"Wow," the kid mumbles, looking over to his mom who's watching, then back to me. "Can I like... get a picture with you or something?"

"Sure."

Gabe's mom pulls her phone out and takes photos of me and Gabe, then Travis gets in on it. I'm surprised to see Danica has her phone out and takes one of me and her son together. Then the boys rush inside to get changed in the locker room and Gabe's mom heads back to her car where she waits during practice.

Danica's eyes narrow, pinning on my face. "You don't look too hungover."

Grinning, I open the door and motion for her to precede me. "Nothing a couple Tylenol couldn't cure."

I follow her through the facility to the practice rink his team has booked for the hour. They only get half the ice, the other half taken by another team. Bleachers are set up and we choose seats near the top, away from all the other parents congregating close to the ice. Some look over their shoulders at me and I know I've been recognized.

I prop my feet on the metal bench below me and rest my forearms on my knees as I watch the kids skating around to warm up. Travis isn't out yet, and practice starts in about ten minutes.

Twisting my neck, I look at Danica on my left. "Does anyone know who Travis's dad is?"

"Not directly from me," she says, putting her feet on the bench beside mine. She leans forward to mimic my position, forearms on her thighs. "I didn't want any unrealistic expectations on Travis. Some people know because he goes to school with a few kids on the team but I'm not sure he's really said who his dad was."

I look back out to the ice. "He seemed a little unsure of himself when I took him to the rink but I think that's merely him getting back into the groove. I was wondering, though, if the coach knew because, yeah... he might be expecting something of Travis he can't give yet."

She doesn't answer but instead leans over and bumps

her shoulder against mine. "I'm grateful you're here. I can do a lot of things for my kid, but I'm a little out of my element with hockey. You're a good friend, Camden."

Angling my head, I bring my eyes to her. "I imagine you'd do just fine if I weren't here but you know I'm really glad to help. You're a good friend too."

She snorts. "I haven't done anything much to warrant that title. You're the one swooping in to help me."

I'm not able to hold her gaze so once again, I divert my attention to the players on the ice. "You've done something no one else has been able to do. You got me to open up about the crash."

Danica slips her arm through mine, hooking us together at the elbows. She gives an affectionate squeeze and fuck if it doesn't feel natural.

Us sitting here like this.

Her tone is teasing. "You didn't open up very much and specifically said you didn't want to talk about the crash."

I smirk at her as I see Travis skate out, my gaze remaining on him. "Hey... I told you I had nightmares and that I never saw a therapist. Even told you a little about my family, which is why I didn't see a therapist."

"Touché," she mutters and then pulls her arm free as she notices Travis on the ice. "But I know better than anyone that it takes more than a five-minute conversation to process trauma and grief."

"Touché," I reply, nudging her playfully with my shoulder. I don't have any intention of opening up wounds that I believe are fully healed. Sure, things might be a little ugly under the scabs, maybe a bit infected. But I can live with that. Seems a lot less painful than ripping at the sores and letting that shit ooze out.

I'll gladly take her friendship. She's easy to be with, not just because she's warm, funny and kind, but because we share something big in common.

The crash.

Would I take more? If we're both feeling this mutual camaraderie, could it be something other than mere friendship? I know I'm attracted to Danica, although I'd only ever admit that to myself. But does she feel the same? I swear there was a moment last night when I felt like she wanted me to close that small distance between our mouths.

I think she wanted me to kiss her but what the fuck do I know? That could have been the beer talking.

For the next hour, we watch Travis's practice and I specifically pay attention to the coach. I looked him up on the youth league website, a man named Dan Kantor who has been coaching kids for several years. By all accounts from watching him, he knows his shit. He knows exactly what kids this age should be able to accomplish and his direction is spot on.

But I do see that he's a little hard-assed and light on the praise. While he's apt to say, "That was good" for a job well done, that's about all the affirmation he hands out. On the flip side, mistakes or substandard play is called out and a spotlight is shone on it. One kid had a bad transition and tripped, falling to the ice. He popped right back up, but the coach made an example of him.

"That right there is the difference in playing for fun or moving on to travel hockey. Your transitions have to be perfect."

And yeah… they do. I'm just not sure they have to be that way at age nine, in a league that most of the kids here are playing in for fun or to learn a new skill.

What makes this coaching dynamic trickier is that some of the parents seem to like the coach's style. The kid who fell got an earful from his dad. After the coach made an example of him, his father called him out.

"Kevin… come on, bud. We've practiced this a hundred times. You can't be making stupid mistakes like that."

I heard a low but distinct growl of disapproval from Danica when we heard that, and while Travis played well and was never targeted by the coach, it clearly upset her to see him do it to other kids. Even if that type of coaching feedback isn't aimed at Travis, he's operating under the assumption it will turn on him eventually and that can be stressful.

When the practice is over, all the kids skate off to the

locker rooms and the parents start clearing the bleachers.

"What did you think?" Danica asks as we traverse our way down the stands.

"I think he's a tough coach. He's not big on positive reinforcement."

"I hate the way he humiliates the kids if they do something wrong. There's a nicer way to deliver the message.

"I don't disagree with you there."

"What should I say to him?" Danica asks, her expression fretful and uncertain. "I don't want him to come down on Travis by thinking I'm a complainer."

"Why don't you let me talk to him? I'll have a friendly chat that I was watching and some thoughts I have. It won't be confrontational."

"Yeah? You'd do that?" she asks in such a tentative way.

I'd probably do anything for you.

I give her a smile of assurance. "You two get out of here. I'll call you later and let you know how it went."

Danica appraises me, seeming as if she has a million questions but doesn't quite know where to start. She looks bewildered, slightly trepidatious and at the same time, a little exultant. I don't know… maybe she's fucking confused as to why I'm helping her, but my offer stands.

"Okay," she finally says with a nod. "I'll talk to you later."

When Danica is out of sight, I head to the edge of the rink where the coach is talking to a couple of parents. I hang back slightly, waiting for them to clear out, but his eyes cut to me over their shoulders.

He clearly recognizes me as the shock is evident on his face but returns his attention to the conversation he's embroiled in. It's thankfully short and as the parents walk off, he turns my way.

I walk up to him with my hand out to shake. "Coach Kantor."

If he's surprised I know his name, he doesn't show it. Merely pumps my hand exuberantly. "This is quite the surprise. Great to meet you, Camden."

Tossing my hand up to the bleachers, I say, "I was watching your practice."

Delight spreads across his face. "That's an honor. What did you think?"

I glance around, seeing most of the parents who were here for this practice have left but others are heading up the bleachers for the next set of kids. When I turn my eyes back, I ask, "Can I give it to you honestly?"

His face shutters and his arms cross over his chest defensively. "Sure."

"You've got a mix of kids. For some this is for fun, while others will want to be competitive. You've got two groups who need different coaching styles, but you're only using one."

"The parents who put their kids in this program do

so wanting me to build them into travel hockey players."

"Not all the parents. Some don't really know what they want at this age. Now granted, you might have a majority of children who are looking to excel—"

"Those are the ones who matter," he says tersely.

"They all matter," I reply, a hard edge to my tone.

The man narrows his eyes. "Do you have a kid on this team?"

"No." I don't say anything else and I'm not about to give up Travis.

"Then you have no say so." He sticks his hand out for me to shake, indicating the conversation is over. "I appreciate you watching but I've got the next practice to get ready for."

"Sure thing, Coach," I say with a polite smile, shaking his hand.

Dismayed by his lack of openness but not surprised, I know that this man isn't going to change. The best I can do is give Travis some advice on how to adapt.

I pull my keys from my pocket as I exit the facility, twirling them on my finger. I consider calling Danica but I'm not sure this is something to discuss by phone.

Instead, I send her a quick text. *Talked to the coach. Mind if I come by to update you?*

Her reply is nearly instantaneous. *Of course. You'll be just in time for lunch.*

CHAPTER 12

Danica

WHEN CAMDEN KNOCKS on my front door, I have to restrain myself from glancing in the ornate mirror hanging over the couch as I walk by. I don't need to be checking how I look, because I'm not trying to impress him.

Liar.

This weird little obsession I have going with Camden as a man, and not as a friend, is driving me nuts. If I'm honest, I think this all started when he showed up to shovel my snow and unfortunately has changed the way I look at him.

He's so damn handsome in a carefree, messy way. It's the shaggy hair that's never quite the same on any given day and the facial hair that's more than a shadow but less than a beard. He's got the hockey player vibe going, which I'm not a stranger to, but he also looks like he'd be a good lumberjack. Throw him in a flannel, some jeans and put an ax in his hand, and well… that is a nice fantasy.

I can blame this on two things.

One, I might be a little lonely. Not only for companionship because I have very good friends to lean on who make my life interesting. But I'm talking about as a woman. I loved sex with my husband. The act of it, the intimacy, the curl-your-toes pleasure. It's been a long damn time since I've had sex and now I'm thinking about it.

The other blame can be cast directly on Kiera. While I had thought Camden hot, I hadn't thought much past that. At the party last night, she had enough alcohol in her to say some crazy-ass things.

Little ideas planted in my head that I know she did purposely.

We were standing at one of the high tops, watching Camden and Bain play pool. I hadn't had a chance to hang with Camden at that point as he was the guest of honor and lots of people wanted his attention.

Kiera made a noise deep in her throat when Bain bent over the table to ready his shot. He was on the far end facing us, and she growled low to me out of the side of her mouth. "Mmm... look at those arms."

I was confused at first. Arms? I mean... what about them?

But then I looked closer and realized what she was saying. Bain was wearing a black, long-sleeve T-shirt that fit him like a second skin and as he stretched over the green felt and lined up his shot—one arm extended, the other cocked back—you could indeed tell he's a well-sculpted man.

And, of course, I immediately thought of Camden. At that moment as he watched Bain, he leaned casually on his pool cue and talked smack to his opponent. Camden's shirt was not tight like Bain's—rather a button-down that fit him nicely, though not like a glove. But he was wearing a long-sleeve athletic shirt the day he helped me in the garage. Moving all those boxes had him out of his Titans' sweatshirt, and yeah... I noticed how well the top fit him and I could tell how much he works out.

It was disconcerting then, and since Kiera pointed it out at the party last night, my imagination has been on overdrive. It's hard because Camden has come through for me time and again, and now I'm over here lusting after him like a teenager who's discovered her hormones.

Camden knocks again and I realize I've frozen halfway across the living room. I scrape away the thoughts of what Camden might look like naked (*I am shameful!*) and center my focus on the real reason he's here.

To discuss Travis and his hockey coach.

I swing open the door, offering him a blazing smile. "Hey... come on in."

He enters, fully at ease and flashes me a disarming smile. "Any chance I could bother you for some coffee?"

"Hangover worse than you let on?" I tease as I lead him into the kitchen.

Camden settles into a kitchen chair. "Something like that. Where's Travis?"

I don't bother with a pot of coffee since I'm not having any more and instead make him a single cup using the Keurig. "Upstairs reading. He has to do twenty minutes a day whether he likes it or not, and trust me when I say, he doesn't."

Camden chuckles and the sound sends a shiver up my spine. Low and rumbling like distant thunder. "I didn't like reading at that age either."

"When did that change?" I ask as I put the cup before him—black, just the way I remember he takes it.

He gives me a sly look. "Never, unfortunately. I used Cliffs Notes to make it through English class in high school."

I gasp in mock horror, holding my hand to my chest. "That's blasphemous to good literature."

Picking up his cup, Camden smirks over the edge. "I was a jock. Wasn't interested in books. I *was* interested in stealing my dad's *Playboy*s out of his closet, though."

I snort, because that's probably a rite of passage for many boys. It won't be for Travis, though. The most he'll get is Mom's old romance books and because of his disdain for reading, I doubt he'll ever be exposed to the juicy stuff. At least not until he gets unfettered internet access as he gets older.

Camden sips his coffee and sets the mug down. "I talked to Coach Kantor for a few minutes. Nice enough guy."

"And yet I hear a little hesitance in your voice," I reply.

"He only cares about the players who have the potential to excel. He's either too close-minded or too lazy to adapt his coaching style to make sure all the kids are benefiting."

I frown with worry. "What should I do? Pull Travis out?"

Camden shakes his head. "I wouldn't. Not yet. Travis is a good player and even if the coach isn't the best all-around guy, he does know his stuff. I think Travis will learn from him if he can adapt to the way he teaches."

"But that man could demoralize him," I muse, worry pressing down on me.

"It's possible."

I feel like he wants to say more, but he doesn't. I'm wondering if he's afraid of stepping on my parenting toes. "You think it's worth the risk?" I ask hesitantly.

"I can't say. He's not my kid. But what I can tell you is if Travis has a passion for hockey, and if even at this young age you can see him always playing, I'd probably let him stay. He's going to need to know how to handle difficult people. No two coaches are the same. The difference between our first coach after the crash and our current coach is night and day. If you can keep Travis's confidence boosted this season, he'll end up learning not only hockey skills, but relationship skills."

Nodding, I let my gaze drop down to the table, mulling all this over. When I lift my eyes back to Camden, I smile sheepishly. "I'm too overprotective sometimes. My heart says to yank him out and find somewhere else for him to play. But my brain is saying you make a lot of sense."

Camden looks me directly in the eye. "Again... not my kid. I'm not a parent, so I don't know what's right or wrong from that angle. I can only tell you what to expect going forward. However, if you want me to talk to him and explain that some coaches won't be nice but that if you can look past that, you can learn something, I'd be glad to."

I hesitate with immediate acceptance. He's already done so much for Travis and me, and this feels a little like I'm pawning off my problems. But I trust Camden, and Travis looks up to him. I know Mitch would approve of him giving guidance to his son.

"If you don't mind," I say tentatively.

"It would be my pleasure," he says, surprising me by putting his hand over mine on the table and squeezing.

It's only for a moment and he releases me just as

quickly.

It was a decidedly friendly move, dripping with fondness, friendship and nothing more.

And I guess that's really all it should be.

I point toward the staircase, hesitantly asking, "Do you... right now?"

Camden shakes his head. "I don't want him thinking I saw something wrong with practice, especially if he wasn't bothered by anything. Let's not create problems if we don't need to."

He said *let's*. As in him and me. The two of us. A team.

"Listen... I've got to get going. I'm meeting some of the guys for a workout." He stands from the table and I follow suit. "See if Travis wants to hit the rink again with me on Tuesday. That will be the day after his next practice and I'll casually bring it up."

"He'd love to practice again." My lips twitch at the memory of when Travis came home the last time. "He couldn't stop talking about you."

Something shutters in Camden's eyes and I know I'm not seeing things when his jaw tightens slightly. It has me immediately backtracking, which includes a lot of babbling. "I know it's a lot, and you don't have to do this. You've already done so much and this isn't your problem. Plus... it's your day off."

"Travis isn't a problem to me, Danica," he says softly. "It's just... I don't want him to think... I don't want to..."

"Don't want to what?" I ask gently.

"I don't ever want him to think I'm trying to super-sede anything he had with Mitch. I'm not trying to replace his wisdom or his advice. I'm only trying to be his friend. I don't want to make Travis feel like he has to guard his memories of his dad because of me. He's only a little kid and—"

I step forward, snatching Camden's hand into mine and holding on tight. His skin is warm, palms calloused as he reflexively squeezes against me. "No, Travis wouldn't think that. And I wouldn't think that. What Travis had with Mitch will never be diminished. We keep his memory alive every day. What you're doing is giving Travis some much-needed guidance in his sport of choice because I don't know what the hell I'm doing. So please... don't treat either of us with kid gloves when it comes to the fact that we very much loved a man who died. There are no ghosts here, only good memories."

I feel Camden's entire body relax through my grip on his hand. When he nods at me, relief clear in his expression, I slide my hand free.

"Well... I better go." Camden turns for the door, looking back over his shoulder. "Let Travis know I'll grab him after school on Tuesday."

"I will," I promise.

"Bye," he says.

"Bye."

I close the door and lean against it, my heart thudding. Those were some deep things we discussed, and part of me wonders how much I was trying to reassure Camden when it comes to a relationship with Travis, and how much of what I said applies to me as well.

Mitch's ghost doesn't haunt me. It's true he was my soul mate and not a day goes by that I don't wish for magic so that he could return to me. But I also know that's not going to happen and my life will go on. That's all part of the healing I've done this past year.

There's a knock on the door, the vibration running through my body and I propel myself off it. I open it to find Camden standing there looking... distinctly uncomfortable.

Shit. I said all the wrong things.

"I'm sorry," I blurt out. "I've made this weird for you, haven't I?"

Camden frowns. "Weird? No. Why would you say that?"

"Because your expression tells me you're uneasy about something. I can see it in your eyes."

Lips twitching, Camden tilts his head side to side with an abashed expression, as if he's trying to find the best way to tell me exactly why he looks nervous. "I am a little uneasy but about something that's got nothing to do with anything we've talked about."

Concerned, I sweep an arm. "Come in."

"No," he says, shaking his head adamantly. "No need. I'm just going to say this, and if it's stupid, tell me, okay?"

"Oh-kay," I drawl, having no idea what could be bothering him.

Camden scrubs his hands over his face before his eyes pin on me resolutely. "Can I take you out on a date?"

My legs feel like Jell-O and I grab the doorframe for balance. "A date?" I ask, repeating the words because surely I heard him wrong.

"It's stupid, right? There's no way you're ready for something like that and it's totally awkward since I was Mitch's teammate and besides that—"

"Yes," I blurt out, a little too loudly to stop him before he rescinds the invitation.

Camden blinks. "Yes?"

A smile breaks wide on my face. "Yes. I'll go on a date with you."

CHAPTER 13

Camden

I'VE BEEN ON dates before.

Of course I have.

Everything from a high school date to the movies to taking a puck bunny to an event hoping to get laid later.

Of note... I always got laid later but that had more to do with the fact that I picked the right women who would give it up.

Never have I been nervous before. I've always had that cocky swagger, knowing my looks, charm and status as a professional athlete is the triple threat women can't ignore.

As I stand on Danica's porch, though, my hands are fucking sweating and my heart is about to thump its way right out of my chest. I have a distinct pressure in the center of my sternum, perhaps the start of an anxiety attack. What the hell was I thinking, asking her out? So many damn things wrong with this scenario and yet, I don't know that I've ever looked forward to spending time with a person more than I do at this moment.

I don't know what I'm looking for specifically, I only know I want to be around Danica in a more intimate way. Tonight that means a quiet dinner in an out-of-the-way restaurant with a table reserved near the back, tucked in a corner so we won't be disturbed.

That's it... good food and conversation.

I hear the hard clack of Danica's footsteps on the wood floor as she approaches the door. When she opens it, my eyes drop first to her feet ever so briefly, and I hold back a groan at the sexy taupe, high-heeled ankle boots. My eyes run up her body. I told her to dress casual and outside of the footwear, she's got on faded jeans and a royal blue turtleneck sweater with a camel-colored blazer. Her brown hair is in loose waves and she's wearing makeup. Her eyes are smoky, lashes long and she's got on a deep berry-colored lipstick.

She looks like a goddamn goddess and it makes me want to run away and pull her into me in equal parts.

"You look beautiful," I say, the words tumbling out before I can stop them. I should have told her she looks pretty, not beautiful. I mean, *pretty* doesn't do her justice, but *beautiful* is really putting myself out there, and that kicks the anxiety up a notch.

Danica blushes, dipping her head briefly before bringing her eyes back to mine. "Been a long time since I heard that."

Not since the crash.

"I'll tell you again before the evening's over," I say, even as I want to mentally slap myself. I never say these things to women.

Because you've never had a woman feel this important to you before.

"You look outrageously handsome yourself." Danica grins, her eyes shining with mischief, but I don't doubt the compliment. She's not the type who would say something she didn't believe. "Now that we got that out of the way, where are we going?"

She grabs a wool overcoat and shrugs into it before stepping out onto the porch. As she locks the door, I say, "To an Ethiopian restaurant I've heard good things about. You said you like to try new things so I thought, why not."

I asked Danica out the day before yesterday. Between then and now, we've volleyed lots of texts. Tiny exchanges, gleaning bits of information, funny memes, GIFs and jokes. Random thoughts I'd text her or she'd text me. I found out during our back-and-forth that she's a certified foodie and will try anything once, so I wanted to take her somewhere unique.

What I wanted to do was call her just to ask her what she was doing and to hear how her day was going. But again, too intimate.

Just too much.

The texts kept it friendly and I'm hoping to fuck we

can continue to be friends if this date ends up being a disaster.

Danica turns and I hold out my bent arm, waiting for her to slip her arm through. It's the most chivalrous move I've ever made in my life, more so than when I walked her out to her car the night of my party. That was late at night in an area filled with bars and drunks. It was a safety issue, but tonight it's more on the romantic spectrum.

Which is so not me, but at this point, I don't know that I'm in control of anything.

Smiling, Danica links her arm with mine and we head down her front steps. I couldn't get a spot right in front of her house, but it's a short walk down the block and the sidewalk is clear of ice and snow. It's a brisk thirty-six degrees tonight and I don't mind that she presses in close. I open the passenger door to my truck and hold her hand as she steps from the running board into the cab.

After closing the door, I walk around the rear of my truck, stepping off the curb and halting momentarily. I inhale deeply. Fuck, I'm wound up. It comes out in an explosive rush from my lungs and I give myself a pep talk.

You're on a date, asshole. You asked her, she said yes. She could have said no. Bain says there's no bro code. Quit worrying, dipshit, and enjoy yourself.

"Yeah... enjoy myself," I mutter as I jog around to the driver's side and climb in. Danica smiles and I smile back, noting my palms are still sweaty as I start the truck and put it in Drive.

"I'm nervous," she blurts.

My head snaps her way as I shift back into Park. "You're nervous?"

She nods with a sheepish duck of her head.

The knot in the center of my chest loosens as I let out a bark of laughter. "Fuck... so am I. It helps to know you feel the same."

Danica laughs. "It's natural, right?"

"God, I hope so." She snickers and the tension melts away. Our eyes lock across the cab of my truck, her face lit from the glow of the streetlamp. "Let's promise to enjoy the night with no worries."

She smirks. "You mean, forget all about our past traumas and the complicated nature of how we know each other? Maybe pretend we just met?"

I beam a smile. "Yeah... just like that."

The trip to the restaurant only takes fifteen minutes and we have no problem filling the time with casual talk. "Where's Travis tonight?"

"At his buddy Jordan's house. I'm sure they're immersed deep into the Xbox as apparently, Jordan got the new hockey video game."

"Is he one of Travis's teammates?"

"Yeah… but they also go to school together."

I glance her way, drinking in her beauty for a second. "Do I need to get you home by a certain time to get him?"

She turns her head to me. "No. He's going to stay overnight. Jordan's mom, Tamara, has become a good friend. Travis does overnights there and Jordan stays at our place often. But I'll pick him up in the morning and take both boys to school."

I'm hesitant to ask my next question, but the curiosity will distract me all night so I get it out of the way. "Does Travis know you're going out with me tonight?"

"No," she huffs out with a nervous laugh. "I told him I was going out with a friend, which is true. Had he asked me *who* I was going out with, I would have told him, but he wasn't curious enough to press me."

"Have you been on a date since Mitch died?"

She shakes her head. "What about you? What's your dating life like?"

I shoot her a glance, turning my attention back to the road. "Nothing serious."

Meaningless sex, sneaking out of a woman's apartment in the morning before she wakes up, trying to dodge claws sinking into me.

The restaurant looks a little sketchy as it's in a strip mall, but the ratings are high and when I called to make the reservation, they were very helpful in accommodating me with an out-of-the-way table.

When we're seated in adjacent chairs at a square table near the back, the waiter provides us with a menu. I lean toward Danica so we can peruse it together, but when the waiter returns, we still haven't decided.

"If I may make suggestions?" he offers. "Ethiopian food is best when it's shared. Put your forks away and use the injera—it's a flatbread—to pinch pieces of the food. I would suggest the Doro Wot and the Zilzil Tibs. They're our most popular dishes."

Danica and I drop our gazes to the menu again to read the description of the food. I look up at the waiter. "Okay… we'll try that. And what beverage do you suggest?"

"I'll bring you some t'ej to try. It's a fermented honey mead made with gesho leaves. A little sweet but pairs perfectly with the spicy food."

"Awesome. And water, please."

"Of course," he says with a slight bow.

"Think we should take some preventive Tums first?" Danica asks.

"Let's be courageous and not."

We both laugh but mine dies when Danica takes my hand in hers, freezing my breath. We're sitting close with our chairs next to each other, and she laces her fingers through mine. Her skin is soft and warm. I stare almost hypnotized at the way they are linked, one of her slim fingers alternating with one of my larger ones, skin slightly more tanned and way rougher.

Danica stares at them too, but then her eyes slide to mine. "I know this is a little weird, and I know neither one of us was really looking for anything. But I also know, deep in my gut, that we've crossed paths again for a reason. Maybe it's only to be friends, maybe it's more. But for right now, I know that holding your hand feels good. It doesn't feel awkward or bad in any way."

Nothing about this scenario should feel right to me, yet I find myself drawing our hands down to rest together on the table, fingers intertwined because touching her feels more than right. I let my gaze rest there a moment, considering that I'm not sure when I last held a woman's hand in an affectionate way.

Certainly never when it felt like this.

I lift my eyes, letting them roam over her face. "I've never talked about the crash with anyone."

She blinks at me in surprise. "Anyone?"

I shrug, letting my thumb graze over the side of her wrist. "After it happened, of course I talked to people about the horror of it. A lot of shared grief with family members and friends. That sort of thing. But I never told a single soul how it made me feel to lose all those people. Never entered into a meaningful conversation about the trauma of it."

Danica remains quiet but her fingers flex, a silent

gesture that she's here and listening.

"Remember I told you that day in the garage that my dad and brothers are military, and they aren't big on feelings."

She nods, another squeeze to my hand.

"I tried one time to talk about it with my oldest brother, Caleb. I've never had a close relationship with my dad... he was too emotionally distant, but I did look up to Caleb."

"What happened?" she asks hesitantly.

"Nothing happened. He listened and then sort of squeezed my shoulder. Said, 'I feel you, brother. But you have to suck it up and be strong. That's what we Poes do.'"

Danica frowns. "That wasn't very comforting."

"We're not that type of family. My dad didn't do a good job letting his boys grieve when Mom died. He said essentially the same thing Caleb said to me... you have to be strong. Then he told me that Mom would have wanted that."

"I imagine your mom would have preferred you'd been hugged instead," Danica says acidly.

That makes me laugh. "Yeah... that's exactly what my mom would have wanted. My dad was all proud, military bearing, the rock upon which our family stood. Mom was the soft surroundings who soothed our hurts when we fell. Without her to balance us..." I don't finish my thought as it's not needed. Danica nods her understanding. "So after the crash, I did what Caleb told me to do. I was strong, and that meant pushing it all down. Not talking about it. Moving forward with my life."

"I'm sorry you didn't have anyone to lean on," she murmurs. "But you have me now."

I swallow hard, pushing past the lump of apprehension in my throat. "I keep dreaming of plane crashes. I had the first one about a month after the plane went down. By then the new team was back on the ice and I was focused on playing hockey. I felt like it came out of left field because I wasn't feeling depressed or anxious or angry or heartsick or any of a million emotions that would be normal for me to have. I was sad for a time, I mourned and I moved on. So it made no sense why I'd have that nightmare. Or why I kept having them."

"It's your mind's way of telling you something," Danica says.

I nod in agreement. "The dreams are all different too. Sometimes I'm on the plane going down with the rest of them. Sometimes I'm on the ground and it drops out of the sky to land on me. Sometimes, it will crash in the distance, far enough away that I'm safe but then the fireball rolls my way, closer and closer until it consumes me."

"Do you feel the same with each nightmare? Are they all terror-based?"

That question befuddles me for a moment. I'd classify them all as terror-based as they're nightmares and they scare the shit out of me. But actually, one of them does feel different.

"The ones where I'm on the ground and the plane falls on me, or the fireball gets me, I'm scared. Panicked."

"And the one when you're on the plane?" she prods gently.

My eyes bore into hers. "I'm relieved. I mean... the free fall scares me and I can feel the lurch in my stomach as we plummet, but I'm surrounded by my team and... it seems okay."

The waiter appears and sets down two glasses of amber-colored wine. It breaks the somber moment and causes Danica and I to pull our hands away from each other. She glances up and murmurs, "Thank you."

When we're alone again, I take my glass and hold it up. She does the same and we tap them together. "Thanks for coming on a date with me," I say.

"Thanks for asking," she replies.

We both take a sip, staring at each other over the rims.

"Mmm," she says with clear delight. "That's delicious."

"A little too sweet for me but I'm glad to have tried it."

Setting our glasses back down, it's me this time who takes her hand. I don't lace our fingers but instead hold her with our palms pressed together. With my other arm on the table, I lean closer to her. "What do you think it means?"

We're not talking about wine or dates. I'm asking her to help me understand and she knows it.

Danica leans in and I can see gold flecks in her brown eyes. "In your dreams... I think you're relieved to be on that plane because you feel guilty that you weren't."

"Yeah." She doesn't tell me anything I didn't suspect already. But somehow, hearing it from her and not from the inner recesses of my mind doesn't make it seem so foolish.

"It wasn't your time, Camden. Whether you believe in God, fate or none of those things... it simply wasn't your time."

My lips curve slightly. "That easy, huh?"

"For the longest time, I was in denial that Mitch died." I jerk at the mention of my friend's name. Her husband. I had forgotten for a bit that he would be in the room during this conversation. Danica grips my hand hard. "But eventually, the only way I could deal with the loss was to realize that it was beyond my control. That there was something bigger at play than I could comprehend. The only way I could accept it was to make myself understand that it was Mitch's time. That might seem callous, but I had to find a way to reconcile the grief in my heart with the need for survival in my gut. So my mind reassured me that there was nothing I could have done to prevent it. It was just Mitch's time."

I cover our clutched hands with my other palm. "I'm sorry, Dani. I hate you went through it. More for Travis because I don't know how a kid could make sense of it the way you did."

She laughs, the sound husky with emotion and affection. "Kids are the most resilient creatures in the world. Many times Travis was my rock and he didn't even know it."

"Here you go." The waiter's voice breaks us apart. He's carrying a plate in each hand and one balanced on his inner forearm. "The Doro Wot, a spicy chicken stew, and the Zilzil Tibs, which is braised beef."

My senses are assaulted by the spices and Danica leans in to inhale.

"Mmm," she hums low in her throat, and my eyes snap from the food to her. That sounded way too sexy. She grins. "Smells divine, doesn't it?"

The waiter motions to the plate of what looks like porous, spongy crepes but slightly thicker. "The injera. Use this to pick up the food but if that gets too messy, no one will make fun of you for using forks."

Danica is the first to reach for the bread, pulling off a

piece about the size of her palm and using it to pinch into the beef. She lifts it to her mouth, sauce dripping, and our eyes lock as she sets it on her tongue. She chews slowly, savoring that first bite.

"Oh wow, that's good. You've got to try that."

She doesn't give me the chance to follow suit, instead tearing another piece of bread and nabbing more beef with it. She holds it out to me, not to take it with my own hand but toward my mouth.

Without hesitation, I open it and let her place the morsel on my tongue.

It's one of the most intimate gestures a woman has ever given me, and I have to admit I'm turned on.

I'm also strangely comforted by it.

I can't even begin to figure out the blend of spices that hit my tongue, but the tender beef and the mild bread melt in my mouth. "Damn, that's amazing."

The waiter offers a slight bow. "Enjoy your meal."

Danica and I dig in, both grabbing bread. "Are your brothers married? Do you have any nieces or nephews?" she asks.

For the next two hours, we eat spicy food and drink honey wine.

We talk about everything.

Except the crash.

CHAPTER 14

Danica

MY *FIRST* FIRST date was over twelve years ago. Mitch asked me to the movies and I didn't know that it was actually a date. We'd been friends for so long and I'd watched him date other girls who were older (and prettier, or so I thought). It never occurred to me that he was interested in any way other than as a friend to hang out with on Friday nights. He wanted to see *Thor* and given we were both Marvel fans, I assumed he thought of taking me after some of his buds couldn't go.

I thought all of that but realized quickly that it was so much more when he walked me to my door at the end of the night. He looked pale, nervous and cagey. I was confused and thought he might be sick.

Turns out… he wanted to kiss me and didn't know how to go about doing it.

He eventually figured it out and our lives changed.

Now here I am, twelve years later, and I'm on my second first date.

It's nothing like the first. From the start, I understand that Camden likes me in a way that's more than friendship. And I have the maturity to understand the complications and the wisdom to know that it's okay for me to want something like this.

Mitch was my soul mate, but now he's not. That ended with his death. I don't pretend to know what my future holds or whether it will be with Camden or some other man. I only know that love is too wonderful to go without and I don't intend to hide from it, thinking that my only shot was wasted when that plane went down.

If I focus on the biggest difference between that *first* first date with Mitch and this second first date with Camden, the two of us facing each other on my front porch, it's that I know exactly what this is.

And Camden isn't nervous the way Mitch was. Sure… I see conflict warring in his golden eyes but his bearing is confident.

Not one to mince words, he says, "I know enough to know that I want a second date."

Simple words to convey exactly what's on his mind.

Because I had more fun tonight than I've had since I lost Mitch, I say what's on my mind too. "I'd love that."

"The trickier thing is that I want to kiss you." My breath catches, because I wondered if this was how the evening would end. "Even trickier yet, I'm not sure if that will get me a return kiss or a kick in the balls."

I hold back a laugh but I can't stop the smile. "There

will be no ball-kicking tonight, sir."

"Good." His tone is gruff but his touch is soft when he steps into me, brushing a lock of hair back from my face to tuck it behind my ear. A shiver rattles my spine. Camden's hand doesn't fall away but instead curls around the back of my neck. He steps in closer and dips his head. "Because I've been thinking about this since you fed me that bite of food and your fingers brushed my lips."

Oh, God. I knew that was such a personal gesture and I'd be lying if I said it didn't make me think of kissing him too.

Camden's words are so damn hypnotizing, I can't think of anything witty in response. It doesn't matter, though, because his face blurs as he closes the distance between our mouths.

The first brush of his lips against mine thieves the breath from my body. In a reactionary inhale, my head swims from the scent of his cologne. The taste of the honey mead on his tongue when it tentatively touches mine makes me even dizzier.

Camden pulls back, staring at me with darkened eyes. I observe innumerable emotions rippling through their golden depths.

Desire.

Hesitation.

Guilt.

My hands come to his chest, resting against the thick sweater and I curl my fingers into the knit to grab tightly. "Don't be afraid," I whisper.

Of all the things I could have said or done to reassure Camden that I am in this with him, I command him to let go of his fears. It's the most powerful thing holding him back.

Camden's hands come to the sides of my neck, his thumbs grazing the skin between the corners of my jaw and my ears. "So fucking tricky."

"It is." I wrap my hands around his wrists as he continues to palm my neck. "And it isn't."

"Tell me more about the part where it's not." His eyes roam over my face, searching for the answer.

"We have history. Both together and apart that complicates things. That's the tricky part. But I'm choosing to stand in the present, not the past. Right now, on this porch with you, I'm forgetting about what was yesterday. I'm only thinking about today... now. I deserve it and I think you do too."

His breath shudders out and along with the exhale, I can see the wariness draining from his expression. Camden's mouth is back on mine, the movement gentle but assured.

I sink into it all the way, pressing into him and moving my hands back to his broad chest. Up over his shoulders and around his neck.

It makes Camden bolder and he slides an arm around my waist. Our bodies press tight and I swear I can feel the thud of his heart against mine as the kiss deepens.

I'm completely and utterly intoxicated by this man... from this very moment. I'm drunk with need to experience more and I mate my tongue more forcefully against his.

Camden growls from deep within his chest, the sound rumbling from his body to mine. His hands are at my hips, gripping me tight and I feel urgency rippling between us.

Tearing his mouth away, Camden mutters, "Jesus fuck."

I'm breathing so hard, I'm panting.

Oh my God... he made me pant, and that's when I notice the ache between my legs that I haven't felt in a very long time.

All from a kiss.

"We're getting ready to cross a line, Dani. And once we do, there's no going back."

My mouth tingles, my blood races and... and... damn it all to hell, I'm turned on beyond measure.

I close my eyes and drop my forehead to his chest. Camden's fingers flex against my hips. Very easily, I could stop this. I could slow us down, even return us to friendship. We can still go back.

But I can't.

I don't want to.

I tip my head, locking my eyes with Camden's. "I want to cross the line. I'm ready to cross the line."

"I don't know." Layered within the hesitation, I hear the truth that's probably painful to admit. He wants to be strong in his actions, assured in himself.

"Tell you what," I murmur, lifting on my tiptoes and pressing my mouth against the hollow of his throat. "I'll cross it first." Camden's hands grip me harder as a harsh breath escapes him. I whisper against his warm skin, moving my lips up to his jaw. "I'm all the way across." To the corner of his mouth. "Waiting for you to join me."

I'm unprepared for the growl that tears free of Camden and slightly scared of its primal nature. It sounds like he's being tortured, but it's just as quickly soothed as his mouth captures mine.

He retakes control, a hand at my lower back and another at my nape, holding me completely hostage. I'm the one drowning now, helplessly being pulled under a strong riptide of longing and lust. Camden is rock solid, though, and I cling to him desperately as his mouth assaults mine.

I'm vaguely aware that my body is plastered against his, having melted into him because that's much easier than holding myself up.

And that's when I notice there's a particular part of

him that's very hard, pushing into my belly and it causes a rush of warmth to surge between my legs, only to recede and leave behind a deep ache.

My hand trembles as I push it between our bodies and shamelessly palm the length of him. Camden hisses into my mouth before he jerks back to stare at me with wild eyes.

"Danica," he warns.

The threat in his tone doesn't scare me but instead turns me on even more. I squeeze him.

"Fuck," he curses, anger flashing in his eyes followed by what might be a promise of retribution. "We've got to slow this down."

"Why?" I ask, nuzzling into his neck before tipping my head to look at him. "Where are the rules? And why can't we have this?"

Camden seems at a loss for words and it's then that I notice he's not holding me anymore. It's like a bucket of cold water square in the face as an awful realization hits.

I stumble back into my door, my hand hovering over my mouth as I stare at him wildly.

His eyebrows knit together. "What's wrong?" he demands.

"I'm acting like a tramp and it's a turnoff," I say, confident in my assessment.

"What?" he asks, and granted… he looks a little bewildered. "I don't think that at all."

"But… you want to slow this down, and I don't know any man who would slow things down with a woman's hand on his dick." Heat flushes my cheeks, and I drop my face into my palms. "Oh God… this is humiliating."

"For fuck's sake, Danica." Camden pulls my hands away by gripping my wrists and then jerks me into him. He peers down at me, jaw set into a hard line. "I don't think you're a tramp. It is not a turnoff what we did. And I only suggested slowing things down because the minute you put your hand on my dick, I knew I was going to fuck you if you left it there."

"Oh," I murmur, then my eyes grow wide as I realize what he really just said. "Oh. Oh… wow. Okay. I understand."

"Do you?" he demands. "Because I am barely able to keep my hands to myself right now. So if you don't want me to end up deep inside you tonight, you need to kiss my cheek and tell me good night."

A shudder runs through my body at the thought of Camden inside me, images of our naked bodies writhing against each other. There's no other response for me. "No way in hell I'm kissing you on the cheek. So you better take me inside and do your worst."

For the first time since we stepped foot on the porch, an easy smile graces Camden's face. "Not my worst. My best."

I smile in relief, winding my arms around his neck again. "Your best, then."

Everything happens so fast that when I reflect on it later, I'll probably agree that there was a desperate edge to what we were both feeling. Despite the assurances to each other, the fevered frenzy by which we crash through my front door in a tangle of arms and legs with our mouths fused probably speaks more to the fear that we might come to our senses at any second.

The way we rush up the stairs, hand in hand with me only slightly in the lead is a clear indication that we want each other so much, time can't move fast enough.

But, oh, the way he tears the clothes from my body only to push me down on my bed and run his mouth over every inch of me tells the story of a man who, no matter how out of control he might feel, wants to make this good for me.

I pull hard on Camden's hair—a benefit to the messy style he always wears—and he lets my nipple pop free of his mouth to look up at me. "I'm dying here. Will you please get your clothes off?"

The world stops with the way he smiles at me. I've seen Camden's mouth curve into all kinds of positive expressions over the last few weeks, but never so blindingly happy as right now. He crawls up my body to lay a hard, fast kiss on my lips and then scrambles off the bed to disrobe.

He looks at me sheepishly when he pulls a condom out of his wallet, setting it on the bedside table but I don't pay it any attention. I'm already lost in the vision before me as he pulls his sweater over his head. Beautifully carved muscles make the statue of *David* look cartoonish by comparison. His dark happy trail of hair below his navel is revealed inch by inch as he sheds his jeans.

And oh my word... my mouth goes dry when I get my first full look at him fisting his cock as he stares down at me with molten lust.

I lick my lips, starting to push up with the intent to crawl across the bed to devour him but he growls at me. "Lie the fuck down, Dani. Not ready to give you this yet."

It feels like flames wash over my entire body, his domineering words turning me on as much as his touches have. Telling me what to do and making it clear that what he chooses to give me will be goddamn beyond magnificent.

I yelp as his hands go to my legs, pulling me down the bed toward him and spreading me wide. I don't have time to be embarrassed as Camden leans over the bed, placing one palm by my head and sliding the other between my legs.

My breath stutters as a long finger presses gently into me. Camden squeezes his eyes shut for a moment, as if he's in pain, but when he opens them, they are full of so much satisfaction.

"Fucking soaked, Dani."

He's done nothing more than kiss me, strip me naked and tease a nipple, and yet I think I might be dripping. Hot embarrassment colors my cheeks but most of my fever comes from his finger now circling my clit.

"Camden," I gasp, feeling ridiculously out of control. I have never been this hyped by foreplay before… primed to get ripped apart. I'm already teetering on the edge and—"Oh shit… I'm going to come."

I swear it's a bark of victory I hear breaking free in a laugh as Camden's finger presses back into me. It's enough to knock the orgasm loose and I cry out as the pleasure seizes my body. I feel my muscles gripping his digit as my back arches off the bed.

I flop back down, gasping as tiny electrical currents pulse through me. I'm panting hard as Camden smiles with pure gratification, his finger now lazily circling my clit.

"Jesus," I rasp as my hand slaps onto his wrist to stop his movements. "I don't know that I've ever come that quickly before."

I'm utterly dizzy with how fast that happened. I'm a little mortified as well. I mean, it's been a long time since I've had sex, but it's not like I haven't had orgasms. I'm a big believer in masturbation.

"I want to watch that again," Camden murmurs, now sliding two fingers into my body.

"No," I exclaim, pulling hard on his hand. "If you don't fuck me right now, I'm kicking you out of my house."

Camden's laugh is rich with affection. He appeases me by pressing his mouth to mine and whispering, "All right. I got you, beautiful girl."

CHAPTER 15

Camden

*Y*OU SHOULD NOT *be fucking doing this.*

I deepen the kiss with Danica, the sweet taste of her tongue and the way she moans making my dick so hard I'm afraid it will break. I ignore the good angel sitting on my shoulder, whispering morality-infused warnings I should not get involved with this gorgeous creature sprawled out before me.

Too many parts of my being are telling me to take what Danica is offering. My cock seems to be running the show, but even my heart is pushing me on. I care for her a lot and while I'm going to chase an orgasm and bring her along for a second one, it's the feeling of closeness that's pulling on me the most.

To share something deep with her.

Reaching out blindly, I grab the condom without missing a stroke of my tongue against hers. I slip an arm under her and haul us both up to a better position on the bed. Danica's legs part and I settle right in between, my hard length nestled against her warm, wet, inviting core.

I could make her wetter.

My mouth on her pussy would do the trick and drive her to another orgasm before I fuck her.

Yeah... that's what I want.

Dropping the condom on the mattress, I drag my mouth from hers. I scrape my teeth down her neck as I palm a breast. I'm rewarded with a moan of pleasure and she bucks when I tweak her pebbled nipple. I blow warm breath as I kiss across her chest, intent on getting that pert bud back into my mouth and eventually between my teeth.

"No," Danica exclaims, her hands halting my progress.

I lift my head, give her a lazy grin. "What's wrong?"

She shakes her head, a wild look in her eyes. "I don't want that."

I cock an eyebrow, my tone dry. "You don't want me to make you come with my mouth?"

Dani rolls her eyes and it's so adorable, it makes me want to surge up and press a chaste kiss to the tip of her nose. "Of course I want that. But next time. I want you inside me now, Camden."

"Impatient," I tease but I'm forced to chase away another intrusive thought.

She's not had sex in close to a year. She's super horny and you happen to be convenient.

No. Fuck that. That's not Dani's nature to use

someone. We have a connection and it's solid enough to propel us straight from our first kiss after our first date right into sex.

Her palm caresses my stubbled cheek and the gentleness of her touch has my eyes colliding with hers. "What's wrong?" she asks. "I felt… something change."

"No," I assure her, leaning my head into her touch like a cat demanding to be petted. "Nothing's changed. But maybe my conscience is piping up a bit. You sure this isn't too fast for you?"

"I'm sure," she says, her eyes flickering with worry. "I'm starting to wonder, though… is it too fast for you? Am I pushing this too much?"

"Stop it," I chastise, stretching to press a hard kiss to her mouth. "I love how into this you are. I love how reactive you are. I love the way you came within seconds of me touching you. And I know I'm sure as hell going to love fucking you."

Danica heaves out what I might term a sigh of relief and I see it echoed in her eyes. I grab her jaw with my hand, force her to keep her gaze on me. "Tell me you want this."

"More than you can imagine."

That's all I need. One more swift kiss and I'm grabbing the condom only to have her tear it out of my hands. She opens it with grace, and I lean to the side so she can roll it on my shaft.

The feel of her hands on me blasts a shudder up my spine and there's a tiny kernel of apprehension that I might not survive this. I don't ever recall my body reacting so swiftly to a woman. Despite my insecurities, my dick has been rock hard since we kissed and it hasn't abated at all.

With a palm to the back of her thigh, I lift her leg and position myself at her entrance. The heat of her pussy burns through the condom and that, coupled with the look of pure lust on her face—eyes glazed, lip between her teeth, her insistent undulations—I lose control.

I drive my hips forward, sliding into her tight channel in one fluid motion that has me nearly blacking out from the intense pleasure. Danica snarls and bites my shoulder.

"You okay?" I ask as I pull back so I can see her face.

"Oh yeah." She groans and rotates her hips. "More."

I thought I was all the way in deep but she's asked for more. I realize… I'm not close enough to her.

Urging her to wrap her legs around my waist, I slip one arm under her back and the other under her neck, giving an all-encompassing embrace as I move inside her. My cheek pressed to hers, I slowly pump in and out, wondering how it's possible that I feel her all over me.

Surrounding me.

Infiltrating.

Minutes ago we were so hot for each other that I thought this would go rough, fast and frenzied. Even with all the tender feelings I've developed for her, lust has overtaken us both.

But now... I want it slow, this gentle rocking that shouldn't feel as good as a hard, passionate fuck, but it does.

It feels better.

"Camden."

Danica's whisper penetrates and I realize I've closed my eyes, pressed my temple to hers and allowed myself to get lost in her.

I lift my head, stare down at her through the sensual haze clouding my head. "Yeah?"

"This feels so good." Her words are drawn out, without hurry.

"Yeah," I agree softly.

Brushing an almost chaste kiss across her mouth, I lift my head to fix my gaze on her. Loosening my arm under her neck, I move it to press my palm into the mattress for leverage. I leave my other arm under her back to keep our bodies pressed as tight as possible.

I've never liked the term "making love." It feels cliché and overused. Besides, what we have between us isn't love.

Not yet.

Maybe not ever.

But this transcends anything I've ever felt for another woman. I don't know if that's because our history is so intertwined with tragedy and survival or if it's like recognizing like.

What I do know is that with this slow pleasure swelling between us by the leisurely pumping of my hips against hers, neither of us in the typical hurry to get where sex normally leads, well… that tells me I need to pay fucking attention to what this is and where it's going.

Time doesn't quite stand still but seems to tick by with an acceptable slowness. All the while I thrust in and out, in and out.

Never in a hurry.

It's only when Danica starts making a throaty noise—somewhere between a moan and a plea—that I know she's close. It's the same sound she uttered the first time I made her come and I'm now pressed to more urgency. I remember how beautiful it was when she broke apart and I'm eager to see it again.

It's only at this point—my desire to give Danica the ultimate pleasure—that I feel my orgasm furling, vibrating, threatening to shake loose.

It seems against my will because while I love the slow fucking, my pace picks up. There's definite provocation as I want to push Danica to release.

Dipping my head, I put my mouth near her ear.

"With me, sweet girl."

"Yes," she pants.

She's still secure in my hold, my arm under her back. I grab her hand, pull it in close to us and lower my body. My hips tunnel as my mouth takes hers. I barely get a swipe of my tongue against hers when my orgasm explodes. My groan pours into her mouth as I plant deep and I'm vaguely aware of Danica bucking under me.

Vaguely aware of her nails digging into me.

Dimly, I hear her calling out, "Yes, yes, yes!"

"Fuck." I curse into her mouth as I grind against her, the orgasm shredding me. "Fuck yes."

I huff out a massive exhale, blinking my eyes against the dimming, which might be me on the verge of passing out from my powerful release.

Danica whimpers and I surge up, looking down at her with worry. She's got her bottom lip in between her teeth, eyes hazy but she manages a smile. "Good God, Camden. You've got a magic dick."

I bust out laughing, loving that she lightened the moment because everything was so deep and heavy only moments ago. In a good way, of course. We both rocked each other's worlds but we can still share a laugh when it's all said and done.

For several minutes, I lie with her on the bed until the racing of two hearts returns to normal. I reluctantly leave her warmth to dispose of the condom and have not a lick of hesitation in joining her under the covers when I return.

Danica moves easily into my arms, resting her head on my chest. Her fingertips stroke the skin over my heart and her warm breath wafts over my skin. I take advantage of unfettered access, sliding my hand over her lower back, her ass… trailing fingers up again to skim down her spine.

With the fire between us quelled, I try to reason out what that is between us.

"Did you tell anyone we were going out on a date?"

Did I sound casual enough in my curiosity?

"No," Danica says softly. "I didn't think to, to be honest. You?"

"No. I don't even know who I'd tell."

She lifts her head and angles my way, a curious expression on her face. "Who are you close with on the team?"

I don't have to think long about it. "I probably hang out the most with Hendrix and Bain. Coen for sure, but he had those months of being an asshole and now he's got Tillie, so we don't do much together."

After a hesitation, Danica asks, "Do you want to keep this secret?"

"I don't know." That's the honest truth. I know nothing because this is unlike anything I've ever experienced. "This feels a little precarious."

"Because I'm a team widow," she murmurs.

"I don't want to be the asshole who moved in on someone I should only be friends with."

"I get that," she replies with a sigh.

"And…" I pause, wondering how best to say this. I'm not afraid to express my feelings—I just want to make sure I'm clear. I shift our positions so we're on our sides, facing each other. "I don't know how to compete with Mitch. I don't know if it's a good idea to even try."

Danica rears up to her elbow to look down at me. "I would never compare you—"

I move two fingers over her lips to silence her. "No. I know you wouldn't do that. Not intentionally. But there will always be differences, and hell… maybe I'd be the one wondering about it."

Her hand rests over my chest, her expression empathetic. "Camden… I can honestly say that not once tonight did I ever stack you up against Mitch. Not on our date, not on our first kiss, and most certainly not what we just did. He didn't even cross my mind until you brought him up. But I can't *not* think about him. I can't control that and it might happen."

"I know." I cup her cheek and rub my thumb over her lower lip. "I'd never ask you to not think about him. I loved him, too, you know."

"I had a lot of firsts after he died." Danica settles back into my arms and I pull her in tight. "My first birthday without him. Travis's first birthday without him. First Fourth of July, first Halloween, Thanksgiving, Christmas. It's almost been a year since the crash and I've had almost all the *firsts* knocked out."

"And I'm the first guy you've been out with. First kiss since Mitch died. First time you've had sex."

"It was fucking fantastic sex," Danica says and I can't help but chuckle, giving her a squeeze. Her voice sounds drowsy. "Will you stay the night?"

"If you want me to."

"I do." Danica yawns and snuggles into me.

Reaching over without trying to disturb our positioning, I'm able to turn out the bedside light. "Then I'll stay." When we're settled, I add, "And maybe we keep this between us for now."

"Of course," she replies. I'm not sure if she wants that particularly or she's merely agreeing because I want it. Regardless, I don't feel comfortable sharing what we have.

CHAPTER 16

Camden

I N FAIRNESS, DANICA gave me fair warning that carpool was a *wait around and do nothing* kind of event. I've got my radio cranked as I sit in the school lineup, waiting to get Travis for drills practice with me.

When we first made plans, I was only supposed to pick Travis up at Danica's house after she got him home from school. But apparently, and this is per Danica and I have no reason to disbelieve her, Travis floated the idea to his mom about me picking him up and we go directly to the rink from there.

I wasn't privy to this conversation as it unfolded this morning but it occurred as Danica was driving Travis and Jordan to school. Her answer was a resounding no because I was already giving my time to take him to the rink.

I only found out about Travis's request when I called Danica midmorning. I was going crazy thinking about her. Last night was absolutely unexpected. The only surety was our first date. I didn't expect to enjoy it so much, I most certainly didn't think we'd kiss and there was never a scenario in my mind where I thought we might end up in bed.

All night long, Danica slept in my arms but I hardly slept a wink. It's not because the position was uncomfortable or because I was in a strange bed, but more to do with the fact that the experience of sleeping with a woman I actually care for was more exhilarating than it was calming.

Danica's not the first woman I've slept in a bed with all night. I've had hookups where you fall into an exhausted sleep and then you go on your merry way after.

However, she is the first woman I've had a true emotional connection with, which made the sex last night a million times better than I've ever experienced.

This morning there was no awkwardness, and in fact, I woke her up with my hand between her legs and my mouth whispering dirty words in her ear. It was different in the early hours compared to the slow mating of bodies last night. This morning it was frenzied, rushed, sloppy and amazing. Danica had to pick up the boys to take them to school and we laughed as we went at it, knocking her headboard into the wall so hard it left a scuff mark.

Yeah... last night and this morning, the memories ran through my head like a motion picture on a loop and so I broke down and called her around ten thirty. She was working, so we kept the conversation short. I think I got what I was looking for in the first thirty seconds— true joy to hear from me. It was enough to push back any regrets or concerns that I made a mistake with her and assured me she didn't have any.

She laughed as she told me Travis wanted me to pick him up from school but she nixed that idea.

"Why not?" I asked curiously.

"Trust me... carpool line is not fun. It's a whole lot of waiting and you have better things to do."

"I don't mind." And I didn't. I had the time off, no other plans and I'm easy to entertain.

Danica didn't give in right away but I eventually cajoled her into letting me pick up Travis. She had to call the school to put me on the permission list and also had them get word to Travis that I'd be picking him up.

It's not that bad... waiting. I arrived early enough I'm only about twenty cars back and I've amused myself on my phone while listening to music. The process is fairly efficient and by the time I pulled up to the spot where Travis waited, I'd barely been there thirty minutes.

Travis was hilarious. First and foremost, he looked beyond adorable in his rumpled school uniform. Exactly how I'd imagine a little boy would look at the end of the day. His hair was all mussed up, his tie pulled loose and hanging crookedly, and there were what appeared to be mud stains on the knees of his khaki pants. I bet Danica spends a fortune keeping his clothes clean.

The best part was apparently Travis told everyone that I'd be picking him up and all his friends were watching. A group of about five or six boys stood a few feet back and rubbernecked at my truck as I rolled down my window.

"Car service for Travis Brandt," I hollered and Travis beamed.

All the boys waved at me, other students craned their necks to see what was so important and Travis strutted to my truck. A teacher opened the back door to the cab and once he was on the running board, he turned to wave to his friends. "I'm headed to the rink with Camden Poe," he called out. "We're gonna play some hockey together."

I grinned behind my aviator shades as Travis dropped into the seat and we bumped fists.

We're at the arena now and gone is the excited little boy who wanted everyone to see he was friends with a professional hockey player. I'm not sure why that's important to him or his social standing because his dad was a Titan as well. I'm hoping it's because he considers me a friend of the family and it's cool to know someone famous.

Now he's a boy—still young—determined to excel at the same sport his dad played. He listens attentively, applies the knowledge I impart and busts his ass to do his best. He'll try the same move over and over again until he accomplishes near perfection.

After an hour, he's drenched in sweat and while he's got no quit in him, I call time. "I need to get you home. I promised your mom I'd have you there by four thirty because you have to get your homework done before dinner."

Travis scrunches up his face. "I hate homework. It's stupid."

"It's necessary," I say as we skate off the ice and head to the locker rooms.

"No, it's not," he counters as he removes his helmet. "My dad went straight into the league when he was eighteen and I'm going to do the same."

Laughing, I ruffle his sweaty hair. "That may be so but you still have to graduate high school, so you still have to do homework."

"Doesn't mean I have to like it," he grumbles.

"Your mom says you do really well at Harrington. I take it that means you're a smart kid, so homework shouldn't be that big a deal, right?"

Travis shrugs. "I guess not." Then he shoots me a grin. "But I'd rather play video games."

"Who wouldn't?"

After Travis changes, we head out. It's the best time for us to talk about hockey so before I unlock the truck, I stop him at the tailgate.

"How was practice yesterday?"

"It was really good. Coach Kantor used me to demonstrate a certain move because he said I was the best." That's not necessarily a bad thing and as long as Travis remains humble, he should be proud his skills are called out. His mouth draws downward and his expression is troubled. "He's kind of mean to some of the other kids, though."

"How so?"

"Well, he's kind of hard to please and some of the other kids—the ones that aren't as good—he gets frustrated with them more. He yelled a lot yesterday and one of the boys cried. He tried to hide it but I saw it and I know some others did too. I don't know that he's going to keep playing."

I grit my teeth and force myself not to give personal opinions about Kantor. But I am vocal about what that means for Travis. "Not every coach—even the ones who know the most—are cut out to coach."

Travis tilts his head. "Why not?"

I lean my arm on my tailgate. "Because coaching isn't about who knows the most, it's about who *can learn* the most."

"That doesn't make sense," Travis says, his brows knitted tight but his tone isn't dismissive. Rather curious, which I like.

The best example I can give him will hit very close to

home, so I'm hesitant. But I remember something Danica said to me the other day.

She told me there are no ghosts. While there are moments of sadness that Mitch died, there are many more happy memories. I've observed that Danica doesn't skirt away from talking about Mitch or the crash in front of or with Travis, so I'm going to go with my gut and assume the same.

"The best example I can give you is the Titans' team. You know our current coach?"

Travis's eyes light up at the trivia question. "Cannon West."

"And before that?"

His face screws up as if he's trying to remember. "Um... I can't remember his name but he was fired."

"That's right," I say in an even tone. "His name was Matt Keller and he was hired to coach the Titans after the plane crash." I pause and observe Travis carefully. Something flickers in his eyes and I can't help but wonder if he's thinking about his dad at this very moment.

Probably.

"Matt Keller was a very knowledgeable coach," I continue, relieved to see interest flare within Travis's expression again. "Had a lot of experience and knew the game as well as any other professional league coach."

"Then why was he fired?"

"Because he wasn't any good at connecting with his players. And when a coach can't reach a player—whether it's teaching them skill, strategy or even just to inspire them to work hard—then they're not doing their job. Coach Keller didn't have the ability to transfer his knowledge in a meaningful way. He wasn't able to excite the team to play their best."

"And Coach West can do that?" Travis inquires.

"He's outstanding. What all coaches should aspire to be. He's managed to build a very successful team this season and it's because he makes his players want to be the best."

Travis considers that for a moment and finally nods. And then he about breaks my heart. "I bet it was hard for you after the crash. You had to get a whole new team and learn to play with them."

I'm speechless. Travis stares at me with an earnest expression, waiting for me to confirm what he already knows. I suffered because of the crash too.

I put my hand on his shoulder and squat down to get eye-to-eye with him. "Yeah… it was tough. Just like I know it was for you."

The kid swallows hard and a tiny muscle quivers in his chin as he nods.

"Your dad was so proud of you. He talked about you all the time. Whenever we were at practices, in the locker room, or on the team plane, it was always about you and your mom. He loved you both very much."

"I miss him," Travis says glumly, and while I hear all the sorrow a little boy who lost his dad a year ago should have, I also hear resolution. An acceptance of the situation. "Mom misses him too."

Fuck, that shouldn't bother me. But whether I like it or not, I have to share space with Mitch. That's whether I'm helping Travis with hockey or dating Danica.

"I know she does." I hope the admission solidifies with Travis that I'm his mom's friend, too, and I'm sensitive to her grief as well. "Your dad was a great man, so there's lots to miss. I know I sure do."

I urge Travis into the back of my truck and turn the chat to something lighter to ease out of the heavy subject matter we left behind in the rink parking lot. We talk about video games, which is easy since I play them too.

When we reach his house, I'm lucky to get a spot right in front. I leave the truck running but get out to escort Travis up to the door. Before we even reach the front stairs, Danica steps over the threshold. It's freezing and she doesn't have a coat on. I refrain from pointing that out because that's coming from a place of possessive concern and I don't want Travis getting a hint of that from me.

Still, Danica's eyes come to me after she drapes an arm over Travis's shoulders. We share an exchange, silent but expressive, and I think we're both saying the same thing.

It's good to see you. You look amazing. I can't stop thinking about last night. When can I see you again?

Danica clears her throat and looks down at Travis. "Have a good time? Learn lots?"

"Yeah," Travis exclaims. "It was so much fun and Camden taught me this sweet little move."

He doesn't mention our talk about Coach Kantor, but honestly, not sure the distinction among coaches is all that important to him. At least I've set the foundation for him to understand that.

I reach my fist out and he bumps it. "I'm glad you had fun. We'll do it again sometime, okay?"

"That would be great."

I beam a smile at him, slide a slightly less brilliant one at Danica with a nod and turn to head down the steps.

"Would you like to stay for dinner?" Danica asks. I turn back toward her, trying to dampen the elation that wells within me. "The least I can do is feed you since you helped Travis."

"I don't want to be an imposition," I say hesitantly, afraid to look at Travis. It's one thing to take him to the rink, but another to sit at his dining table at his mom's invitation.

"I've made plenty, so no imposition," Danica assures me. "Only has about another half hour until it's ready."

"Awesome," Travis says and he does a fist pump.

"Camden can play video games with me."

Danica smirks and turns her son toward the door. "Camden can relax with a beer and talk to me while you take a quick shower and start your homework."

"Awww," Travis grumbles as he steps into the house. "That's no fair."

I throw a thumb over my shoulder. "Going to shut off my truck."

Danica doesn't follow her son inside but waits on the porch for me. When I bound back up, I glance at the stairs behind her framed by the door. "Is he up there?"

She tilts her head. "Um... yeah."

"Good. Been dying to do this." My hands go to Dani's face and I pull her in for a swift but deep kiss. Her hands grip my belt and she pulls us closer together. Her tongue touches mine and my body reacts.

Swiftly.

With a yearning groan, I pull away from her and she steps back, smiling devilishly. "Come on inside. You can keep me company while I cook."

"I'll help," I say as we enter the house.

She glances over her shoulder and winks as we walk to the kitchen. "We can probably sneak in another kiss or two before Travis comes back down."

Fuck yes. That sounds better than anything she might be making for dinner. And while I know that's all I'll have tonight—because if it weren't complicated enough that I'm dating my dead teammate's wife, I also have to navigate the fact she has a child—I'm strangely satisfied with just that.

CHAPTER 17

Danica

AIMING THE REMOTE at the smart board, I depress the button and a new slide appears on the Power-Point I'm presenting to Brienne. Our kickoff gala for the new foundation named in her brother's honor is the day after tomorrow and it's fallen squarely on my shoulders to plan the entire event. I've been working on it for over a month and I'm presenting it to Brienne for one last eyeball to make sure she doesn't see anything that needs changing.

I've provided her with the ballroom layout for this invitation-only event along with a proposed agenda of festivities that will encourage future sponsorships, recurring donations and volunteers.

Two hundred and fifty invitations went out and we've had two hundred and thirty-two RSVP their attendance. I've worked with the venue's event director and we've got twenty-five round tables arranged in a well-thought-out pattern that provides perfect views of the stage, the large drop-down screen where marketing videos and testimonials will roll, and a podium from which speeches will be given. I'm one of the speakers and I feel sick about it but I'm not only the new director, I'm one of the inspirations that led Brienne to start this foundation. My personal story is important for everyone to hear.

"This is my final draft of the agenda." I'm seated beside Brienne at a table in her office and I use a laser pointer to highlight an area of the slide. "Verify this is the order of the speakers you want. And if you change your mind and want to remove me, I won't argue."

Brienne snorts. She wants me to be the face of the foundation since I'm a prime example of why it exists but she knows I'm scared to speak in front of all these rich people. I'm not an introvert by any means and I could get up in front of a crowd of my peers. But most of these people are nothing like me and it's overwhelming. I also don't want to let Brienne down.

She ignores my last-ditch effort to stay off the stage, instead nodding at the slide. "I think we serve the first course immediately after I speak so people can eat as we run through the speakers and videos."

"Easy peasy to do that," I say, jotting notes in my spiral planner. Brienne gives me hell that I don't use the iPad she bought me for such things but I love the feel of pen and paper. "All the videos have been through post-production review and they are amazing. Do you want to see them ahead of time?"

"Yes," she says, giving me a lopsided smile. "I want to keep crying to a minimum so it's best I see them in advance."

"I've got extra tissues in case, although I'm afraid I'm the one who's going to be a snotty mess. I'll forward them to you."

The videos are of other widows, widowers and family members who lost loved ones in the Titans' crash. Stone will also be one of our speakers, and of course I'll be up there talking about what it cost Travis and me to lose Mitch, not just monetarily but emotionally. It's going to be a rough night.

Brienne angles her chair toward me and covers my hand with hers. "I'm proud of you, Danica. You have impressed me so much and this gala is going to be a huge success."

I blush but don't try to hide it. Brienne went out on a limb by giving me such an important job and any compliment is like her hanging the moon for me. "Thank you. I want to do the best possible job."

"You're doing better than the best possible," she says, staring at me with a look that says I should believe her.

I nod, a grateful smile on my face. "I'll send you the final seating chart and videos. Let me know if you want any changes."

I was given the final RSVP list yesterday and I

worked to spread out all the players among the tables. That's why the big donors are coming—to rub elbows with the Titans. I intentionally put Camden and me at tables on opposite sides of the room. I was afraid I'd steal too many glances at him and make a fool of myself.

Even as I think that, a warm giddiness takes hold. The last few days with him have truly put joy in my heart. Last night the stolen kisses when Travis wasn't around and the banter among the three of us at dinner had me all up in my feels. It felt right to have him at my dinner table and it melted me to see the easy back-and-forth between him and Travis.

And of course, I cannot stop thinking about the time we spent in bed. I feel my face heat up at the memories, but Brienne will probably think it's leftover blushing from her compliments.

There's an insistent knock and without waiting for Brienne to welcome whoever it is, the door bursts open and Jenna Holland flies through.

Jenna is the media liaison for the Titans, a job Brienne personally hired her for last year as she built the new team. She and Brienne are close friends and by virtue of us all working together, I've gotten close to her as well.

"Look," she practically shrieks as she runs over and shoves her hand between us.

I don't have to look hard. The glint of a massive

diamond on Jenna's left ring finger catches my attention.

"Oh!" I exclaim in awe, taking her hand to look at it closer.

Brienne yanks her hand from me and holds it up for inspection before lifting her gaze to Jenna.

She sees what I see... a woman who's utterly in love and filled with so much excitement she might implode.

Brienne and I fly out of our chairs and hug Jenna, who is clearly a newly engaged woman.

When we release her, Brienne demands, "Details. Now."

"I'm so sorry to burst in on your meeting," Jenna says, her voice quavering as she holds her own hand to gaze at the ring.

"Whatever," Brienne says with a wave of her hand. "Give us the details."

"It was perfect. Exactly how I'd want to be proposed to. It was over pancakes this morning. Gage got up early and made them... my favorite kind with blueberries. He had set the kitchen table with nice plates and linens, had coffee and fresh juice. I was still half-asleep when he forced me out of bed to come eat and there it was... a black box right beside my plate."

"And," I prompt because that's totally swoony but clearly there's more.

Jenna rests her hand on her chest and sighs. "It was all down on one knee and the most beautiful words. He didn't even get them all out before I knocked him over. Just crashed right into him, flattened him to the floor while screaming yes."

"And then what?" Brienne asks, truly intrigued by the romance of it all. I know enough about Brienne to know she's about as unromantic as you can get, or at least she was until she fell in love with Drake.

Jenna's cheeks turn a raspberry color, which only heightens the difference in her skin tones because of the scarring from her jaw down to her neck. "Um… well… I kissed him and he sort of kissed me back, and it was a really good kiss, you know? The type that kept us on the floor and…"

Brienne and I snicker.

Jenna gives a sheepish shrug. "I didn't get to even look at the ring until a bit later."

With joy-softened eyes, Brienne pulls Jenna into another hug. "You got one of the best ones out there."

"Yours isn't so bad either." Jenna laughs as they break apart.

By all accounts, both Gage and Drake are good men.

Mitch was a good one too. One of the best. A stunningly strong stab of pain hits me right in the middle of my breastbone, robbing me of air. Pressing my hand briefly to my chest, I turn away from the women, focusing my attention on my laptop to exit out of the presentation. It's been a while since I've felt that… the keen sense of loss.

"Anyway," Jenna says with a giggle, "I'll leave you two alone so you can finish whatever it was you were doing. I'm going to my office where I will log on to my computer and then stare at my ring all day." Jenna levels a pert wink at Brienne. "You might need to dock me a vacation day."

"I'll come talk to you later," Brienne says and then I hear the door close behind Jenna.

I turn to face my boss and ask, "Anything else we need to go over?"

"What's wrong?" she asks, hands on her hips and that no-nonsense look she wears very well.

Plastering on an innocent expression, I say, "Nothing. Why?"

Brienne merely watches me, refusing to address my lie and waiting me out. I know how stubborn she can be, so with a sigh, I give her the base version. "I'm so happy for Jenna. Truly. But it made me really miss Mitch."

"Oh, honey," Brienne coos as she moves to me. Her hand goes to my shoulder. "I'm sorry. I know things like that have to be hard."

"Yeah… I know. I love seeing you and Jenna happy and in love. I remember that feeling so well. All the butterflies, giddiness… the excitement of being near your man. Having someone to watch out for you." I level her a knowing look. "Someone you can have crazy sex with on the kitchen floor." Brienne's eyebrows shoot high and I laugh. "You know what I'm talking about."

"I do," she replies with a gentle smile. "And you might not believe it, but you'll have that again one day."

A flood of memories assault me and they're not of Mitch but rather Camden. Our date. Our first kiss. Laughing with him at dinner last night, stolen kisses while he helped me with the dishes and Travis finished his homework. One very hot kiss on the front porch when he left. The orgasms he gave me.

Today... it was his call first thing this morning to hear my voice and I suddenly realize... Camden is all those things I just described to Brienne. I've been nothing but butterflies and giddiness since our first date, and there was probably a bit of it going on before he asked me out.

"Actually, I think I have found it again," I admit.

Brienne's mouth drops open and she stares at me with astonishment. She finds her voice and asks, "With who?"

I pinch the bridge of my nose and give myself a quick pep talk. Once I let the cat out of the bag, this becomes very real. Exhaling, my hands fall away and I look Brienne dead in the eye. "It's Camden."

"Poe?" she exclaims. "Camden Poe?"

"Yes." That one word comes out laden with guilt. "It's wrong, right? It's gross and a betrayal to Mitch and everyone will hate me—"

"Stop," Brienne snaps and my mouth slams shut. "Does he feel wrong to you?"

"No."

"Gross?"

"No."

"Do you care what people think about you?"

"Not really, but I do care what they think about Camden."

There… that's the real issue. Camden is the one with all the doubts because of his relationship with Mitch.

Brienne uses her hand on my shoulder to push me down into my chair. She resumes her seat and leans toward me. "Start from the beginning and tell me everything."

So I do.

I tell her everything, minus the details of the night we spent together, but she's clear on the fact that we've been intimate. She nods, makes a few comments like "That makes sense" and "I get that."

When I finally dry up, she asks the most important question of all. "How do you feel about Camden?"

Again, all the memories from the past few weeks as we solidified our friendship and then became lovers, how he's helped Travis with hockey and showed up out of the blue to shovel snow for me. I could focus on how amazing he is in bed and how he's made me feel things I thought were long dead, but when it boils down to it, it's his kindness that has me all googly-eyed over him. "I like him a lot, Brienne. I know it's new and we're still getting to know each other, but I don't feel like I've got anything holding me back. I loved Mitch. Still do. But I'm ready to live a full life again. You helped me see that I needed to do that. I guess you sort of made me see possibilities again when you offered me this job."

"Good," she says with an emphatic nod. "That's all that matters. And Travis?"

My stomach pitches because I might be ready to move on, but is he ready for me to do the same? "I don't know. I need to talk to him. Camden has been helping him with hockey, and Travis really looks up to him as a friend"

Travis was crushed that Camden couldn't stay and play his hockey game with him last night. He said a doleful goodbye but was heartened by Camden's promise that they'd find time to play soon.

Travis was upstairs in his room using the thirty minutes I allow him each night when Camden called. He'd just made it back to his place.

"Hey, super cool mom," he drawled when I answered the phone. "Will you let Travis play hockey with me online?"

"You can do that? That's a thing?" I had no idea.

Camden laughed. "Yes, it's a thing."

And sure enough, it was. My son flipped out when I went upstairs to tell him and was so overjoyed, I let him play an extra half hour with Camden. I'm not sure I understand what was going on, but they were on the same team and communicating through headsets. I watched for only a few minutes and left them alone, although I was dying of curiosity.

Later, after Travis was asleep, Camden called me. "You've got an amazing kid," he said.

I agreed with him and we talked for almost an hour.

"I don't know where you went just now," Brienne quips, "but that smile on your face tells me a lot."

I flush hot and shake my head with a laugh. "Sorry… I was thinking about Camden."

"I'm happy for you, Danica." Brienne takes my hand in hers. "Don't you dare have regrets."

"No," I rush to assure her. "I don't have regrets at all. I really like Camden and I don't know… I guess I hope this will turn into more. But I'm not ready to let this out yet. I think Camden is still unsure about some things."

"With the team?"

"Yeah, and he has to work through that on his own. I'll follow his pace."

"Nothing wrong with that." Brienne squeezes my hand gently. "You've got me cheering you on."

"I'm so glad to have you as a friend." I stand, packing up my laptop and planner in my leather satchel. "Let me know of any further changes and I'll update the agenda."

Brienne stands too. "Want to grab some lunch later? I'll see if Jenna wants to come too. Maybe Kiera can meet us."

It's with true regret that I decline. I've enjoyed our lunches and getting to know other women associated with the team. "Um… I can't today."

"Plans already?" she asks with enough innuendo that she knows exactly why I can't join her.

"Something like that." I wink and head out of her office.

CHAPTER 18

Danica

I CAN'T BELIEVE I'm this nervous, but my hands are shaking as I ring the doorbell to Camden's condo.

We have a lunch date planned, but I'm not sure if his invitation was code for sex or if we're actually going to eat.

I'm bolstered by my talk with Brienne a few hours ago. She validated my desire to test the waters with Camden. She made me feel confident that I can still hold Mitch close, can still even mourn him, but also find happiness with someone else. I'd suspected it, but damn if it's not better when someone else says the same thing.

The door swings open and Camden is there looking unlike I've ever seen him before. He's usually in warm-weather clothing—jeans, sweaters, boots and the like. But I'm guessing he hasn't been outside today as he's wearing workout shorts and his gray T-shirt stretches slightly over his chest but loose through the abdomen. I notice so many things in that first glance. His arms are amazing—pure porn in my mind—with cut muscles and dark golden hair from elbow to wrist. His skin is tan, but not like he's been in a tanning bed. Just a normal healthy glow from whatever his ancestral roots are. That same golden hair catches my attention on his legs, equally muscled.

It's not like I haven't seen those body parts before, because we did have sex and I saw him slide out of bed the next morning. But for some reason, he's as sexy with parts of him covered up, hinting at the mystery of what's underneath.

Although not an absolute mystery.

Best of all is what he's got going on from the shoulders up, his beautiful, light brown to dark golden hair that he wears wildly untamed. His facial scruff is a bit longer than normal, almost thick enough to be a playoff beard. I'm guessing these last handful of days off he didn't feel like shaving, but I didn't notice how much it had grown out until now.

Camden rubs a hand along his jaw as he lets his gaze slide down my body and then up again. I'm wearing a brown tweed wool skirt and espresso-colored tights. A mustard-colored turtleneck is hidden under my puffy winter coat. There's nothing sexual about my outfit, but the way he's eating me up makes me hot and self-conscious.

He steps back, sweeps his arm to welcome me.

"Come on in, little girl," he growls low, adding to

the *wolf preparing to eat the lamb* vibe I'm getting.

Stepping past him, I shrug out of my coat. He's there to take it from me, hanging it on a rack in the corner. "I thought you invited me over for lunch. I get the distinct impression I might be on the menu."

Camden steps into me quickly from behind, a hand on my hip and his lips near my ear. "It's a possibility."

I have to suppress a shiver of desire and I hope the possibility becomes reality. I don't have the nerve to make the first move.

I take in Camden's condo, noting with a bit of astonishment how neat it is. It's spacious, the living room filled with plush furniture that invites you to sink in and watch a movie. No walls separate the living area from the dining and kitchen but rather it all flows together. I love the kitchen with its white cabinets and quartz countertops accented with black wrought iron pendant lighting.

Camden's lips move from my ear to press a soft kiss on my cheek. "I'm glad you were able to come and eat lunch with me."

I'm a tiny bit disappointed when he moves past me into the kitchen where I see he's laid out food. He flashes a crooked grin as I take it all in. "I'm not the best cook so I ordered some stuff. I hope you're okay with that?"

Setting my purse on the edge of the counter, I survey the sandwiches neatly arranged on plates next to tubs of pasta salad and fruit salad. "I think you know me well enough by now to know I enjoy all kinds of food. Maybe a little too much at times."

Camden hands me one of the plated subs and motions toward the salads to help myself. I scoop a spoonful of fruit salad as Camden asks, "What do you mean by too much?"

I give a half shrug as I add pasta salad to my plate. "You know… we women have to watch our figures. Blah, blah, blah. I don't watch mine very well."

Camden doesn't say anything and the silence draws my gaze to him. His eyes are boring into me. "I think you're perfect. So whatever it is you're eating, I would tell you to keep on doing it."

I blush as my eyes go back to the pasta salad and I decide on a second spoonful. "You're sweet to say that."

"It might be sweet, but it's also honest."

Those words send my heart into a reckless gallop, not only because he said something sweet but because I hear the truth in his tone. It's refreshing and endearing, and it does nothing but deepen my feelings for him.

After we have our lunches and are settled onto side-by-side stools at his counter, Camden asks, "How's your day been so far?"

"I had a good meeting with Brienne and we went over the last-minute details for the gala Friday night."

Camden slaps his hand to his forehead. "I had forgotten all about that. I need to make sure my tux still fits."

"Why wouldn't your tux fit?" I ask as I toy with a spiraled noodle.

"I've packed on a bit of muscle this year using a new training regimen. It should be okay, but I need to make sure."

"We can try it on now if you want and I'll give you my expert opinion."

Camden studies me, his lips twitching. "You're not just saying that to get me out of my clothes, are you?"

I decide to throw caution to the wind. "Maybe."

Desire flashes hot within Camden's eyes and the fork he was holding clatters to his plate. He spins fully on his stool to face me, hands going to my knees.

"I had the best intentions. It was a gentleman's request to invite you to lunch today, and I assumed I'd feed you and send you on your way back to work. I think I'm going to fuck you instead and I'll pack you a doggie bag to go."

I nearly choke and my eyes bug out of my head. "Are you serious?"

The determined look on his face sparks a throbbing between my legs. His tone is gruff. "I never joke about fucking."

Before I know what's happening, I'm over Camden's shoulder and getting an upside-down view of his apartment as he carries me back to the master bedroom.

My world flips again as he tosses me on the bed. I catch glimpses of sleek, blond wood furniture with clean lines accented by taupe-colored walls. A pristine white comforter on the bed feels incredibly soft in my hands as I grip it.

Camden comes to the edge and takes off my shoes. Brown leather Mary Janes with gold buckles. He doesn't spare them a second glance, merely tossing them over his shoulder. His hands slide underneath my skirt to pull at my tights and then my legs are completely bare.

"How do I get this skirt off?" he asks as his gaze burns into me.

"How about I work on the rest of my clothes and you ditch yours?"

Camden grins, a competitive light shining in his eyes. Before I can even reach the zipper at the back of my skirt, he's got his shorts and T-shirt whipped off and stands there gloriously naked and semi-erect.

"Damn... that was fast," I mutter, my hand stilling at the zipper while rolling to my side. I think I'm probably in a decidedly unsexy pose.

And I can't move. I'm mesmerized by how beautiful Camden is. All of that golden skin and defined muscle. My eyes catch on the thick length of his cock and I love that he keeps himself well-trimmed.

Apparently, I'm taking too long, because Camden's hands are at my hips and he's flipping me over. He finds the zipper and works it down, pulling my skirt and panties right down my legs. Then he's hauling me up to my knees so he can whip off my turtleneck. He doesn't waste time taking off my bra, merely pulling the cups down to expose my breasts. My nipples get sharp pinches between his thumbs and forefingers as he nuzzles my neck. I buck and then press my ass into him, feeling the thick length of his shaft against my lower back.

It all happens so fast. Once again, I'm flipped so I'm staring at the ceiling. Camden pulls my legs roughly apart and falls onto me, his mouth immediately on my pussy. It's an ambush and I'm not prepared for how good it feels. I moan, lacing my fingers in that soft hair and pulling on it hard. My hips rotate against the onslaught, his tongue and lips playing my body perfectly.

Camden isn't quiet in his endeavors. He sounds like a man starved who's gorging on his first meal in forever. He sucks at my clit and pumps his fingers in and out of me. It's almost embarrassing how he coaxes a ridiculously fast orgasm, and a hoarse scream rends the air between us. My hips jerk so violently my pubic bone catches him in the chin.

Chuckling, Camden crawls up my body and presses his mouth to mine in a deep, toe-curling kiss. Lifting his head, he stares down at me in triumph. "You're like a bomb just waiting to be detonated. I wonder how fast I can make you come again."

He starts sliding down my body, but I lock my hands behind his neck. "No way. You said you were going to fuck me and that's exactly what I'm expecting."

Camden appraises me with his lips curving upward. "Look at you, Danica. Using all the dirty words."

And once more, my body is moving so fast, I'm dizzy. He flips me to my stomach and without even giving me time to take a breath, he pulls me up by the hips so I'm on my hands and knees. It's a commanding move, and in this position I know what he wants.

Camden's hand strokes my lower back and his tone is so gentle. "You have such a beautiful, luscious ass. I'm going to enjoy fucking you from behind so I can see it."

I can't tell if he's trying to spar with me, both of us throwing out dirty exclamations. But I give it right back. "As long as when you do fuck me from behind, you do it hard."

Camden snarls with challenge and pulls away from me to rummage around in the drawer of his bedside table. Out comes a condom, and it takes him no time to get it on his dick, now fully hard and thick.

Settling in behind me, Camden asks in what one might consider an ominous intonation, "Are you sure you want this rough?"

I can barely breathe from the suspense. "I'm sure."

I brace myself for Camden to slam into me, but instead, he works his way in gently. I'm sopping wet from the orgasm, and my body stretches easily to accommodate his girth. He's in no rush, but I know he's affected by his harsh breathing. He curls his body over mine, splaying one hand across the center of my chest and the other between my legs.

He punches in the rest of the way and I scream with how good it feels. Camden groans, his hand plucking at my clit as he begins to fuck me from behind.

I'm overwhelmed with sensations, the play of his roughened fingertips between my legs and the length of him inside me hitting something that makes my eyes cross. It is the absolute perfect storm he's unloading on my body and I feel another orgasm boiling.

How the hell does that happen so fast?

Camden thrusts into me, hitting me at the deepest point every time. He does it over and over and over again… relentlessly and beautifully. He's barely a handful of strokes in when my fingers reflexively curl into the soft comforter. "Jesus… getting ready to come again."

"That's it, baby," he grunts with each punch of his hips and then I explode. It's his name that falls out of my mouth along with gibberish, which I hope he understands translates into *this feels really fucking good.*

Before my orgasm can even work halfway up my spine, Camden straightens and puts both of his hands on my hips. If I thought he was fucking me hard before, I was wrong. He pounds into me mercilessly, which either knocks loose another mini orgasm or extends the second one. My arms shake with the effort to hold myself up while Camden uses my body in a way it's never been used before.

Not cheaply. Not without care. But with an intense focus and pure determination that turns me on.

"You feel so fucking good, Dani. So fucking good."

Camden continues to drive into me. The pleasure is so intense I feel like I'm on the verge of blacking out and then my arms give way. Flopping onto the mattress, I'm an absolute puddle… unable to move.

In no way deterred and still giving me the pounding I demanded, Camden fucks me harder and harder by merely lifting my hips enough to give him leverage. The sound of slapping skin and his muttered curses are music to my ears, a testament to his desire for me.

"I'm going to come," he warns in staccato breaths.

But I don't want him to come. I want him to keep going on and on because I feel so completely dominated and cherished at the same time.

Camden slams in but he doesn't pull out again. He rotates his hips and grinds against me, his entire body falling onto mine as he shudders out his release. "Goddamn, that's good."

His sweat-soaked skin is plastered to mine and his hips continue to roll against me, sucking out every bit of pleasure.

Lifting onto his elbows so he doesn't crush me, Camden brushes his mouth over the back of my head. It takes a while for his breathing to regulate and then he presses a kiss between my shoulder blades as he slowly slides free.

I mourn the loss of fullness inside me but then my gut pitches when Camden utters a strangled curse. "Shit."

My head whips around and I look at him over my shoulder. He's staring down at his dick, the look on his face one of pure horror.

I scramble around and face him, fear suffocating me. I see what he sees. The condom has a long tear in it down the length of his dick. The end is still intact, filled with his semen, but we both see the milky white substance on the skin where it's torn.

"Damn it," Camden mutters, his gaze lifting to mine. "Tell me you're on birth control."

"I am. My periods are irregular, so I've been on it ever since I had Travis."

Camden falls back onto the bed with a dramatic sigh. "Thank fuck."

I settle onto my hip, my hand pressed down into the mattress near his shoulder. Hovering over him, I tease, "Gave you a little heart attack, didn't it?"

Camden doesn't laugh or smile. He runs a hand over his face, his eyes staring fixedly at the ceiling.

"Are you mad?" I ask him tentatively.

His eyes snap to mine and he leans up on an elbow so we're face-to-face. "I'm mad at myself. I've never lost control like that. That was really rough, Danica. I broke the fucking condom. Did I hurt you?"

I shake my head hard, my hand on his cheek. "No. Not at all. I loved every bit of it, Camden, and I want you to do that to me again. It was amazing."

Camden heaves a sigh of relief, letting his forehead drop to mine. "Really?"

"So amazing," I reiterate. "You can fuck me senseless anytime."

Lifting his head, he smiles tenderly and brushes my hair off my face. "If you say so."

"I do." I give him a push to his chest. "Now... put some food in me so I can get back to work."

Camden doesn't budge, his expression turning serious again. "I'm safe."

My brow furrows in confusion. "Safe?"

"I've always worn a condom when I've been with another woman. I've been tested for STDs at every yearly physical. You know... the condom tore, so I didn't want you to worry."

Odd... I wasn't worried. "I appreciate you saying that. You know I'm safe too, right? I mean... there was only Mitch."

"I figured," he says, leaning down to brush his mouth across mine before pulling me from the bed. "Come on... let's get you fed."

CHAPTER 19

Camden

THERE HAVE BEEN countless studies on the psychology of professional athletes. What is that extra "something" they have that propels them to elite status?

Sure, you must have talent, which needs to be developed, and you must have strength, which comes with hard work. But those two things alone, even if mastered, will never ensure your success.

For me, there's something centered deep within that I have to tap into. It's a layered well of confidence, ego, desire and pure determination to prove to myself that I'm the best I can be. I bring that mentality to every aspect of my life because being a professional hockey player isn't just stepping out in front of adoring fans screaming my name. It's every minute of every hour of every day. It's the way I eat, sleep and work out. It's the way I meditate and the care I extend to my body. It's the loyalty to my teammates to play my best for them and it's the fans you never want to let down.

Somewhere in this past year, I've lost something.

This season hasn't been my best, and Coach West has been trying to figure me out. There's absolutely no physical reason I should be a second off a pass or allow someone to get the jump on me.

Which means it's a mental issue, and there's no doubt my psyche has taken a bit of a beating since the crash. My mistake was not giving my mental health the same care and hard work that I give the rest of myself as an elite athlete.

The mistake wasn't made right off the bat. I did quite well when we built the new team and my play was excellent. In hindsight, that was a combination of pure adrenaline and a driving need to keep my mind occupied that led to my game play staying elevated. If I couldn't think about the crash and what I'd lost, I could operate in a bubble. By hyperfocusing on the new team and my career, I shoved the dark tragedy down deep.

It worked until it didn't.

Summer came, and without the hectic pace of an active season, I had time to think and that wasn't such a good thing. I began to tabulate all the things I had truly lost. By the time our season rolled back around, I had gotten too much into my head, and it showed in my game performance. All of it culminated in me missing a practice, something that embarrasses me deeply. It also put me at a crossroads. I could continue as is, possibly ruining my career, or I could confront my demons.

While I'm not averse to therapy, I'd rather not do it. That's probably just some male jackassery, thinking myself tough enough to figure this out on my own.

Tonight as I step onto the ice for our game against the Carolina Cold Fury, I can tell I've got my mojo back. Physically, I feel stronger… faster. But honestly, I think that stems from the fact that my headspace has calmed. Everything seems on point, every pass I make crisp and on the money. My spirit seems connected to the game and I enjoy the feel of the nerves causing my stomach to flip and pitch. I'm hyped up to get the win. The game no longer seems oppressive but rather euphoric.

And it's all because of Danica.

There's absolutely no other explanation.

And I'm not talking about the amazing sex, although that does make me feel really good. But for the first time since the crash, I've opened up to someone about my feelings. She has made me feel so comfortable by acknowledging that I was allowed to be hurt by the loss. That I don't have to be so strong and that it's natural to have some guilt. I think one of the things that has helped me the most, though, is seeing how Danica has flourished despite her losses. Travis, too, for that matter. It's not to say they're not missing Mitch because I know they are.

But watching Danica reinvent her life has been an eye-opener for me. She had to learn to take care of herself and Travis financially. She had to make big decisions and let go of a lifestyle she was accustomed to. She gave up all her luxuries to keep her kid in a good school. She got a job without really knowing what she was doing or if she would be successful. Danica did all of this while mourning the loss of her husband. If she can be this strong, so can I.

I admire her so fucking much and I'm not an idiot. I know that part of the reason she's been able to do the things she's done is because she's been open about her pain, embraced others in the same situation and she's accepted help, care and love from like individuals. She had a support system that I didn't take advantage of and I'm thinking it made all the difference.

Because I like her so much and because she's such a genuine, down-to-earth woman, it's not been difficult to talk with her about the crash. Granted, I've had to ease into it, but when I have a shitty day from a rush of survivor's guilt, I can tell Danica without judgment. She doesn't think me weak but rather self-aware, which is strength. At least that's what she told me.

As I skate around the rink for our warm-up, I know I should be in full game mode, but I can't help when my thoughts drift to Danica. She's not here at the game because it's a school night.

But she did tell me something that has me feeling like a strutting peacock. "All of my cheers tonight are for you."

Those were her last words before she gave me a goodbye kiss and left my apartment yesterday. I know when that puck drops in fifteen minutes, she'll be glued to her TV along with Travis. Knowing that I've got a personal cheerleader, someone who is going to be proud of my successes and supportive of my failures makes all the difference in the world out here on the ice. I know without a doubt I'm going to have a great game tonight.

◆

THE CROWD AT Mario's is shoulder to shoulder. We defeated the Cold Fury 4–2 and yours truly had a goal and an assist. After the game, Coach West clapped me on the shoulder and said, "I don't know what the fuck has changed in your life, but whatever it is, it's working."

It's Danica, Coach. That's what's changed.

But I can't tell him that. I can't tell any of these people celebrating with me here tonight. I'm going to assume that if this thing continues with Danica, we'll have to come out to others. We're not there yet, and that's only because all of this is so new. Danica, I'm sure, will have no problems but I'm still feeling a certain amount of guilt because of who Danica is.

A member of the Titans' family before the crash.

Wife to a player.

Wife to my teammate, linemate and friend.

I'm confident there's going to be judgment. I don't know how much or who it will come from. And I don't want to cause waves on this team. We're going into the latter half of the season rolling like a locomotive, plowing down our opponents. We have momentum and a spirit within us that can make us contenders for the Cup this year. And if my team thinks it's wrong of me to be with Danica and it hurts the team mentality because I dented the morality, I'll never forgive myself for crushing everyone else's dream.

Someone gives me a light punch to my biceps and I turn from the bar where I just ordered a beer.

It's Bain, his hand held out. "What's up, star of the game?" I grasp it sideways and he pulls me into a half hug. "You were on fire tonight."

"It sure as shit felt good." I grab my beer and follow Bain through the crowd.

It's always been a blast to celebrate with my team and the fans after a win. Mario's is our main hangout, although sometimes we go to Stevie's bar.

We reach a sectioned-off area the owners created for us filled with high-top tables where we can share beers and not be swarmed by fans. It's sort of worked out that we're mostly left alone when we're in this group space, but we all take turns stepping into the throng and hanging with the fans. After I drink this beer, I'll go do some pictures and autographs, which I actually enjoy.

Most of the team is here but noticeably absent are the coaches. They don't typically hang with us, although sometimes Gage will, and that's only because last season he was a teammate and captain of our team. I imagine he's not here mainly because he put a ring on Jenna's finger yesterday and they're celebrating alone. Drake is also absent, and that's not unusual for a home game. He's a single dad to three boys and prefers to get home to them and Brienne.

We join Hendrix, Stevie, Stone and Coen at a high top. There are more congrats and backslaps, and I offer one up to Coen who scored two goals tonight.

"Where are Harlow and Tillie?" I ask.

"Harlow's in the middle of a trial and working," Stone says, looking glum.

"Tillie's back in Coudersport, packing up for the movers," Coen adds and then looks at me pointedly. "You got the invitation for our housewarming, right?"

"Yeah, man." I think I did. I vaguely recall an email about it.

"Well, you haven't RSVP'd yet, asshole. We have to know how many are coming so we can prepare."

"All right, dude. Chill out. This is my confirmation… I'm coming. When is it?"

"Next Saturday." Coen turns his fierce look on Bain. "And you're coming?"

"Wouldn't miss it for the world," Bain says, but I can

tell by the look on his face he's not quite sure if he saw the email either.

But neither one of us would miss it because it's a big step for Coen. He and Tillie bought a house together, and it's a sign of how committed they are.

I wonder if Danica was invited. Coen had been going to the support group meetings this year and his friendship with her has strengthened. While Dani would never tell me anything Coen or any other member of the group shared with her in confidence, she's told me on more than one occasion how much she loves talking to Coen and getting to know him better.

Yeah... surely he invited her. So I'll be able to see her.

Because it's not like I can bring her as my date. That's the can of worms I'm not interested in opening right now.

Or should we open it?

I pull out my phone and send her a quick text. *You awake?*

I am, she replies.

"I'll be right back," I say, not really to anyone at our table but I assume they heard me.

I wind through the crowd to the exit and as soon as I step outside, I dial Danica. It's freezing out here, so I huddle against the building until she answers.

"Hey, you," she says softly when the line connects.

"You played amazing tonight. I'm so proud of you."

I try to ignore how good her words make me feel, like a little puppy jumping for joy. "Thanks. Travis make it through the entire game?"

"Conked out in the middle of the third period," she says with a low laugh. "But when I put him to bed, I told him you won."

I can imagine his reaction. I've come to learn this week just how geeked out Travis gets with hockey. We've played online together a few times, most recently last night. Travis had some sort of school function they had to go to, which is why I couldn't see Danica, but after they got home, he and I played together. I never thought something like that would be so fun, but we play in a server with kids Travis's age and most of them are trash-talkers to the max. None of them know who I am as Travis and I agreed to keep it secret, just so people wouldn't get distracted.

It's hilarious when I'm the one trying to sound like a kid dumping on another and I don't understand half of what they're saying. Some kid last night let loose a few curse words at Travis, and I kind of lost my shit on him. Told him I'd kick his ass if he didn't lay off. Apparently, Travis told Danica and she texted me later a rolling eyes emoji with *Try to be the mature one, okay?*

"I thought you were going to Mario's tonight," Danica says, cutting into my thoughts about her kid.

"I was. I mean I am. I stepped outside to call you."

"That's nice," she murmurs. "I was getting ready to go to sleep."

I rub hard at the back of my neck. Danica under the covers, all warm and snuggly, is something I'd very much like to see right now. I fucked her so hard yesterday, we'll both be feeling it for days to come, but it wasn't enough to take away the ache for her. If she invited me over right now, I'd ditch everyone and go.

But she won't because she can't. We can't do anything like that with Travis in the house and we both know it.

I try to sound casual when I ask about what I really want to know. "Are you going to Tillie and Coen's housewarming party next Saturday?"

"I think so," she says, and I can hear the smile. "I'm trying to set up a babysitter. I assume you're going."

"Yeah." And I'm feeling all kinds of weird about it. How will I act around her when surrounded by my teammates? Do we ignore each other?

I guess we'll have a practice run tomorrow night at the gala. That will be such a huge event, I probably won't even see Danica other than in passing. But an intimate team gathering at Coen's house? Well, that's going to be tough.

"So listen…" Danica says, but the tentative tone sets me on edge, "I'm going to be staying at the hotel tomorrow night after the gala since I intend to have a few drinks. Travis is staying overnight at his friend's house."

My shoulders relax even as my dick jumps. "What are you suggesting?"

"Well," she drawls coyly and I can almost envision her twisting a lock of hair around her finger. "Maybe you can do a sleepover with me."

"We'd get no sleeping done," I point out.

"Of that, I'm sure. But I know we can find plenty to keep us occupied." God, she has no idea all the things I want to do to her, and tomorrow we'll have all night to figure it out. "I have to leave early in the morning to get Travis to hockey practice."

"Care if I come?" I ask. We're at a weird stage where I don't know if it's cool to ask such things. "I could see how he's playing and give him some advice if—"

"I want you to come," she interjects. "Not to help Travis but because I want to spend time with you."

"Then I'm there." We have a game that night, and I need to be at the arena around two, which raises the question, "Do you and Travis want to come to the game Saturday? I can get you tickets. Since it's an afternoon game, maybe we can go out for dinner or something after?"

"That would be awesome. I know Travis will go bonkers when I tell him."

"It's a date, then."

An unconventional date with a woman and her kid, but a date all the same, and I can't wait.

"I'd better head back in before everyone wonders what happened to me. See you at the gala tomorrow night."

"See you tomorrow night."

CHAPTER 20

Danica

WHEN BRIENNE DECIDED to throw this gala to launch the Adam Norcross Charitable Foundation, she breezily said we have about two hundred and fifty people. That amount sounded outrageous to me at the time, and now that I'm in the ballroom and see how many people that actually is, my nerves are slightly spastic. I haven't had to do much since I arrived tonight. While I'm the one who organized this event, it's one of Brienne's assistants, Molly, who's walking around with an iPad and ear mic handling last-minute details and helping people find their tables.

The venue is beyond lovely and I know that Brienne is shelling out close to a hundred grand for the evening's festivities.

The extravagant ballroom has a stage on one end and a dance floor with a DJ on the other that will see plenty of use later tonight. Multi-tiered crystal chandeliers hang from the ceiling, dimmed to emit the barest of golden glows. The tables are covered with white linen and adorned with beautiful floral centerpieces that sit low to not obstruct anyone's view of their dining companions. Tiered candles flicker in the middle, adding a small bit of extra light by which to converse.

The food Brienne wanted is being catered by a chef who owns a Michelin-starred restaurant here in Pittsburgh. Everyone will enjoy a sumptuous five-course meal while speakers talk onstage about our foundation. We'll start with an appetizer of seared scallops with a truffle sauce, followed by a light and refreshing salad of mixed greens, heirloom tomatoes and crumbled feta cheese. The main course is a choice between a succulent grilled filet mignon with a red wine reduction or a buttery poached lobster tail, served with a side of roasted asparagus and truffle mashed potatoes. There's also a vegetarian dish of penne with fire roasted vegetables. Dessert is a decadent chocolate mousse cake with a raspberry coulis. My stomach rumbles at the thought of such a meal, especially since I've been so busy today, I haven't managed to eat anything more than a piece of toast this morning and a protein bar at lunch.

The bar is open and the prevailing theory is that alcohol will loosen the purse strings. Brienne has every conceivable liquor, mixer and garnish available. There is an extensive selection of specialty drinks, including classic martinis, margaritas and cosmopolitans. I was impressed as hell that Brienne worked with someone to create an original drink for tonight's event, a signature cocktail of champagne, elderflower liqueur, and fresh strawberries. It's being brought out by white-gloved waitstaff on trays to pass out to guests.

Brienne has mercifully kept me by her side since we arrived, a relief because I have no clue how to mingle in circumstances like this. Most of my work for the foundation has been behind the scenes, but tonight I'll become the face of it. While I'm incredibly extroverted when I'm in comfortable circumstances, I don't feel like I fit in this world and maybe I never will. Brienne has been introducing me to everyone and although I can't remember a single person's name, it's helped ease me into the evening.

It's interesting that Brienne introduces me merely as Danica Brandt, director of the foundation and never as the wife of Mitch Brandt. I think she does that so I'm seen as a businesswoman first and foremost and not as a widow to be pitied.

Everyone will know soon enough as I'm scheduled to give the opening remarks, during which I'll invite Brienne to the stage so she can boldly ask people to open their checkbooks.

Despite my nervousness and in between meeting people, I'm still trying to get a glimpse of Camden when he walks in. He's a definite as he did indeed try on his tuxedo and found it still fit, even with the extra muscle he's packed on this season. I was at home when he texted me. *It's a little snug so I won't be eating a lot.*

I like snug, I replied.

He sent me a laughing emoji and promised me that I could peel him out of it later. Despite all the nerves, I'm looking forward to my first event as the foundation's director, but I might be looking forward to the evening with Camden a little more. His schedule is heating back up with games and our moments alone are stolen.

A hand circles my wrist and I can tell by the soft skin and delicate fingers it's not a man. I turn to see Kiera smiling at me. We lean in for a hug, then she holds me at arm's length to check out my gown.

I've attended my share of black-tie events throughout my time here in Pittsburgh and while I love to dress up for a party with full hair and makeup, I've never been the flashy type. For example, Brienne is in a silver lamé gown with a plunging neckline, the formfitting bodice and skirt accented with all-over crystals. She glows like a diamond.

I know I can carry off something like that, but I don't like to. I prefer to be comfortable in formal wear so I chose a simple sleeveless black silk gown ruched at the waist. The collar cuts across the base of my neck and the material feels divine against my skin. It's so light it floats when I walk. A modest slit stops above my knee and shows the barest peek of leg.

SAWYER BENNETT

"You look fabulous," Kiera said.

Arching an eyebrow, I give her a critical look. "Pot calling the kettle black."

She's a sexy bombshell who will have almost every man in here tonight sizing her up. She chose a cherry-red gown with a daring neckline similar to Brienne's. Her dress fits like a second skin with a side slit that goes above her mid-thigh.

I smirk at her. "I can only imagine what Drake is going to say when he sees you in that outfit."

I find it more than hilarious that her brother is so overprotective because Kiera certainly doesn't need such oversight. She's a strong, confident and sexually open woman. If she decides she wants one of those players, it doesn't matter what Drake says. She's going to get him.

On more than one occasion, she's dropped her voice to me and said, "Mmm... I'd like to get a piece of that."

And she's the type to get the piece if she wants it.

Kiera rolls her eyes at my mention of Drake. "One day my brother will learn that he's not the boss of me." She flourishes that statement with a dismissive wave and then asks, "Are you ready for the big speech?"

I wrinkle my nose. "In a million years, I will never be ready for this speech."

Kiera's hand slides to take mine and she gives it a reassuring squeeze. "Speak from the heart. It's what you do best and you're going to be fine."

As if Brienne's assistant was waiting for Kiera to say those exact words, I see her up at the podium as she taps the microphone. "If I can have everyone's attention, please. We will be starting in about five minutes, if you can make your way to your assigned tables."

Brienne turns from her current conversation to glance at Kiera and it's apparently the first time she's seen her tonight. They hug and Brienne exclaims, "That dress is amazing. Please tell me I can borrow it sometime."

Kiera laughs. "I love the irony of this. Drake will hate it when he sees it on me, but he's going to love it when it's on you."

"That's because he knows no one would dare leer at me when he's by my side, but he can't keep his eyes on you twenty-four seven," Brienne quips.

Kiera snorts. "What my brother doesn't know won't hurt him."

Brienne winks. "That will be our secret."

Giving me a last good-luck hug, Kiera disappears into the crowd and Brienne leads me to the main stage. Behind it is a massive drop screen that has been running pictures of the Titans people who died in the crash. Every once in a while, I catch a glimpse of Mitch as he flashes by. It doesn't make me sad tonight but makes me feel more secure. As if he's watching over me. I know he would be so proud of what I'm doing right now.

"You good?" Brienne looks at me with genuine concern. She knows how nervous I've been.

An anxious laugh pops out of my mouth. "No. But I'm going to do this and I'm going to make you proud."

Brienne's expression turns triumphant. "That's my girl. I knew I picked the right one for the job."

From my clutch purse with its long gold shoulder chain, I pull out the index cards I jotted my notes on. I've been working on these remarks for a while now, but I've managed to condense it into a few key phrases to prompt me. I know it will be more natural than reading a typed speech. I set the clutch on the edge of the stage to retrieve after I'm done.

Brienne's assistant waves me up to the podium and I take a deep breath. I let it out slowly and reassure myself nothing horrendous will come out of my mouth.

"Good luck," Brienne says.

Up on the stage, I find an immediate benefit to the lighting. It's focused directly on me, which leaves the rest of the crowd shrouded in dark shadows. This gives me a tiny boost of confidence because I can sort of pretend no one's out there.

I throw a short prayer up: *Please don't let me pass out.*

Taking my notes to the podium, I trace the front of the first card as I look at the words written there.

You've got this, Dani.

Leaning toward the microphone a tad, I say, "Good

evening. And welcome to the Adam Norcross Charitable Foundation Kickoff Gala hosted by Brienne Norcross and"—my voice rises to a crescendo—"your very own Pittsburgh Titans hockey team!"

The ballroom erupts into thunderous applause and I wait several seconds for it to fade. I smile out at the shadowed audience and when it quiets again, I continue. "I know everyone is excited to be here, but some of you might be wondering who the heck I am. My name is Danica Brandt, and my husband Mitch was a Titan. I lost him when he went down with the plane on February 20 of last year."

It's so silent in the ballroom that it almost feels surreal. With the audience in the shadows and no noise whatsoever, it's easy to believe I'm all alone.

But I'm not.

"I'm the director of the Adam Norcross Charitable Foundation because somehow, Brienne thought I'd be great for the job." I twist my neck to look at Brienne offstage and she grins at me. Turning back to the crowd, I say, "It was a big leap of faith. I had no higher education and no work skills. I was a mom first and foremost, and Mitch was the breadwinner." I take a breath and rather than look at the index cards, I push them to the side. "After Mitch died, I was utterly lost. Not only was I mourning, but I had a grief-stricken son to support, emotionally and financially. Sure... we received life insurance proceeds and the Titans generously fulfilled Mitch's contract through the end of the year. We had some retirement accounts, but those were off-limits. And… we did what a lot of professional athletes who make good money do. We lived a grand lifestyle. But here I was with limited financial means that would dwindle fast, so I had to make quick, sharp decisions. The only problem was, I had no clue where to turn. I couldn't even fathom what I needed to do.

"Now, I'm a lucky woman because Brienne—who I met in a support group for those of us who lost loved ones in the crash—stepped in and guided me all the way, not just in giving me a job but in helping me figure out how to survive on my own with a young son. She helped many of the widows in the same way. Throughout the months following the crash, Brienne realized there was a great need for a charitable organization to help widows and widowers who've lost the main income-earning person in their family. It was through these talks and meeting with other survivors that Brienne formed a vision, and here we are now."

I glance around again knowing I can't make eye contact with anybody because it's too dark. I hope they all feel exactly how important Brienne is to me. "I wouldn't be standing before you tonight if it weren't for Brienne Norcross. She single-handedly brought this team back from extinction. She made it viable and provided this city with a new roster of players who have energized and invigorated the nation.

"But she's so much more than that. I am lucky to call her my friend, my employer and one of the best people I know. If everyone will please join me in welcoming Brienne Norcross to the stage."

I feel the wave of people as they get to their feet, their applause almost deafening. Brienne glides onstage waving out at the crowd as she moves toward me. She takes me by the shoulders and kisses my cheek, whispering, "That was fucking fantastic."

Relief and giddiness wash through me as I realize my part is done and I can enjoy the evening. "Knock 'em dead."

Brienne's remarks are inspiring, and I wait for her offstage with Drake who appeared sometime when I was at the podium. When she exits, the lights come on and the servers file out with the salad course. There will be speakers throughout the evening while everyone eats, the goal for our guests to open their wallets and donate. We're using a fundraiser app that donors can download at the tables to make their pledges. After the food, there will be music and dancing.

Drake puts his hand around the back of Brienne's neck and pulls her in for a soft kiss. "You were amazing, Ms. Norcross."

"Why, thank you, Mr. McGinn," she says with a

flirty bump of her hip against his.

Putting his arm around Brienne's back, Drake says, "You were great, too, Danica. Very moving."

"Thank you," I reply, always a little in awe of the big goalie who looks like he eats nails for breakfast but is a total teddy bear with Brienne.

"Well, shall we eat?" Brienne asks. We say our good-byes and head off in different directions to find our tables. As I wind my way through, I purposely glance over to where I know Camden has been seated, but he's not there. Frowning, I look left and right, wondering if a mistake was made in the seating or even worse, maybe he didn't come.

When I reach my table, I release a tiny huff of disappointment only to have my attention taken by someone standing there.

It's Camden.

And oh my God, does he look incredible. It's not just the tuxedo but he shaved and his hair is tamed, and while I don't like that as much as scruffy Camden, the clean-cut version is very, very nice.

"What are you doing here?" I ask because this is most certainly not his table.

He shrugs and moves to pull out the chair next to me. "I go where I'm told and Brienne's assistant said this was my seat."

"Oh," I murmur in confusion and settle into my

chair. Camden helps me scoot it in and then takes his seat again. "Okay."

I glance around the table and note no other players here. I don't know a single person, although I met the older gentleman with snow-white hair sitting across from me earlier with Brienne.

We make introductions and everyone congratulates me on my position and my opening remarks. But the table is large and the room is loud with all the chatter, so one-on-one conversations are hard except with the people next to you.

I talk to a lovely lady to my left throughout the salad course. She's a retired cardiac surgeon at UPMC and her late husband was good friends with Brienne's father. While I'm talking to her, I'm happy to note the rest of the table engaged with one another. That includes Camden, who is talking to a very beautiful woman sitting on his other side. Granted, she's in her mid- to late-forties, but she's exquisite and that age gap truly doesn't mean a thing. I push down the spark of jealousy, knowing he's only being polite.

I think that's all he's being.

When the waitstaff comes to take away our bowls, Camden covers his mouth as if wiping it clean with his napkin and leans toward me. He says in a low voice that only I can hear, "You look amazing tonight."

My face heats with the compliment, and I hate that it

also reassures me, which means I had a moment of doubt. Maybe it's natural for me to feel insecure. It's been a long time since I've dated and I have a vague recollection of apprehension at the start with Mitch. Of course we were teenagers and pretty stupid, but I imagine some of it applies here.

The remainder of the dinner is a bit of a blur. The food is delightful and the conversation at the table waxes and wanes as we listen to various speakers. Two other Titans widows share their stories, and Brienne invited the widow of a US soccer player to speak as well. Her story is fascinating because she has a disability that prevents her from working and so an organization such as this can really give her a helping hand.

I have a hard time not tearing up when Coen walks to the podium. He speaks on behalf of the three surviving players—him, Hendrix and Camden. It's very moving as he reveals their personal losses and how hard they've worked to rebuild the team, all while feeling guilty for moving on. I struggle not to reach for Camden's hand, but I see from the glow of candlelight that he's fixated on Coen's words. It's more validation to him that survivor's guilt is a very real thing that can cripple you if you're not careful.

Gage speaks as well, focusing most of his attention on the amazing things Brienne did to rebuild the organization. He was an integral part of that as a player and now as a coach. His words concluded with a standing ovation for our beautiful and determined leader.

Lastly, Stone wraps up at the podium, talking about losing his brother and taking his place on the team. "It was so confusing," he admitted to the crowd, "and even to this day, I struggle with gratitude for what I have."

All these testimonials have been carefully orchestrated to pull at heartstrings and get donors to show their generosity. That's the entire purpose of this event and everyone knows it. Before the evening kicked off, all guests were provided a QR code on a tiny placard at their seats to download the donations app. As the evening progresses and money is pledged, we have a running tally on the drop-down screen onstage.

As we eat and listen to the speakers, I'm still hyperfocused on Camden next to me. He's wearing cologne that does funny things to my belly and anytime we grab a moment of conversation, I feel the intensity of his interest in what I'm saying.

After dinner is finished, the party starts. A DJ spins the latest and greatest dance tunes and the parquet dance floor fills. An open bar keeps everyone having fun and the wallets opening wider.

I, unfortunately, have to drift away from Camden and make my circuit around the ballroom to speak to people, accepting congratulations for the appointment to the directorship as well as talking about the importance of the organization. But I always see Camden here or there, chatting with various guests. Our eyes meet and lock, and we have a second or two where messages are exchanged. *I can't wait to spend time with you alone.*

Brienne and I bump into each other at the bar as I get a glass of wine and she orders a martini. I can't help but ask, "Did you have anything to do with a change in the seating arrangements?"

"What do you mean?" she asks, her cool eyes on me.

"Camden got seated at my table." My tone is droll and she knows I know it was her.

The bartender hands her the martini and she plops a twenty-dollar bill in his tip jar. She merely winks at me and walks off.

I turn to watch her but my field of vision is taken up by Camden standing there. My heart leaps at the sight of him.

He inclines his head and holds his elbow out to me. "May I have this dance?"

CHAPTER 21

Camden

DANICA'S HEAD WHIPS left and right as she glances around. She looks like the kid who got her hand caught in the cookie jar, and I can't help but chuckle.

"Relax, Dani," I say, looking around and noting that no one is paying us any attention. "Nobody would think twice about a Titans player asking you to dance. It's the nice thing to do. We're all friends."

It's funny that I'm the one reassuring her since I'm the person who keeps worrying about how this will look to others. But I decide not to worry about it because right now, I'm simply asking a friend to dance.

She smiles and slips her hand into the crook of my elbow. I lead her to the dance floor already full of couples swaying to a slow song I don't recognize. I only know the melody is slow and this is the best opportunity I have to get her to myself.

I take her hand in mine and place my other lightly on her hip. All very appropriate. There's space between us... a purely platonic meeting for two friends on the dance floor. I hate it because I want her to lean into me, place her head on my shoulder and let me inhale her delicate citrus scent.

We can't do any of that, but at least we're in our own little bubble and we're able to talk candidly.

My voice is thick as I casually look around the ballroom and mutter, "I want you to know, that dress is driving me crazy."

Startled, she glances down between us, as if she somehow lost swaths of fabric or something. Her eyes rise to meet mine. "Really? It covers a lot of me."

"It covers you in all the right ways," I counter. "I don't know if you know this, but whatever that thing is made of shows off your curves to perfection."

"Aah," she teases, a subtle play of a smile on her lips. "It's the whole mystery of what's underneath."

"There's no mystery, Dani." I lean in slightly and growl near her ear, "I've seen every inch of your beautiful body. Hell, licked most of it." She shudders in my arms and I can't fucking help myself. "I need to kiss you."

Danica jumps, looks around. "But... we can't."

"Not here," I agree as I release her but just as quickly, I tuck her hand back in the corner of my arm. "Follow me."

This is me throwing caution to the wind. I walk casually from the ballroom, not wanting to make a scene. What I want to do is throw her over my shoulder and run her up to her room for a quick fuck, but I'm not asshole enough to do that.

I see the bathrooms down to the left and head that way. We walk past the two unisex doors and take another left. Danica doesn't say a word, but I notice I'm walking faster and she's jogging slightly in her sky-high heels.

There's nothing down this hallway, so I go back the other way. Past the bathrooms again, past the main hall leading to the ballroom and we take another left turn.

Various doors sit to the left and right and I put a hand to each one. All locked. I growl in frustration but see another hallway up ahead.

Fuck it... we're far enough away from the ballroom no one would ever see us back here.

"Come on," I mutter and step up my pace.

Danica laughs, clutches her dress to lift the hem and runs along with me. I glance back over my shoulder, see no one following us. As soon as I turn right into that hallway, I'm going to slam her into the wall and kiss the fuck out of her. I'd like to hike up that dress but I won't. Not yet.

Too much risk for that, but a kiss will hold me over.

We fly around the corner in a wide arc only to come to a skidding stop as we take in... holy fuck.

Bain and Kiera are there and he has her pressed into the wall. He's got one of her legs hiked around his hip and the other gripping her jaw to hold her still for what looks to be a bruising kiss.

Danica gasps loudly, her free hand covering her mouth as her eyes widen in shock. Neither Bain nor Kiera jump apart but they do end the kiss and turn their heads our way almost lazily. Kiera looks playfully wicked as she grins and Bain looks nonplussed.

But then both glance to where Danica and I are holding hands. My inclination is to let go or make excuses that she hurt her ankle and I was helping her to a bathroom and we were lost.

Instead, Danica pulls away from me but not to hide the fact we were clearly looking for some private space of our own. She marches right up to Kiera, grabs her by the hand and pulls her away from Bain.

"Come on," she says and drags Drake's sister along with her, away from the catastrophe of hooking up with Bain.

Kiera looks over her shoulder at Bain and blows him a kiss. Danica marches with purpose past me, not sparing me a glance but I note her cheeks are red. The two women disappear around the corner and I can only imagine their conversation.

My head turns to Bain who casually moves my way.

"Dude," I drawl with a shake of my head. "What the hell was that?"

His eyes flash impishly, his smile unrepentant. "I could ask you the same."

I don't let him distract me. "Drake will fucking kill you if he finds out you're trying to get carnal with his sister."

"Not trying," he says as he strolls past. I walk along with him back toward the ballroom, neither Danica nor Kiera in sight.

"You've already…?"

He doesn't reply, leaving me to guess if he's pulling my leg. "What were you and Danica doing sneaking off?"

"We weren't sneaking," I protest in a low growl. "We're friends."

"You're full of shit," he says but then stops to turn toward me. "I told you once before, there is no bro code in effect. You're free to see Danica if you want."

Without admitting anything, I grumble, "Not everyone will think like you."

"That's true," he says, and that's not something I necessarily wanted confirmed. "There may be some who don't see it that way, either on the team or among the fan base. But what the fuck does that matter?"

"That's an awful cavalier attitude," I muse, preferring to throw the heat back his way. "Sort of the way you're being with Kiera."

Bain shrugs. "The difference between you and me is I don't care what anyone else thinks. I do things to make myself happy. You should too."

His eyes bore into me as he silently awaits my admission about my involvement with Mitch's widow.

But it's not my place without talking to Danica, and the only thing Bain or Kiera knows is that we were holding hands.

"I'll catch you later," I say and pivot away from my teammate. I brace for him to follow me or force me to talk, but he lets me go.

♦

I EXIT THE elevator on the eighteenth floor and follow the signs to room 1827. Danica texted me a few minutes ago that she was there and waiting. After catching Bain and Kiera in a compromising position, effectively precluding the steamy kiss I was after, I retreated to the ballroom. Kiera and Danica were in there talking for a few minutes before they split and went their separate ways. I headed straight for the bar to order a bourbon to calm my nerves.

I was bothered about finding Bain with Drake's sister, as it could cause strife among the team. Drake has made no bones about wanting everyone to stay away from Kiera. But I've also got to deal with the fact that Bain is now rightfully assuming there's something between Danica and me. I'll have to answer for that.

For an hour, I waited for the event to conclude and I stayed far away from Danica, instead hanging out with a few of the single guys—Boone, Foster and Kirill.

Danica couldn't leave the event until every last guest had gone home. I also couldn't loiter around waiting on her because it would be too obvious. As such, I eventually settled into a dark booth in the back of the hotel bar. While waiting for Danica, I surfed on my phone and sipped at a club soda.

I'm wound tight when I knock on the door. Eager to see Danica, kiss her, slide inside her body, sleep all night with her. I'm also a little tense over my run-in with Bain. It brought to the fore the mountains that Danica and I still face if we want to be together. It's getting... complicated.

Danica answers the door still wearing the black silk gown that, in my opinion, is the most perfect thing she could ever wear. She's ditched her heels so the hem of the dress pools around her bare feet. Her hair had been up in some sort of loose swirl on her head, but now it's flowing around her shoulders and my fingers itch to slide through the soft locks.

"Hi," she says with a coy smile.

I smile back. "Hi."

She motions me in and I brush past her, noting she has a small rolling suitcase sitting on a luggage rack. It's open and hanging over the edge is a piece of sapphire-blue lingerie. I wonder if she's going to put that on for me.

I hear the door click shut and I turn to face her.

"Some night, huh?" I say.

"Some night indeed," she murmurs with a rueful smile as she comes to stand before me.

"What's the deal with Bain and Kiera?" I ask.

Her face scrunches up and she tilts her head left, then right, as if she's mulling over how to answer. Walking over to the bed, she sits and pats the area beside her. I settle down, our thighs touching, and I take her hand.

Her fingers compress lightly on mine. "They're sleeping together."

"I figured that out by the way they were kissing," I say with a mirthless laugh. "How long has this been going on?"

Danica shrugs. "She was a bit tight-lipped. All she said was it's a fling and they're having fun. She was far more interested to know why you and I were holding hands."

"What did you tell her?"

"The truth," she says as if she can't believe I would even ask such a question. "What did you tell Bain?"

I rub my hand over the back of my neck and look at her sheepishly. "Kinda brushed him off. It's none of his business."

"No, I suppose it's not," she says quietly.

"I guess it's not so bad that Kiera knows," I muse as I nudge my shoulder against hers. "I mean, y'all are good friends and it's not like she would tell anybody, so it's pretty contained."

Something flickers in Danica's eyes and it puts me on edge. "She's not the only one who knows, Camden. I told Brienne."

I surge off the bed, releasing her hand as I spin to face her. Panic presses down on me. "You told Brienne? She'll tell Drake. He'll tell the rest of the team."

Danica slowly rises from the bed and crosses her hands over her chest in a very defensive pose. Her eyes narrow on me. "First, Brienne would never say anything without my permission. But I guess I'm wondering, why are you so freaked out about it? Are you ashamed to be with me?"

"Fuck no," I blurt, lunging at Danica and forcing her arms away from her chest by grabbing her hands. "I could never be ashamed of you. But I do wonder if I should be ashamed of myself. I'm fucking walking all over Mitch's grave by seeing his wife. I'm a douchebag."

A myriad of emotions crosses Danica's face, but it ends with empathy. She tugs her hands free, presses them into my chest and tips her head back to lock eyes with mine. "You are not a douchebag. You are not walking on Mitch's grave. Have you been thinking this the whole time?"

"Well, yeah. Haven't you? Haven't you been worrying about if this is the right thing to do?"

Danica's expression goes slack and she steps away as her gaze cuts over to the window. She's not looking me in the eye when she whispers, "Nothing about you feels wrong. Except for the fact that you think it feels wrong."

I growl in frustration because I'm not explaining this right. I put my hands to her cheeks, forcing her gaze back to me. "I don't think we're wrong. On the contrary, nothing has ever felt more right in my entire life. But that's what I feel. I don't think other people are going to understand, Dani. This is so fucking complicated."

"I'm sorry," she murmurs regretfully. "I'm sorry you're so conflicted about this. And I do understand. I completely see how this might put you in a tough position. The only thing I can tell you, Camden, is that you're going to have to figure out your feelings. I don't feel wrong about this. I might have been uneasy at first, but the one thing I keep coming back to is that Mitch wanted me to be happy. We had conversations about what life might look like without each other. We were both firmly in agreement that we would want the other person to move on and be happy. Whether that was with another partner or not. We loved each other so much that we would never abandon that commitment with death. Loving each other meant letting the other person have no guilt about moving on to another. I know Mitch would be disappointed if I didn't seek out something for myself."

I brush my thumbs over her cheekbones, a faint smile filtering through the worry. "You forget... I knew Mitch too. Knew him well. Without a doubt, I know he would want you to be happy."

"So let's not worry about what other people think."

I lean down and brush my lips over hers. "It's not that easy, Dani. If it was just me and you living in a different reality, I wouldn't think twice about it. But I'm a Titan and part of what makes this team successful is the underlying respect and loyalty that we have for each other. Look at Bain and Kiera... they're two consenting adults and should be able to do whatever the hell they want, but it's going to cause a major ripple if they're caught. Drake will be livid, and it will change the team dynamic. I don't know if I can risk doing that to my teammates. It only takes one or two of them to look at me and you and say we're wrong and that I've stabbed Mitch in the back. And if that happens, everything we've worked so hard for could be in jeopardy. I know that sounds dramatic, but you've been in this community long enough to know that what I'm saying is true."

Danica closes her eyes as if she's trying to process the onslaught of worry I've unloaded on her. When she opens them again, they're filled with understanding. "I never thought of it that way. But I do see what you're saying. So, what do we do?"

Dropping my hands, I turn my head and nod toward

the door. "You can tell me to leave. You can tell me it's over."

Danica shakes her head. "Not an option."

My knees almost buckle from the relief of those three words. "Then I say we hold the course, see where this thing goes, and we'll figure out what to do as we go along. But we keep this to ourselves."

I can tell by her expression that she's not actually on board with this. In its crudest fashion, I'm essentially asking her to be my secret side piece. I'm denying her the ability to be a full part of my life and I hate myself for it.

But not enough to leave her alone.

CHAPTER 22

Camden

ANOTHER GREAT GAME under my belt. No goals, but I got an assist and also single-handedly stopped a breakaway—cleanly and without penalty—to make sure we stayed ahead to win the game. I felt in control, my mind connected to the game and a fire in my belly that's been absent for longer than I care to admit.

Knowing that Danica and Travis were in the crowd watching at my invitation produced more nuanced feelings. My adrenaline pumped knowing they were cheering me on, but I also worried that it might have been too much pressure on them.

They came to watch Mitch at almost all of his home games, and while I know they've been to a few games this season, it's not a huge part of their lives. I'm not sure if I complicate this for them. Danica and I are lovers. Travis and I have become friends and he looks up to me. Are they feeling disloyal to Mitch today? Or are they thinking about him at all?

Danica would tell me we're sharing space—the good

memories of Mitch and the current memories with me. It's still all very confusing, but the one thing I'm proud of is that I pushed those thoughts out of my head when I stepped onto the ice. Until that final buzzer sounded, I didn't worry about Danica and our illicit relationship, or whether I'm trying to be something to Travis I shouldn't be, or even the worst thought that sometimes plagues me about whether I can ever measure up to Mitch.

Of course, now that the game is over and I'm heading out to meet Danica and Travis at a popular restaurant that specializes in great burgers and even better milkshakes, those insecurities are creeping in. But I let them float about my mind because I have to deal with them, and one thing Danica has taught me is that it does no good to push things down and ignore them. That was my mistake after the crash... trying to be like my dad and brothers. To suck it up and be strong.

It's funny, but I've talked more about the crash, the losses, my emotions and feelings in the past four weeks since reconnecting with Danica than I have in the past year. I can talk about my survivor's guilt without overwhelming panic crushing my chest. Last night after the gala, after we wore each other out in bed, we lay on our sides facing each other and talked things through. I mused about how scary and uncontrollable fate was and that you never knew when your time was up. She pointed out that fate can be kind, as it saw fit to stop me from joining my team that day. A frustrating knee injury that thoroughly pissed me off kept me off that plane.

Fate was exceptionally generous to me and I know that. The difference between before and after meeting Danica is that I was never able to be grateful for it. I've felt too guilty to admit how fucking fortunate I am.

"It's okay to be glad to be alive," Danica said, and then she said something else I'll never forget. "I, for one, am very glad you weren't on that plane."

Those were some forceful words, shocking me to my core. Validation that I have the potential to be someone important to her. Maybe as important as Mitch one day.

The burger joint is a short walk from the arena and I'm going to meet Danica and Travis there. I could've had them meet me in the family lounge on the same level as the locker room, but that would be outing ourselves and we're not ready for that.

When I enter the restaurant, my gaze sweeps the place. It's crowded because it's dinnertime, our game an afternoon one. People recognize me instantly and I have a fleeting moment of panic that maybe this was a bad idea.

I'm a Titan getting ready to sit down and have a meal with a Titan widow and her kid.

I spot Travis first—he's facing me from a booth in the back. His smile is huge and he's waving with both arms. Danica sits next to him, as beautiful as ever, and despite my unease, just seeing her settles something deep inside me. It's a blanket of calmness and I decide to embrace it.

Winding my way through the tables, a few people tell me "Good game" and someone takes a photo of me as I walk by. Travis slips out of the booth to rush up to me. "You were awesome tonight, Camden."

I'm shocked when he throws himself against my side for a hug and my arm comes naturally—protectively— around him for a squeeze, then a ruffle of his hair. "Thanks, kid."

He pulls away and turns to go back to the booth, and I see he's wearing Mitch's name and number on his jersey. It's an older jersey, worn from many washings. My heart thumps, a moment of sadness for Travis mixed with immense awe at his resilience and ability to embrace his past and future.

He slides in next to his mom and I realize she's wearing Mitch's jersey too. While I have the same flash of sorrow for her, awed that she calmly coexists with what's behind and what's in front of her, an extra emotion digs at me.

A bit of jealousy.

Or maybe it's a desire to have her wear my jersey.

I push it away and plop down opposite them in the booth.

"You were amazing tonight," Danica says. There's

not a lot of gush to her words the way there was with Travis, but her praise is all in her eyes. I can see it clear as day that she's proud of the way I played, and I have to force myself not to puff out my chest.

"It was a team effort. We're on a hot streak, for sure."

I'm not being intentionally humble. I've never believed one man makes a difference in this sport. Sure… we've got some superstar players like Coen, Stone and Drake who will be at the top of the stats at the end of the season, but they're only as great as the team around them who provide defense and scoring opportunities. We're running like a well-oiled machine.

Danica taps her foot against the side of my leg and the smile she levels at me tells me I'm a superstar to her. I have to drag my eyes away and force my focus on Travis. "What did you think of that penalty Casperson took in the third period?"

Travis lights up, eager to share his knowledge and analysis. He gives me an impressively succinct argument as to why it was a stupid penalty—and it was—along with a better play that could have been made to stop the breakaway. The kid has hockey in his DNA, but he's smart as hell. Not many children who play can think at that level. Those who can are destined to do well because once you marry the savvy with the physical prowess, you have an elite player.

The waitress comes and takes our drink orders. Danica joins me in a celebratory beer and then we order burgers. Travis is the center of attention in our little threesome. He's incredibly extroverted and likes eyes to be on him. He's funny, gregarious and a pleasure to be around.

I use an opportunity when Travis has his mouth full of food to ask his mom, "What do you have going on this week?"

Nicely innocuous question, hoping to get a feel if we might be able to sneak in some time together. We have another home game tomorrow, a day off and then we're gone for the rest of the week. Tillie and Coen's housewarming party is on Saturday when we return.

"I have meetings Tuesday," she says, dipping a fry into ketchup. "Potential sponsors I met at the gala. But I'm probably going to work from home the rest of the week."

Harmless answer to Travis if he's listening but coupled with the expression on her face, it tells me that on Monday I might be able to snag some time for lunch at her house. I manage to slip her a wink unnoticed and she dips her head with a knowing smile.

When we're nicely stuffed, the waitress brings a dessert menu. Travis isn't a milkshake fan so he opted for a brownie sundae. Danica and I both passed, although I ordered a second beer.

Danica nudges Travis. "I need to use the restroom."

Travis slides out of the booth and Danica scoots out, taking her purse with her. "Be right back."

I've moved farther into the booth so I can turn at an angle and rest my back against the wall, my arm on the table. Travis folds his arms and leans forward a little. Because he's only nine, he looks diminutive in that position, but the expression on his face is hard and unyielding.

It gives me a moment of pause, but it's his words that almost send me into a panic. "Do you like my mom or something?"

My eyebrows fly up so fast, I'm surprised they don't shoot off my face. I sit straight up and turn toward him. "Excuse me?"

"Do you like my mom?"

Every instinct based on denial kicks in. "Yeah... sure. We're friends, so of course I like her."

Travis rolls his eyes and if I wasn't so nerve-wracked, I might even laugh. "I'm nine years old, not stupid. I see the way you two look at each other."

Deflection.

"What do you mean?" I ask tentatively, picking up my beer to take a sip.

I get another eye roll. "You look at her like you might want to kiss her?" I choke on the ale, eyes watering. "And she looks like she wants to kiss you. I remember what that looked like when my dad was alive."

Oh shit. Fuck. Fuckity fuck fuck fuck.

"Um… well… I think…" My mind is blank and while I want to be truthful with him, I don't want to be insensitive. I'd also very much like his mother in on this conversation, but she's in the damn bathroom right now.

"It's okay if you like each other," he says, and I blow out an embarrassingly loud and obvious breath of relief. Travis ignores it. "I mean… you're cool and my mom thinks you're cool. And I don't want her to be lonely, so I want to know if you like her. Like in the kissing way."

"In the kissing way?" I ask, feeling myself flush hot.

Travis grins at me. "I know things. Kissing means you like her romantically. It's more than friends."

I deflect a little longer but more than being afraid to answer the question, I'm now insanely curious about something. "How do you know things? Is there someone at school you like in a kissing way?"

Travis screws up his face. "No way. I'm too young for that." No, you're really not. I remember kissing Amelia Slater in third grade on the playground. It was on a dare but I had liked her and wanted to kiss her. "Besides… this is about you, not me."

My lips twitch at his earnest bearing and how deftly he brought that back around. "Okay… got it."

"So…," he prompts. "Do you like her? Because it's okay if you do. I mean, I'm cool with that."

There's no thought of denial, deflection or word

trickery. I tell him how it is. "I like her a lot."

Travis grins, then spots something over my shoulder. His smile still in place, he says in a low voice, "Mom's coming. We'll keep this between us men."

I hastily take another sip of beer so I don't laugh at how unbelievably fucking cute that was. When his mom reaches the table, Travis says, "I have to go to the bathroom."

"Okay," Danica says pleasantly, tossing her purse into the booth and sliding onto the seat. As Travis walks away, she turns to me, "What were you two talking about?"

"What do you mean?" I hope my expression looks innocent enough.

Danica smirks... a mom who knows when she's being bullshitted. "You were leaning in toward each other like you were telling secrets."

I know better than to try to hide stuff from such a person and Danica is more than formidable.

"Your son," I say with a jerk of my head toward the bathrooms, "just called me out. Wanted to know if I liked you in *the kissing way*."

Danica slaps her hand over her mouth to stifle a laugh, her eyes exhibiting both amusement and horror. It drops away just as quickly. "What did you say?"

"I played stupid at first, but your kid is as smart as you. After much berating, I admitted I liked you a lot and then you reappeared, so that was the end of the conversation."

"Was he okay with it?" she asks curiously. I note she doesn't have an ounce of fear or hesitation in her tone, almost as if she trusts her son will have her back.

Which he does.

"He said he was cool with it."

Danica cuts her eyes toward the bathroom, likely to be sure Travis is still there, and reaches over to slide her fingertips across the back of my hand. "I'll talk with him later tonight and let him know I like you in the kissing way too."

I look over my shoulder at the bathroom and lean closer to her. "Since we have Travis's approval and all, think we can do lunch together Monday?" I lower my voice. "I could come to your place. Bring you food and we can spare maybe ten minutes to eat and fifty minutes letting me see how many ways I can make you scream?"

Danica flushes and it makes her prettier. "I'd like that a lot. But what if I want to make you scream instead?"

Jesus, the thought of how she would accomplish that tightens my groin. "I don't scream," I say, pointing out my manliness.

She leans across the table and lowers her voice. "No, you don't. You make a growling noise. But I bet I can make you pant."

My throat is dry but I refrain from sipping my beer to wet it. Our time is limited before Travis gets back and I want to hear all I can to hold me over until Monday. "And exactly how would you do that?" I rasp.

"With my hot, wet mouth on you." Her eyes lock hard on mine and once again, a finger trails over my hand. Her voice is like velvet. "I'm going to make you see stars, Camden."

Her eyes cut past my shoulders and she leans back, withdrawing her hand. "Travis is coming."

"Fuck," I say, shifting in my seat because my pants are way too tight. "Thank God he ordered dessert because I'm not going to be able to stand up anytime soon."

Danica flushes again, but I see pride in her expression. She shoots me a wink and then turns to Travis with a smile as he slides into the booth beside her.

CHAPTER 23

Danica

M Y DOORBELL CHIMES and I suppress a yip of excitement, instead letting the joy at seeing Camden buzz through me like fizzy champagne. I shuffle-run my way to the door, my fuzzy bunny slippers preventing a full-out sprint. I swing it open and drink him in.

For those few seconds, I appreciate his male beauty, followed by the anticipation of what will come out of his mouth. Every single word is important to me.

His gaze makes a luxuriously slow slide down my body, taking in my loose braided pigtails because I was too lazy to blow it out, a ratty Guns N' Roses T-shirt, gray leggings and lastly… my slippers that have floppy bunny ears, googly eyes and bent whiskers. My feet were cold.

When Camden's eyes slide back up, they lock on me as his mouth curves into a lecherous smile. "I don't know that I've ever seen you look hotter. After we eat, I'm taking those bunny slippers off and I'm going to wreck you hard."

I reach up and rest my hand on the doorframe, putting the other on my hip. My voice is raspy, seductive. "Special just for you. And I thought we agreed, I'll do the wrecking."

Camden bursts out laughing and steps into me. Wrapping a hand around my back, he hauls me in for a hard kiss before leaving his lips against mine to whisper, "Seriously. You're beautiful and you can wreck me anytime you want."

"You're sweet. And I'll wreck you as often as you like."

Then my hand is in his and he's leading me to my kitchen as I shuffle along behind him so as not to lose a slipper. He sets a grease-stained white paper bag on the table and the smell of cheese steaks wafts from it. Shrugging out of his coat, he tosses it on a chair and moves to my fridge to pull out two bottles of water.

I grab plates, napkins and forks so we can catch any good stuff that falls out. Settling down into adjacent chairs, our legs press against each other. We huddle over sandwiches and fill each other in on our lives from the past few days since we had burgers with Travis.

The Titans had another home game yesterday that Travis and I watched on TV. Camden invited us again as his guests, but I declined since it was a school night. I tell him about the fundraising events I've been putting together and I run more ideas by him, using him as a sounding board before I present them to Brienne. We discuss college and I explain about the 529 plan I set up today so I can start putting money in each month for tuition. That wasn't something Mitch and I had done. Hell, we didn't even know about it because in our minds, the money would always come in, and we figured we'd have enough to send Travis anywhere he wanted to go. It was stupid and shortsighted, but now that I have a job, I can afford to set some aside each month.

We talk about Travis and the fact that he hasn't mentioned his conversation with Camden about liking me.

In a kissing way!

I decided not to bring it up because I'm still unsure of what we have going on. The only thing Travis knows is that Camden likes me and apparently, he's okay with that. He doesn't know the intricacies of dating someone for the first time since Mitch's death or the social implications of Camden and Mitch being teammates. That's all more than his nine-year-old mind can process right now, nor should he have to reconcile that at his age. Until Camden and I find sure footing, I'll wait to see if Travis mentions it.

"You excited about the road trip coming up?" I ask.

He nods as he finishes a bite of his sandwich. When he swallows, he says, "Yeah. We're on fire right now and we want to test that momentum out in opponents' arenas. That's where playoff championships are won or lost... in how well you play on the road and without your fan base behind you."

"The team has really stepped it up this year. It's phenomenal when you consider how the team was patched together."

"I think that's all Coach West." The respect is evident in his tone. "We've got the same talent we had last year, but he knows how to inspire."

"He's become a solid support to me over the last several months."

"I'm not surprised," Camden says, bumping his knee affectionately against mine.

Cannon's loss of his wife to cancer several years ago makes him uniquely experienced in how healing happens over the long haul. He's so easy to talk to, and you can tell that's because he's genuinely interested in helping others.

I find Camden to be that way too.

My doorbell rings as I'm bringing my cheese steak up for another bite, so I set it down and wipe my greasy fingers on a napkin. Scooting my chair back, I head for the front door to find the UPS man there.

I'm not expecting anything so I'm surprised when he hands over a package addressed to me that requires a signature. The return address brings a smile to my face.

"Thank you," I say as I sign his electronic pad.

I carry the lightweight box into the kitchen and Camden asks what it is.

"No clue. But it's from Mitch's mom. She sends gifts to Travis all the time, but this one is addressed to me."

I set it on the counter and move back toward the table.

"Open it," Camden says, nodding at the package. He must sense my curiosity and excitement.

I stare at him a moment, unsure if it's rude to take part of our lunch hour to do so, but he nods again at the gift, a firm expression on his face.

Decision made, I grab scissors from the utility drawer and cut along the packing tape. Balled-up pieces of newspaper surround what I immediately see is a scrapbook. Mitch's mom, Cora, loves the hobby and has chronicled our lives over the years in these books. I run my hand lovingly over the front, done in a blue-and-purple-checked fabric with an inset picture of me and Mitch. We were young... the newest of friends.

I feel Camden behind me and then his hand is lightly on my waist as he looks over my shoulder. "What is it?"

"A scrapbook." I start to push it away but his other hand comes around to lay on mine, halting my movement.

"Go ahead and open it. Let's see it."

I hesitate because I know inside is full of memories.

I'm sure Cora found a box of photos and put them together in a lovely story of some portion of our lives, most likely chronicling how we grew to love each other.

I lift my face to look at Camden, and he smiles with encouragement and understanding. "Go on. Unless you don't want me looking, then—"

"No, I don't mind. There's nothing to hide and nothing that's private."

"Then go on." He moves to my side and leans forward, crossing his forearms on the counter.

"Okay," I say with a grin and open the book.

The first photo is of Mitch facing the camera and holding up a homemade card. I recognize it instantly and still have it. I was seven and he was nine. It was for my birthday—my parents were having a neighborhood party for me. His mom insisted he make the card as she was trying to get him to explore his artistic side—which did not exist—and not focus so much on hockey. There's another picture on the same page of me and Mitch at my birthday party. He had gotten me a book as I often had my nose stuck in one.

"Mitch looks like you were going to give him cooties," Camden remarks as he takes in my arm over his shoulder, cheesing for the camera, and Mitch leaning away. We were buddies but sometimes I could be annoying, given our age difference.

I laugh because that's exactly what it looks like.

The next photo is of a tree house Mitch's dad built into a huge oak tree in their backyard. We're both hanging out the window, looking down at the camera. I think his mom took that photo. We were ten and twelve.

I point to a trapeze bar that hung from a low branch. "I was swinging upside down on this and fell. My pinky finger caught a root and broke. I was crying and Mitch was telling me to suck it up. Said he got hurt in hockey all the time. I was so mad at him that I didn't talk to him for two weeks."

Camden chuckles. "I don't think boys are all that adept at understanding of those types of things."

"He was pretty dense," I say fondly.

I flip through a few more pages... cute shots of us playing in the tree house, riding our scooters in the neighborhood, splashing around in the above-ground pool at my house.

I turn the page and my breath catches. It's a photo of us in our teens. I'm sixteen and Mitch had just turned eighteen. He was taking me to the senior prom, and I had stars in my eyes over that man. He was going to play professional hockey and everyone knew it. His prior girlfriend, Jenny Witten, hated me because I had his attention, and she and a bunch of her girls surrounded me that night when Mitch went off to get us drinks. They were bullying me, throwing nasty insults that truly didn't touch me. I had Mitch and she didn't.

He approached and heard the things she said and I'd never seen him so angry. He announced right then and there to everyone who could hear that he was in love with me and anyone who said an unkind word would pay for it.

That's how I found out he loved me... an announcement to everyone at prom.

"Pretty dress," Camden comments. Mitch is slipping a corsage of gardenias on my wrist. He knew they were my favorite flowers.

"Yes," I murmur, smiling inside with fondness because Mitch hated the smell. Through the years, he bore it, though, because of my love for them.

Camden watches over my shoulder as we study the photos. The last page holds a picture that marks the beginning of our adult relationship. My high school graduation. Mitch had been playing in the league for two years and I was the envy of all the girls. He came to my grad, bringing me a huge bouquet of gardenias, which I'm convinced he stole from someone's yard because they don't usually sell them in flower shops that I've ever seen. He scooped me up in his arms and swung me around. My cap had fallen off my head, but I held tight with one arm around his neck and the other clutching those flowers. Our future started for real that fall when I enrolled at Pitt and the rest is history.

As I close the scrapbook, I realize I'm weighed down

by a tiny bit of sadness. Each photo holds a happy memory, but looking at them in succession only highlights all I've lost.

"Are you okay?" Camden asks as I move away from him to the sink. I wash my hands to take a moment to process my feelings.

"Yeah." My voice is thick with emotion, though. "Just a little blue is all."

I rinse my hands, dry them off with a paper towel and when I'm tossing it in the garbage, I realize that he didn't reply.

Turning to face him, I find him leaning against the counter, hands tucked into his pockets. His expression is uneasy. "I don't know what to say to you. I don't know if it's my place to say anything. I worry you're not over losing Mitch and I don't want to be insensitive."

I settle against the opposite counter, my arms folded across my stomach. The space between us seems overly expansive. "You don't need to say anything, Camden. Sometimes I get a little sad. I don't mean to do it. I can't control it. It comes and then it goes. You need to be okay with it."

"I am okay with it," he says gently. "I never want you to dampen your emotions regarding Mitch. But I'm an outsider here and I think I always will be. You two had so much history together, it's daunting. Every time you're sad about Mitch, there's a part of me that wonders if it's because I'll never be enough."

I scrub my hands over my face and let out a harsh, pent-up breath. Holding out my arms, I shake my head with no good answers. "I hate that you feel that way. I can only promise you that's not what I'm thinking. Yes, I miss Mitch sometimes, but you know what? I miss you too when we're apart."

That seems to settle him because his chest deflates as if he was holding his breath. My heart hurts for his uncertainty and the best way for me to soothe that right now is first with touch, then with words. I move across my kitchen and into his arms. I'm relieved he embraces me, allowing me to rest my head on his chest.

"When Mitch died, I was drowning in grief. My tears were as common as breathing." Camden's arms jerk slightly, then tighten. A measure of support. "But eventually, the tears dried and happiness returned in small doses. Then it came in big flushes. Travis was usually at the center of any joy those first few months, but I knew I had to give him a normal life. I kept my tears for when I went to bed so he wouldn't share in my burden. With time, things changed. I found myself in bed at night, not crying over Mitch but smiling over something Travis said or did. If he had an amazing moment at school, it's what I was thinking about when I closed my eyes. It got better and better. Every day that passed another stitch closed up the hole in my heart. And one day, I felt complete again. The tears were gone and I was happy."

I push back against Camden's hold and tip my head to look at him. "But it doesn't mean I don't still have moments where my grief rears up. I can't control that and I don't want to. I embrace those emotions because it's part of who I am. I need you to embrace that about me... that I'm a woman with deep feelings."

Camden's eyes flick between my own as if he's trying to figure out a puzzle, but I don't know how to be any clearer. I'm about to offer further reassurance when he speaks and I'm not expecting the directional change in the conversation.

His hands come to my face. "I haven't had a nightmare since we reconnected. I know part of it is that you've gotten me to open up about my emotions and talk about the crash. But the greater part was seeing how you embraced the experience and learned from it. Grew from it. I'm trying to model myself after you and that's the greatest gift you've given me."

I smile up at him because that sentiment is about as lovely a thing as anyone has ever said to me.

But my smile slips a bit with his next words. "On the flip side, coming to know you better and caring for you more deeply as each day goes by seems to increase my worry. Maybe it's not knowing if we're good for each other or maybe the timing isn't right. There's the fear of judgment and I'm trying my best to work past that, I promise you. Mostly, by getting involved with someone as amazing as you... I'm at risk of getting hurt. For as much as you've helped me grow, I could go in way deep with you and find out that you're not ready. All my bad dreams now are of falling for you and then losing you."

Once again, my heart hurts for him. Camden is as traumatized by the crash as any of us, and I am quite sure I'm as much a complication as a gift to him. I wish I could give him the assurances he needs, but I'm flying as blind as he is.

The only difference is, I'm willing to take the risk.

I can't make him ready to do that, though. I can only wait for him to work through these things on his own and offer my hand, hoping he'll be ready to take it one day so we can step out together.

I snuggle back into his chest and give him the only promise I can make at this time. "I understand how you're feeling."

But I can't offer a solution.

CHAPTER 24

Danica

HAVING THROWN THE condom away in the bathroom, Camden slips back under the covers and pulls me into him spoon-style. While the sex between us is fucking amazing and only gets better every time, I have to admit, I enjoy the cuddling after. Camden wraps himself around me ever so perfectly and I could drift off to sleep in this warm cocoon or I could lie here and talk to him for hours.

We ended up here because I'm wanton and I own it. Camden's been gone most of the week with two away games in Houston and Vegas. We hadn't made any solid plans for when he got back. Tillie and Coen's housewarming party is tomorrow evening, and while we've both RSVP'd, we haven't even discussed how we're going to play it.

This morning I woke up with an intense need to see Camden. To talk to him and honestly, to have him in my body. I find myself craving sex with him and because our time is limited between my job, raising Travis and

Camden's travel, I decided to be bold.

He flew in late last night from Vegas, but I know he's generally an early riser. I sexted for the first time in my life. Put on the sexiest bra and panties I own—refusing to dwell on the fact that Mitch bought them for me—and I took a picture of myself in the mirror. I had my hair pulled over my shoulders, popped my booty out and gave as sultry a look as I could before snapping the picture.

I sent it with a simple message. *If you come over, I'll take the day off work. I don't have to pick up Travis until three. I'm waiting.*

It was bold and daring and my heart raced in terror that he'd text back and say he had plans. Instead, I got nothing.

No response. No indication he'd read the text. Not even a pop of a bubble that he had started a reply.

After ten minutes, I started feeling foolish and put on a robe. After thirty, I got dressed for the day—a T-shirt and leggings, my standard work-from-home attire.

I'd barely sat down at the kitchen table to open my laptop when the doorbell rang. I didn't need to see through the small panes of glass to know the looming figure out there was Camden.

Scrambling out of the chair, I kicked off my bunny slippers, whipped my T-shirt over my head and shimmied out of the leggings. I was out of breath by the time I reached the door.

When I swung it open, I intended to give him a sexy pose, but I didn't get the chance. Camden merely hauled me over his shoulder, his large palm coming to rest on my bare ass as the back of my panties were nonexistent, and carried me up the stairs. He's so strong he took them two at a time.

In my bedroom, he tossed me on the bed and stripped off his clothes. I went to my elbows to watch hungrily. Prepared with a condom in hand, he first spread my legs wide and used his mouth to bring me to a cataclysmic orgasm. Then that condom was rolled on and he was inside me and it was exactly what I needed.

Not wanted.

I needed it. Him. This.

Now we're cuddling and it feels amazing to experience this intimacy. We live in small snatches of time together and because Travis is a big part of my life, lazily lying in bed is a luxury I'll never take for granted.

"You tired?" I ask as my fingers stroke the hair on his arms.

Camden nuzzles the back of my neck, his hand spread across my lower belly. "Give me about ten minutes and I'll be ready to go again."

I snort with laughter. "I mean from the road trip."

"Oh." His abashed chuckle is adorable. "Yeah... little tired."

"You can take a nap if you want. I can work and

wake you up later."

"No fucking way," he growls, his hand moving lower down my belly. "I've got you for another four hours at least, three if we decide to eat food. I'm not letting you out of this bed."

"Just going to fuck me for four hours, huh?" I ask, wondering if that's achievable.

"Not going to stop touching you for four hours," he corrects me.

I adjust so my arms come over his and squeeze him tightly. I burrow back into him deeper, relishing the heat from his skin and the smell of our sex in the air.

"That lingerie did me in." His voice is lazy, replete but playful. "Do you wear stuff like that often?"

I wince over my answer before it comes out of my mouth. "Not unless someone is going to see and appreciate it."

And now everything is awkward. It's clear that I've only ever worn sexy lingerie for Mitch before and he can probably deduce that the bra and panties were part of my seduction wardrobe for my dead husband.

Tears spring to my eyes as I try to imagine how Camden is feeling. I want to turn around to face him… see the truth of how much that hurt, but I'm too chicken.

But then Camden does something I know I'll never forget as long as I live.

He makes it easy on me. His hand slides a little lower, fingertips playing at the edge of my pubic mound. He puts his lips near my ear. "I loved that picture you sent me. Turned me the fuck on. My next day off I'm going to buy you a dozen outfits like that and demand you wear them all the time for me."

I nearly cry out in relief that he accepted the fact that my life with Mitch and my new relationship with him might intersect. If I thought I was falling for him hard before, I'm absolutely tumbling with no control because Camden made that easier on both of us. It gives me such hope for a future with him.

Desire overwhelms me and I push his hand right between my legs. "Let's see if we can beat that ten-minute mark you set."

Camden growls and sinks a finger inside me as I feel his teeth on my shoulder. It's pure bliss and I let myself fall into it.

♦

WE'RE NOT CUDDLING now, but this might be even better. We just got done eating pizza in bed and now we're sitting up against the headboard, our heads bent over his phone as we watch TikTok together. I learned not long ago that Camden is slightly addicted to it, but what's surprising is the content he's curated for his feed. It's not hockey or sports or even celebrities. I'm amazed that he follows TikTokers with content focused on food, animals, art and life hacks.

Lifting his wrist, Camden looks at his Apple Watch. "It's getting close to time to pick up Travis."

I lean over to look and see it's almost two thirty and I'll have to leave in about fifteen minutes. I need a quick shower because four hours in bed with Camden has left me well used.

My mouth involuntarily curls at the memory of some of the things we did and a pleasurable cramp hits me between the legs.

Yeah... sex with Camden is so good, I'm afraid if I compare it to Mitch, I might be torn apart by the guilt. So I don't let my mind go there.

I started to slide from the bed but I forgot there was something I needed to talk about. I turn toward Camden. "Have you given any thought to Tillie and Coen's party tomorrow?"

His eyes cloud over with what I've come to recognize as unease about our relationship. "Um... yeah, I have. And I don't think this is the time to out ourselves to the team. You know, it would take away from Tillie and Coen's spotlight and—"

"Say no more." I cut in by placing my fingertips against his lips. "We'll barely look at each other or talk unless it's in a group setting and it appears we are nothing more than casual friends."

I wince internally because I know that sounded a

little pathetic. I rush to cover and paste a smile on my face. "It'll be fine. I'm sure you and I can have a wonderful time, and there's no need for us to act weird. Everyone knows we were friends before the crash."

"For sure," he agrees, sounding a little too relieved I'm not pushing for anything. His hand goes to the back of my neck and he presses his forehead to mine. "We'll figure this out, I promise."

I can't nod in agreement.

I can't say "I know" because I refuse to put faith in anything at this point.

I can only hope.

Lifting his head, Camden brushes his mouth against mine. "Any chance Travis is having a sleepover tomorrow night?"

My mouth curves into a smile against his before pulling back to look at him. "As a matter of fact, he is."

"Want to come to my place after the party?" he asks.

"I'd love to."

I shove away the tinge of bitterness that I cannot have more with Camden. He's everything I could ever want except that he wants to keep this a secret. I think back to Mitch, proclaiming to everyone at senior prom that he loved me, and I long for that type of commitment from Camden. It's not only that I want it... I'm afraid I need it.

Frankly, it doesn't feel good that he's not fully invested in me when I've gone all in.

CHAPTER 25

Camden

COEN AND TILLIE bought a gorgeous house in Sewickley and we're all here to celebrate it. This is a big deal for several reasons, the most obvious being that last season, Coen was a complete and utter asshole to everyone. Some leeway was granted because he was one of the Lucky Three, but honestly, he was so unlikable that sympathy didn't go far.

But something happened to the man over the summer when he holed himself away in the tiny town of Coudersport after deciding to leave the sport. He came up against the bright and bubbly artist, Tillie Marshall, who didn't take his shit. She refused to be cowed by his surly attitude. I don't know the entire story or how things progressed, but suffice it to say, Coen fell madly in love.

At the start of this season, it was tough on the guy. Tillie had a home and business back in Coudersport, which is three and a half hours away from Pittsburgh. Since the season started, they've been managing a long-distance relationship, but Coen suffers when she's gone. Everyone can see it. While he smiles these days, it's only truly bright when Tillie's in town.

I'm guessing it's been as hard on Tillie as it's been on Coen because she decided to move to Pittsburgh permanently and travel back to Coudersport as needed for her business. All I know is that Coen's been on cloud nine the last few weeks since they closed on their house and moved in.

Coen and Tillie's new place is only about a twenty-minute drive to the heart of Pittsburgh but it feels like a world removed from the city. Their seven-thousand-square-foot house is made of brick, stone and copper-covered dormers. It sits on five secluded acres and has an attached apartment that they're converting into an art studio for Tillie.

The party is in full swing when I arrive and I have no clue if Danica is here. I only know I'm probably going to spend a good deal of time craning my neck for a glimpse of her. It fucking sucks having to play it cool with our relationship in public. I look at all the couples—my teammates like Stone, Coen and Drake—who have found love in the last year, and I envy their ability to have their women at their side. It's not something I ever coveted before. I've been to plenty of parties and get-togethers, and I've always been happy hanging out with the single dudes. Tonight, I'm feeling a bit empty because I want to talk to Danica, laugh with Danica and touch Danica. I want everyone to know that I cherish her and that she's mine.

After snagging a beer, I join a group led by Coen who gives a tour of the place and I'm eventually deposited back with the single guys. I end up joining Kirill and Boone, my usual posse, minus Hendrix who's off in the corner talking with his girl, Stevie. Bain hasn't arrived yet, but I'm sure he'll hang out with us once he gets here. With half an ear on Kirill and Boone discussing which truck is better—Chevy or Ford—I keep surveying the house and the movement of guests, looking for Danica.

When I do locate her walking in the front door, I have to restrain myself from going to her. She immediately sees Jenna and with a smile on her face moves to her for a hug. Jenna takes her by the hand and leads her off toward the kitchen, which flows from the main living area where I'm standing.

Forces beyond my control are pulling at me so I follow behind, nodding at friends, teammates and their significant others. I tip my beer, trying to drain it completely so I have a good reason for being in the kitchen to get another. It's not that I'm going to talk to her, but I want to be near her.

Danica is holding a wineglass and waiting while Tillie fills it. Her back is to me and it allows me to take in the rest of the scene—tons of people standing in pockets of two to five.

Coen appears and joins Tillie and Danica in conversation. Despite my better judgment to stay away for fear of revealing my true feelings to all, talking to Coen seems like safe territory and allows me to at least be near Danica. So I wind my way through, fortuitously able to grab a beer from a large metal bin filled with ice on the counter.

Coen and Tillie see me first, but Danica turns, following their attention.

Tillie beams at me. "Hi, Camden... I'm so glad you could come."

"Wouldn't miss it." I step into Tillie and kiss her cheek. "Your new house is beautiful."

Even though my heart is pounding like a steel drum, I give my regards to Danica. I want to say something charming but not so much that Coen and Tillie might suspect we're more than friends. Maybe an inside joke we share, but even that would give away that we're more than just acquaintances.

I'm sure Danica can sense my unease and her smile is uncertain. I can't risk anyone knowing, and I'm afraid one word out of my mouth will be coated in the tender feelings I have for her.

So I merely lift my chin toward her. "Hey."

"Hey," she says, her smile sliding a bit.

Grabbing another beer from the bin, I jerk my thumb over my shoulder. "I only came in to grab beers for me and Bain. He's waiting on me."

"We'll catch up in a bit," Coen says, and Tillie nods effusively.

Danica, though… Christ… she looks hurt by my brush-off. I hate that, but she knows we can't out ourselves. She's going to have to trust that by playing it cooler than cool, it will be safer for both of us.

I turn away from what might be recrimination in her beautiful eyes and move through the kitchen. I head downstairs to the basement, which is Coen's man cave. I'm now stuck with two beers since I have no clue if Bain is even here.

Spotting Coach West and his girlfriend, Ava, I decide to go say hello but then veer off as Brienne and Drake join them. Brienne knows about me and Danica, and I'm not in the mood for probing looks or the shuddering thought she might come right out and ask me about it.

I finally land at a table where Stone and Harlow are sitting with Foster, who brought a date. He introduces me, but I immediately forget her name as I'm too worried I've hurt Danica's feelings. Should I go back up and talk to her? Can I do it and contain my feelings?

I decide it's too risky and keep my ass planted in the chair. Eventually, I loosen up, but that's probably due to the three beers. Danica remains upstairs and I start to feel better about the situation. She's probably keeping away from me the way I am her. It's all moot, anyway, since we'll be together later when she comes to my house. We made plans to leave the party earlier rather than later so we could have time together. Next week is solidly packed with away games. We're in New York on Sunday and Monday, Boston on Thursday and Carolina on Saturday. We'll have some quick stops back in Pittsburgh in between, but it will be hectic, and I doubt we'll get to see each other between practices, her work and of course, caring for Travis in the evenings.

But tonight we've got hours together and I intend to get my fill of her in all ways. I'll make sure she knows how I feel about her then, in the privacy between us.

For the next hour, I engage in casual conversation with those at the table, but then Coen comes down the stairs. "Can I get everyone to come upstairs briefly for an announcement?"

I raise my eyebrows at Stone who shrugs his shoulders. We all dutifully make our way out of the basement and crowd into the massive living room that spills into the kitchen and dining area. Coen and Tillie stand together in the middle, his arm around her waist. He's got a beer in his other hand.

"Tillie and I would like to thank you all for coming to our housewarming to celebrate this new journey we're on. I'm personally most grateful for all the presents you brought." There's a wave of laughter and Tillie pokes a playful elbow into Coen's ribs. He merely leans down and gives her a swift kiss, which then turns soft and tender before he pulls away. He stares at her for a long moment with so much emotion, the collar of my shirt feels tight. As if he has to tear his gaze from her, he looks around the crowd. "But we really didn't invite everyone here today to look at our beautiful new house. I wanted everyone to come so they could look at my beautiful new wife. Tillie and I eloped last week."

For a moment it's so quiet you can hear a pin drop, and then all of a sudden there's a roar of congratulations, wolf whistles and applause. The newly wedded couple share another kiss, this time him bending her backward as someone yells, "Get a room."

Laughing, Coen lets his wife up and pulls her in for a one-armed hug, raising his beer with his free hand, as if he just won the biggest prize in the world.

Guests swarm the couple and they eventually get pulled apart and drawn into different conversations. Danica stands on the other side of the room from me, and I keep glancing at her as we talk to various people and wait our turn to offer congrats to Tillie and Coen. Every once in a blue moon, her eyes meet mine then quickly move on. I'm convinced she's playing the same role I am... let's ignore each other so we don't tip anyone off.

Still, nothing about tonight sits right. It's torture being in proximity to Danica, unable to talk to or touch her, even if it's only to hold her hand. And deep down, I know that I'm the one pushing this secretive agenda. Danica would be fine with me walking over to her right now and kissing her the way Coen just kissed Tillie.

Coen eventually makes his way over to me, and I give him a bro hug. I have no clue where Tillie is, but Danica is at the kitchen island, chatting with Kiera whose presence I notice for the first time.

"Congratulations," I tell him. "You know that the team had voted you as most likely to elope, right?"

Coen snorts. "Of course I knew that. Where do you think we got the idea?"

My eyes drift over to Danica once again and this time, she's looking right at me. God, I could fucking stare at her all day.

"You two have become good friends," Coen says.

Whiplash is almost a certainty as I look back at him. "What?"

Coen nods toward Danica and my eyes helplessly slide to her. She's talking with Kiera again. "You and Danica. You've become good friends."

I hate myself as soon as the words are out, denying the truth. "Not really. I mean… she's great and we've had some in-depth talks about the crash, but nothing more than that."

"Yeah... Tillie lost her parents in a car accident. It made it easier to talk to her about the plane disaster. You know... having something so awful in common."

I nod. I know exactly what he means. Seeing how Danica stayed strong for her son and remade her life has been a significant catalyst for me, helping me move forward past my grief and guilt. I never addressed it the way I should have eleven months ago.

"They were a close couple," Coen says in a low voice, and it's because he's still looking at Danica that I realize he's talking about her and Mitch. "Together since they were kids. I admire her, but honestly... how do you get past something like that? I'm not sure I could get past it if I lost Tillie."

If I thought I couldn't feel worse tonight, I was wrong. Coen just unwittingly gave me a huge reason why I shouldn't be with Danica.

Because maybe she'll never feel the same for me that she did for Mitch. I shake my head, forcing that thought away. I'm past those doubts. Danica has assured me, and I have to trust her in a way that I can't exactly trust myself, to take the next step.

Christ, I'm an asshole.

I'm a mess.

An assholish mess.

I want to tell Coen that yes, people can move on. I want to tell him that Danica has decided to move on.

With me.

But I don't.

"Listen… I've got more rounds to make. I'll catch up with you later." Coen and I fist-bump and then he walks away.

I check my watch and see it's still a half hour before Danica and I agreed to leave—separate from each other, of course. I'm to head out first and she'll follow about fifteen minutes later.

Meandering across the living room, I join Baden, Sophie, Gage and Jenna. Gage was my teammate last year and is now a coach. Since he made the transition, there's a line of respect we don't cross, but at these types of gatherings, no one's a player and no one's a coach. We're all simply Titans.

I get sucked into a conversation about *Ted Lasso*. Baden's never seen it and we're astounded and give him shit. I feel someone at my elbow and move to the left to make room for another person to join the conversation.

It's Danica. My body reacts immediately, in painful ways that pull me in different directions. Her arm brushes against mine and I smell her shampoo, and it makes me want to devour her in front of everybody. This is doused quickly by my panic that everyone in this group will see my feelings in my expression and bearing.

I barely spare her a glance and look across the room. Kirill is standing all alone at the kitchen island, nibbling on carrots and dip. "Hey... I'll be back. I've got to ask Kirill something."

No one pays me any attention except Danica. And I don't so much see as feel her hurt that I didn't give her more than a brief glance. That I'm leaving as soon as she arrives.

I'm only able to suck in a relieved breath when I reach Kirill.

"What's up, man?" he says, and I grab a carrot, swirling it in the dip. I fucking hate carrots.

"Not much," I mutter and twist my neck to look over at Danica. To see how badly I've either pissed her off or hurt her.

But she's not where I left her.

My eyes scan the room and the carrot drops out of my hand and into the dip when I see her walking out the front door with her coat on and her purse hitched over her shoulder.

"What the fuck?" I grouse, looking at my watch. She's leaving earlier than we'd planned and before me.

I don't rush to follow but follow her I do. Casually winding my way through people, I even manage a quick joke to Bain about arriving so late and deciding to join us. He smirks, but he's forgotten as I exit the house.

From the front porch, I scan left to right for Danica. The cars are parked on both sides of the street. I spot her half a block down.

Without hesitation, I jump off the porch and cut across Coen's front yard. I hurdle a low line of shrubbery into the neighbor's yard and manage to intercept Danica. My hand takes her wrist. I love how delicate her bones are and how soft her skin is. "Why did you leave so early? Is everything okay?"

She tugs her arm away and while her tone is even and calm, her eyes are harsh and unyielding. "No, it's not okay. I can't do this, Camden. I thought I could but I can't."

I thought I had some panic moments in the house but clearly not. Right now, I feel like I might hyperventilate. "Can't do what? I don't understand."

"I can't be with you and not be with you. It's not okay that you can't even stand next to me in a group and have a normal conversation. I might have been able to pretend we were just friends if you could've pretended as well, but your absolute ignorance of me is unbearable. You lying to get space from me is inexcusable."

I'm hot and want to tug on my collar. "What? What do you mean?"

"You said you were grabbing beers for you and Bain and walked away. That was a lie. Bain wasn't even there yet."

I frown in puzzlement. "How did you know that? You'd just arrived yourself."

"Never mind how I know," she snaps angrily. "I just know, okay?"

Holding up my hands, I surrender and knowing I'm being overly obtuse because I'm on the defense, I ask, "Okay. I still don't understand. Did I do something wrong here?"

She blows out a breath and looks off to the left, refusing to meet my eyes. "You didn't do anything at all."

"And that makes you mad."

Danica faces me. "No, that makes me sad. It makes me sad because I can't be falling for a man who doesn't have the courage to want to fall for me."

"I am falling for you," I insist. I step into her, cup her cheeks and bend my head to peer at her. "I'm there, Danica. I'm not trying to hurt you, but it's a precarious time for this all to be happening. It's bad timing."

"For you," she says evenly as she steps backward, causing my hands to fall away. "But not for me."

I feel awkward so I shove them in my jeans pockets, vaguely noticing that it's starting to snow. But I don't feel the cold. "What does this mean? You don't want to see me anymore?"

She takes in another deep breath and lets it out so slowly, maybe to prolong a very painful answer. "I can't get in any deeper with you. My feelings are already too tied up, and after tonight, they're now bruised. I can't live half a life with you, not only because it hurts me, but ultimately, it will be too confusing for Travis. He can't see us together and happy, then watch us act as strangers around the team or others." I wince, because I understand how fucked up that sounds. "If we continue like this and he sees you're one way with me when we're alone and then you completely ignore me when we're around others, it will confuse him. Fuck... it confuses me. I'm not about to let Travis see his mother made to feel like she's not good enough. I'm not ever going to let my kid think that's right."

I stumble back from her, those last words landing like physical blows to my chest and twisting my guts into painful knots. Is that what I'm doing to her?

It's startling after all those painful truths that Danica takes my hand and holds it gently. "I know you're conflicted, Camden. And I absolutely understand your reasoning behind us staying a secret. You're not wrong... I know this could cause unrest within the team, and that scares you. So hear me... I'm legitimizing your feelings. But I'm also going to legitimize mine. We're at two different places in our lives and this is where our paths diverge."

I know she's right but fuck if I'm going to admit it out loud. So I remain silent.

Her hand slips from mine and my gaze falls away from hers. "If you decide you're able to give more... to make this real... you know where to find me."

I nod, my mind racing with a million conflicting thoughts. I don't reply, but it's when I notice cold snow hitting the back of my neck that I look up and see she's gone. I scan down the block and there's no sign of her.

CHAPTER 26

Danica

THE HEEL OF my foot taps restlessly as I watch the door for Kiera. It was a last-minute invite, but she didn't hesitate to accept when I asked her to meet me for breakfast. I think the nature of my text ensured she'd come.

I'm all fucked up in the head and need a sounding board.

She merely replied, *When and where?*

I chose a quaint tea and pastry shop near the arena, an area of town she's familiar with. Kiera only moved here three months ago and is still learning the city. The tea shop has the added benefit of serving chamomile, which hopefully will ease my nerves.

I chose Kiera rather than a handful of other friends I'm close with because she already knows about me and Camden. When Camden and I stumbled on her and Bain a little over a week ago at the gala, we became a group of four having illicit relationships within the bounds of the Titans' team. I pulled Kiera away from Bain, dragged her back to the ballroom and tried to get the down-and-dirty details. It had to be quick since we were surrounded by people.

"How long has this been going on?" I asked because the way they were embraced indicated they had carnal knowledge of each other already.

With a big grin, she informed me that she had sex with him on New Year's Eve and they've been "casually banging each other since." I wanted more details, but she asked, "What's going on with you and Camden?"

I never thought to lie or downplay it but I told her it was complicated and we were trying to figure it out. We were then pulled apart as Brienne wanted to introduce me to someone making a very large donation. I've not been able to talk to Kiera about any of this since that night.

Rubbing at my tired eyes, I lament my lack of sleep. Parting ways with Camden was one of the hardest things I've had to do in my life. It feels like a rough-edged dagger has been stabbed straight through my heart and then twisted for maximum punishment.

It was probably delusional, but I'd hoped his desire to be with me would outweigh his fears. It's a sore rebuff that it didn't. I've never been through a breakup before—Mitch having been the one and only I'd ever dated. All I can say is it sucks and I'm not handling it well.

Kiera breezes through the door, unwinding a deep

purple scarf from around her neck and unbuttoning her brown wool coat. Only two other customers sit at a table on the opposite side of the room so her eyes land on me quickly.

Her face is already soft with empathy as she approaches. Shrugging out of her coat, she tosses it across the back of her chair and plops down. I nod at the cup of tea I'd ordered for her and the plate of scones between us. She wrinkles her nose and ignores them both, leaning forward. "What's going on?"

I shake my head, my gaze dropping to my tea that I haven't touched yet. It's hard to find the right words. Nothing seems adequate to describe what's happened between me and Camden, so I lift my eyes and admit, "I ended things with Camden last night and I feel awful about it."

"So un-end it," she replies as if that's the most obvious answer.

"I can't go backward."

Kiera sighs and picks up her tea, takes a tiny sip and grimaces. She's a coffee person and I know this about her, but this shop only sells tea. It's for tea snobs. "Start from the beginning. All I know is you like Camden and he likes you, so catch me up."

"It's a bit more than *like*," I say gloomily.

"On your part?"

"I think on both our parts." My fingers trace the

pattern of little roses on the saucer. "The feelings have gotten strong, but it's complicated, for him more than me."

Kiera pushes the tea away and picks up a scone. Holding it before her mouth, she says, "Let me guess… he feels he's in Mitch's shadow and can't handle that."

I shake my head. "On the contrary, no. We've had those talks and yes, I think he had some insecurities in the beginning, but he trusts that I don't compare them. Camden knows what I had with Mitch was amazing, and what I have with him is amazing too."

"Then what's his problem?"

I lift a shoulder. "He wants us to see each other secretively. He's not ready for the team to know about us. Thinks it will cause waves and people will judge and not understand."

"So what? I mean… if y'all have feelings for each other and they're genuine and deep… what does it matter what anyone else thinks?"

"It doesn't matter to me. I'm confident that I should be able to move on with my life in any way I see fit. I loved Mitch with all my heart and I love his memory. That will never change. But I'm allowed to be happy again, and I will be. I'm just afraid it's not going to be with Camden."

"The whole teammate thing is the complicating factor," Kiera muses, then nibbles on her scone. She licks crumbs off her lips. "I wonder if he's talked to any of them. I mean, I know for one, Drake would never have a problem with you two dating. I bet most would be fine with it."

"I think you're right, especially since most of Mitch's friends…" I trail off, not needing to say the words. The fact is, this is a new team with only Camden, Hendrix and Coen remaining from the original Titans roster. If anyone would think Camden is crossing a line he shouldn't, it would be one of those guys.

"It's nobody's fucking business who we allow into our hearts, Danica."

"I know. I agree."

"Camden should know it too."

"He knows it," I say quietly, telling her the thing that hurts the most. "He knows it and believes it, but he's too afraid to go for it."

"Then fuck him," she grouses. "Metaphorically, of course."

I settle back into my chair, crossing my arms over my stomach. "I can't be mad, though. I understand why he's nervous about the entire situation. It's a legit worry."

Shaking her head, Kiera drops the rest of the scone onto the plate. "Those things are dry as fuck." She takes the napkin and wipes her fingers before dabbing at her lips. "I'm confused. Are we mad at him or not?"

I can't help but laugh. "I'm not mad. Disappointed.

Also understanding. Sad. Worried I made a bad decision in parting ways."

"Now I understand why you said you're fucked in the head."

I pick up my tea and sip. When I settle the cup back on the saucer, I voice my biggest fear. "What if... what if the reason he doesn't want anyone to know is that this isn't serious for him? I'm... convenient."

I hate that tears prick at my eyes. Last night at the party, the way Camden acted made me think that I'm just a convenient fuck. That I misread the feelings and our connection.

It made me feel used and cheap and that's the real reason I bolted from Tillie and Coen's house.

"Do you really believe that?" Kiera asks quietly. "Because you're a good judge of character, Danica. I don't know that you could miss something like that, and Camden seems like a nice guy."

I shrug because I don't know what's real anymore. "I told him if he changes his mind... he knows where to find me."

"Well, there you go." Her voice is overly cheery. "He'll come around."

"And if he doesn't, then I'll know that it wasn't as special as I thought it was."

"So what's the plan?" Kiera asks, crossing her arms on the table. "Do we set you up with someone hot and rub it in his face? Drive him wild with jealousy so he knows what he lost?"

My snort is loud and unladylike. "While that does sound fun, you know I'm not the type to do that. I think I'm going to have to move on from the loss, the same way I did after Mitch died. While it's two different circumstances, it still hurts."

Kiera takes my hand and squeezes. "I'm sorry. You don't deserve this and I know you're not, but I'm mad at him."

I flex my fingers against hers, a silent thank-you for her support. When I pull away, I ask, "You still casually banging Bain?"

Her eyes flash mischievously. "Every chance I can."

"Is that going anywhere?"

"Nah," she drawls with a wave of her hand. "We're just having fun and neither of us is interested in commitment."

"Are you both seeing other people too?" I ask. Because I'm not sure how playing the field works from a woman's perspective. Never had experience with serial dating, and it's the stereotype that men are the ones who sow their oats.

"Who needs other people? Bain is a beast and more than enough for me to handle."

My jaw drops slightly, not only from the shocking nature of her words but the raw lust in her voice when she talks about him. If the feelings I have for Camden—both physical and non-physical—had a sound, that's what it would be.

"Does Drake know or have any clue?"

Kiera dips her head and levels a look at me that says I've asked a stupid question. I hold up my hands in placation. "There's no sense in him knowing since it's not going anywhere. I'm sure we'll fizzle soon."

"Doesn't sound like you'll fizzle the way you called him a beast," I mutter.

A small smile plays on her lips, but she doesn't confirm or deny my observation. Instead, she flicks my cup with her finger. "Finish your tea. Let's go shopping... a little retail therapy."

A small flush of happiness washes through me but I know it's merely recognition that a few hours with Kiera will provide my heart a much-needed break from hurting.

CHAPTER 27

Camden

BACK-TO-BACK WINS IN New York against the Vipers and the Phantoms, respectively, means there's a jubilant, rowdy atmosphere in the locker room. My teammates are all joking around as we finish our showers and get dressed. The bus will take us straight to the airport for a short stop back in Pittsburgh for one day and then we're on to road games in Boston and Carolina.

I laugh when appropriate, quipping when I can and handing out high fives and fist bumps. Doing everything possible to make sure my outside doesn't match my inside.

I'm unsettled and not able to get my footing. I'm feeling the exact way I felt the morning Coach West showed up on my doorstep when I missed practice, except now I have the added burden of pain from losing Danica. I've played like shit the last two games and Coach will be talking to me, of that I'm sure.

With a towel wrapped around my waist and another over my shoulders, I walk to the cubby assigned to me.

The Phantoms' arena is new and their locker rooms are plush. I kick off my slides and sink my bare feet into the carpet.

A loud crack rends the air and what feels like a sharp, electrical sting hits my right ass cheek. I jerk forward and turn to see Bain there holding the towel he's snapped me with.

"You asshole," I growl, rubbing my tender butt.

He grins and makes to flick it at me again. I jump backward and warn, "Do it and I'll kick your ass."

"Lighten up, dude. We just beat the Phantoms. We beat the Vipers. We're at the top of our division and second in our conference."

He's given me very good reasons to turn my frown upside down, but I don't fucking feel like it. I'm in a bad mood because I miss Danica and I'm pretty sure I might have fucked up my life by letting her go. I turn my back on Bain and reach into my cubby for my duffel. I drop the towel and grab a fresh pair of briefs, pulling them on. It's always been the rule that we arrive on game day in dress suits and we usually leave in the same. But on nights—like tonight—where we're headed home late on the plane, we're allowed to dress casually, as long as it's Titans' gear. I brought a pair of track pants, a T-shirt and sweatshirt, and hopefully I'll sleep on the short flight back.

Did I mention I've been sleeping like shit the last few

days?

Hendrix's cubby is to my left and he appears, giving me a quick glance. "Good game, man."

"I played like shit," I mutter. I don't see it as I'm digging through my bag for my deodorant, but I feel Hendrix and Bain sharing a look over me.

And then another sharp sting hits my right ass cheek and I whirl on Bain who's backing up from me warily, gripping the towel that he just snapped at me.

"What the hell is wrong with you dude?" I take a menacing step toward him and the towel whips like a snake as he unleashes it again. I jump back as it cracks, only slicing the air and not touching my skin. I stare at him with wide eyes and my teeth gritted. "I'm so going to kick your ass."

He cracks it again, causing me to back into Hendrix. "Why don't you tell us what's wrong, let us help fix it, then I can stop doing this?"

I glare at him and the fucker whips it again. It comes perilously close to my hip, covered only by my briefs, and I roar like an infuriated bull. I charge at Bain but Hendrix has me by the waist, jerking me back and then slinging me away. "Calm the fuck down," he orders.

I'm vaguely aware the locker room has become quiet and as I look around, everyone's staring.

Hendrix points at Bain. "Put the fucking towel down. It's not funny anymore."

Bain tosses the towel in the bottom of his locker and reaches for his bag. "Just want the guy to open up. Figured poking the bear might get him to blurt out what's wrong."

I ignore Bain, finding my deodorant and layering on a good amount. Bain and Hendrix are silent on either side of me as we dress. For some reason, as mad as I am at Bain for goading me and demanding to get in my business, I'm now even more irritated that they're not bothering me at all. I'm going to guess that means I'm in a fucking bad mood no matter what.

"I'm playing like shit because I've got something on my mind," I mutter as I pull on my track pants.

Hendrix and Bain both turn toward me and move closer. I've opened the door now and there's no closing it.

But fuck it. I lost Danica because I was afraid to let anyone know about us. Bain already told me there was no bro code, but I thought he was being funny. At least this won't come as a huge shock to him.

"I've been seeing Danica." Hendrix's eyebrows shoot up but Bain remains impassive. "And it was getting really serious, but we broke it off."

Now Bain's eyebrows move, except now they draw inward with worry. "Why?"

"Because it's too complicated," I say with a huge sigh.

"And you're regretting the decision?" Hendrix asks.

"Yes," I say, then immediately change my mind. "No. It was the right thing to do."

Bain scoffs. "Bullshit. If it makes you feel like shit, makes you play like shit, then it wasn't the right thing."

"I'll feel better eventually," I retort. "I'll get over it."

"I'm sorry, buddy," Hendrix says, squeezing my shoulder.

Bain crosses his arms across his chest. "Ahh," he drawls with a knowing look on his face. "I get it."

"Get what?" I snap.

"Danica was constantly comparing you to Mitch," he says with a smirk.

"No, she wasn't doing that," I snarl.

"She doesn't want you around her kid?" he guesses.

"Travis and I get along great."

"She's too mired in grief and can't give you her all?" Hendrix asks tentatively.

I shake my head, shooting him a glance. "No... she's ready to move on."

"Then she's feeling weirded out about you and Mitch knowing each other and wants to keep things secret?" he tosses my way.

"No," I growl with frustration. "Danica is great with everything. She's solid. Sure, she has moments of sadness about Mitch, but she says he wanted her to be happy. They'd talked about those things. And even Travis likes that I like his mom."

Bain moves to stand before me, his expression thunderous. "Then what the actual fuck, dude? You have an amazing woman who, as far as I can tell over the last several weeks, has brought you out of your funk. You care for her and her kid. She's ready to give her all to you and you break it off? Are you stupid or something?"

"It's not stupid to worry about the welfare of the team," I snap. Bain blinks at me and looks to Hendrix who shrugs. I suck in a breath and after letting it out, my voice is slightly calmer. I glance around to make sure no one's been listening. "I'm worried that this could negatively affect the team. There might be some who think it's fucked up I'm with Mitch's wife."

"Widow," Bain corrects me bluntly. "She's not his wife. She's a widow and Mitch is dead."

I wince because that's a harsh reminder, but Bain didn't know Mitch. He wasn't part of that team.

My gaze goes to Hendrix. "I agree with Bain. I don't think there's anything wrong with it."

I turn around slowly and look at all my teammates. They're talking and laughing and enjoying easy camaraderie. They all truly care about each other, just the way it was with the team I had before the crash.

Giving my attention back to Hendrix, because he knew Mitch well, I ask, "Are you sure I'm not doing anything wrong?"

"Does it feel wrong when you're with her?"

"Nothing has ever felt more right," I say.

"I don't care if anyone has a problem with it," Bain cuts in, leveling me with a harsh stare. "If she's that good for you and you for her, fuck anyone in this locker room and fuck any fan who has an issue with it. You cannot bend your life to fit—"

"I don't want to hurt the team. I don't want some people to have bad feelings about it. I don't want to throw off this momentum we have going."

"They won't be upset," Hendrix says. "They'll be happy for you, man."

"How can you be so sure?"

His hand comes back to my shoulder. "Because I am, and Bain is, and because they love you the way we do."

Bain grimaces and holds up his hands. "That's way too mushy for me, but yeah… what he said."

I laugh, feeling the tension leave my body. Both of the guys grin back at me.

"You need to go for it," Hendrix says and Bain nods.

"Just go for it?" I muse as I take in my friends and see the truth of what they're saying written all over their faces.

Bain gives me a light punch to the shoulder. "Go for it. As soon as we get back to Pittsburgh, you can—"

Something propels me and I find myself standing on top of the bench that runs down the aisle of cubbies. I put two fingers in my mouth and let out a shrieking whistle. Everyone turns my way.

When I know I have everyone's eyes on me—including the coaches who are changing out of their suits into comfortable clothes for the trip back—I say, "I have an announcement."

My eyes land on Coen for some reason, the other member of our Lucky Three. He doesn't know about me and Danica the way I brought Hendrix into the loop, but as I see his easy smile, I know deep in my heart, he only wants what's best for me.

I sweep the crowd again as they move in closer with curiosity. Coach West's already changed and wearing a pair of jeans and a thick sweater. His arms are crossed over his chest, but his head is tilted and he smiles with interest.

"I've been seeing someone for several weeks. It started as a friendship, then turned into something more. Something deeper. And I recently ended things with her because I thought my being with her would complicate things for the team." Everyone looks up at me in confusion. "I'm seeing Danica Brandt."

I wait... expecting a reaction. Waiting for someone to say something, but everyone stares at me, waiting for me to continue my story. "I ended it a few days ago, but I'm thinking I made a very bad decision. I was afraid to let you all know. Afraid it would cause bad feelings and hurt the team. But I've very recently been convinced by a few of you that I shouldn't give her up. They told me not to give a fuck what anyone thinks, but I do care. I care a lot about this team and I want us to remain cohesive. We're a family, and I don't want to cause waves if any of you think it's wrong of me to date her. If you do, I'm hoping we can talk it out man to man. I'll tell you then what I'll tell you now… I'll take very good care of her and Travis. I'll do Mitch proud."

I pause, taking everyone in. Some of the guys stare at me with open mouths, others smile. I swear I see Kirill dab at his eyes.

"I think it's great you're with Danica." My head whips toward the voice… the most important one. Coen. He gives me a thumbs-up. "I think you two make a great couple and Mitch would approve."

Someone in the back whistles… Andrei Komokov. "Go for it."

Someone else yells out, "We all approve."

"But hurt her and we'll kick your ass," another says, the obligatory big-brother act.

One by one, the guys come up to fist-bump, bro hug or slap me on the back. They offer words of support and congratulations. Coen mutters, "I thought I saw something there at the housewarming party. At least I know I wasn't crazy."

When everyone is back at their cubbies, I feel someone walk up behind me. I pull my T-shirt over my head and turn to find Coach West standing there. "That was some speech."

"It was from the heart," I say.

Coach nods. "That it was." He turns to walk away but not before saying, "You two make a really cute couple."

CHAPTER 28

Danica

"**G**O, TRAVIS... GO!" I scream from the stands as he accepts a pass from a teammate and shoots down the boards. It's only a practice scrimmage before their first game next week, but I'm about to jump out of my skin with excitement.

Mainly from the fact that Travis was so hyped up today he was bouncing around like a rabbit all morning.

I'm out of my seat, hands clasped hard and my breath held deep in my lungs. I exhale on a whoosh when Travis tries to get a shot off but tangles up with another kid as they scrabble for the puck. I plop back down.

A woman sitting on the bleacher bench in front of me leans back and touches her hand on my knee. "Is it going to be like this all season? Because I'm not sure my heart can handle it."

Laughing, I give a rueful smile toward the ice. "I think we're in for several years of heart attacks and heartaches."

"But the smiles on their faces are worth it," she says.

"Yes, they are," I agree softly.

It warms me to my bones that Travis is finding joy in the same sport his dad played. He might have gotten off to a bit of a rocky start but with a few extra practices with Camden and—

Stop it.

Stop thinking about Camden.

I force myself to concentrate on my kid, looking adorable at this stage of his young career. Sometimes he looks in command and other times he looks wobbly. It's all part of growing strong, learning the sport and pulling on that DNA I know he has from Mitch. I can't wait to watch every second of it.

The coach blows the whistle and gathers the boys in. I don't know what he's saying but he pats a few of the kids on the helmets. Travis hasn't mentioned any further negativity going on, so maybe Camden's talk with—

Stop it. Stop it. Stop it.

The kids skate off the ice for the locker room and I grab my purse, sidestepping down the bleachers. It will take Travis a few minutes to get changed and I walk slowly to the front of the complex, chatting with a few other parents.

Someone taps me on the shoulder and when I look back over it, I see one of the dads there. He points toward the front lobby area. "Aren't you friends with

Camden Poe?"

My heart gives a wild, painful thump of confusion as I turn that way. Sure enough, Camden's standing there with the sunlight from the double glass doors painting him into a silhouette. I can't quite see the expression on his face, but he's definitely staring at me.

Or rather the group of people I'm walking with.

As we get closer, I confirm that his gaze is leveled with mine and within his eyes I see a request to come talk to him. I say goodbye to the parents and turn toward him, trying to quell the gallop of my heart, blinking against the prick of tears.

I didn't realize how bad it would hurt to see him.

I'm nervous as I come to stand a few feet away, my hands clutching at my purse straps over my left shoulder. "What are you doing here?"

He stands casually, hands in his pockets. "Came to see Travis's scrimmage."

"Oh." The disappointment that he's here to see my son and not me is almost crushing.

"He tried to ping me a few times this week to play online with him, but honestly... I didn't know what to say. Didn't know what you'd told him about us, if anything, so I told him I was too busy on the road trips."

"He hasn't asked," I admit.

Camden's head drops as he nods. When he lifts his gaze, I'm stunned by the worry I see there. "How are you doing? Are you okay?"

"No," I say truthfully. "But I will be. One day."

He nods again. "I'm not okay either."

It's difficult not to throw myself at him, but I'm very confused as to why he's here. "I'm sorry."

"Don't be," he replies, and for the first time, the curve of a smile appears. "I've already taken steps to rectify the situation."

His tone hedges on playful and a tiny kernel of hope blooms within me. "Oh yeah? What did you do?"

"Stood up in front of the entire team after the Phantoms game and told them that I had been seeing you."

My eyes flare and my mouth hangs open. "You did?"

One side of his mouth lifts higher than the other, popping a dimple. "Yeah… in hindsight, it's quite embarrassing, but the feedback was beyond positive."

"And what exactly was the feedback?"

Camden steps closer. "One hundred percent well wishes with one unknown voice from the back threatening to kick my ass if I hurt you."

I drop my gaze so he can't see my responding smile because I'm not sure I'm ready to buy into his charm yet. However, I'm forced to look up when I feel his fingers on my chin. "I'd already hurt you, though, so the warning was a little late."

I shake my head. "You did what was best for you."

"I did what was best for a coward, not what was best

for me. But like I said… I rectified that. The entire team knows how I feel about you, and there are only two more things I need to do."

He's trying to rectify a poor choice? My throat is dry, voice raspy. "Two things?"

"The first… the most important… is to apologize and ask you to give me another shot. You said you'd be waiting if I changed my mind, so I'm hoping in the last few days you haven't found yourself another feller."

I can't help but giggle. "Feller?"

"I'm trying to be charming," he says, moving all the way into me and taking me by the hips. "But seriously… I'm ready to jump all in with you, Danica. It was stupid of me to have those fears."

"No." I shake my head furiously. "I understand where you were coming from."

Camden bends his head to get closer to me. "Of course you do. Because you're amazing and I want to be like you when I grow up."

"The fact that you're standing here in front of me right now means you're kind of amazing too."

His hands move from my hips to my face, and he dips a little closer. Beautiful eyes lock onto mine. "You and I have a tether between us. The crash bonds us in a way no two people would want to be bonded, and yet I cannot imagine my life without you. I'm falling in love with you, Danica, and I don't want to hide it anymore. I sort of want to scream it, actually."

"I'm falling in love with you too," I reply as I close my eyes briefly. When I open them, I admit, "I might even already be there. I can't remember what it was like to come to that realization. It was such a slow build with Mitch over many years." I wait for him to tense up but he only smiles in understanding. "With you, I'm sucked into a tempest of emotions and it feels volatile and wonderful all at once."

"I've never been in love before. I only know I've never felt this way about anyone. I never imagined I could ever feel this way. You're the first thing I think about when I wake up, the last thing I think about before I close my eyes, and there are a million times more in between. When I'm near you, I feel like I'm about to come out of my skin and at the same time, when you touch me, I'm so at peace, I don't think anything can bother me. I don't know if that's what love is, but it should be."

Tears truly sting now and I blink them back. "I think you know exactly what love is."

I expect a kiss but to my dismay, Camden lifts his head to look at something behind me, only to give me his regard again. "All the hockey parents are watching us."

"Oh God," I say, starting to fall into him... to bury my embarrassment in his chest.

His hands cupping my cheeks don't let me move, though, and instead, he tips my face to kiss me. His lips are soft, his tongue gentle as he makes me see stars.

When he pulls back, he asks, "Am I forgiven?"

"For what?" I ask numbly, my lips still tingling.

His roguish smile tells me he finds me amusing and his lips on my forehead say he loves that about me.

Camden pulls away as some of the kids come out of the locker room, meeting up with their parents and walking out. Taking my hand, Camden says, "One more thing to do."

He leads me closer to the locker room door just as Travis emerges. His eyes immediately land on Camden and widen. A smile breaks free as he takes him in, then his gaze drops to where our hands are clasped.

To my relief, the smile doesn't waver but his eyes flick between the two of us. "You're holding hands."

"We are," Camden says, holding them up for a better look. "You okay with this?"

He nods, his cheeks turning a little red.

Camden drops my hand and squats in front of Travis. "You know I like your mom, right?"

He nods again, his smile disappearing as things have turned serious.

"I have to be honest, buddy... I more than like her."

"You mean you love her?" he asks hesitantly, his gaze shifting over Camden's shoulder to me and then back again.

"Yeah. And I know this might be a little weird and totally out of left field, but I love you too. Always have because you're Mitch's kid and I loved him. I want you to know that I'm here for you... whatever you need. You and your mom are a package deal to me. I need to have you both, okay?"

Another nod. Seems the cat jerked the poor child's tongue clear out of his head. But then he recovers and asks, "Can we go have ice cream to celebrate?"

Camden cranes his neck to look back at me. "What do you say, Mom? Can we do ice cream?"

"We can do ice cream," I say with a faux huff of annoyance.

Straightening, Camden reaches his hand out to me and I lace my fingers with his. He drapes his other arm across Travis's shoulders and we walk out of the hockey complex together.

Bain Hillridge is new to the Titans and he's building relationships with his new team, both on and off the ice. If only he could keep his hands off his teammate's little sister. GO HERE to get all the details on Bain!

sawyerbennett.com/bookstore/bain

Go here to see other works by Sawyer Bennett:

https://sawyerbennett.com/bookshop

Don't miss another new release by Sawyer Bennett!!! Sign up for her newsletter and keep up to date on new releases, giveaways, book reviews and so much more.

https://sawyerbennett.com/signup

Connect with Sawyer online:

Website: sawyerbennett.com

Twitter: twitter.com/bennettbooks

Facebook: facebook.com/bennettbooks

Instagram: instagram.com/sawyerbennett123

Goodreads: goodreads.com/Sawyer_Bennett

Amazon: amazon.com/author/sawyerbennett

BookBub: bookbub.com/authors/sawyer-bennett

About the Author

New York Times, USA Today, and Wall Street Journal Bestselling author Sawyer Bennett uses real life experience to create relatable stories that appeal to a wide array of readers. From contemporary romance, fantasy romance, and both women's and general fiction, Sawyer writes something for just about everyone.

A former trial lawyer from North Carolina, when she is not bringing fiction to life, Sawyer is a chauffeur, stylist, chef, maid, and personal assistant to her very adorable daughter, as well as full-time servant to her wonderfully naughty dogs.

If you'd like to receive a notification when Sawyer releases a new book, sign up for her newsletter (sawyer bennett.com/signup).

Milton Keynes UK
Ingram Content Group UK Ltd.
UKHW020733030823
426269UK00015B/721

9 781088 197806